ONCE
A MYTH

Once
a
Myth

Goddess Isles
Book One

by

New York Times Bestseller
Pepper Winters

Once a Myth
Copyright © 2020 Pepper Winters
Published by Pepper Winters

Published: Pepper Winters 2020: **pepperwinters@gmail.com**
Cover Design: Ari @ Cover it! Designs
Editing by: Editing 4 Indies (Jenny Sims)

Dedicated to:

My readers.
You've been with me from the beginning.
From darkness to tragedy and everything in between.
Dark Romance, Grey Romance, Rom Com, and Tear Jerkers.
Thank you.
Thank you for your time reading my words.
Thank you for adventuring into my pages.

Prologue

ONCE UPON A TIME, a teacher surprised us with a pop quiz.

I was seventeen.

It was my last month of school.

The test comprised of a single question.

What is the worst thing that happened to you, and how did you survive it?

When the class sneered at the seemingly random query, our teacher smiled, and said, "You think this is a stupid question, but really, it's the most important one you'll ever answer. Why? Because the worst thing to ever happen to you probably hasn't found you yet. You're young. You're fanciful. You're naïve. But to know that your life will have battles, arms you for the trials ahead. And the answer that you write on this silly piece of paper will be there, in the back of your mind, keeping you company while you face it."

I groaned with my classmates.

I joked with my friends.

But I did the work required.

I thought long and hard and scribbled:

The worst thing to happen to me? When Max got drunk and abandoned me at the bonfire party last year. In the middle of nowhere with intoxicated teens everywhere, I was lost and lonely. A guy tried to feel me up. He pushed me against a tree, and the fire glowed behind him while he touched places he shouldn't.

How did I survive it? By being brave and kneeing the bastard in the balls. By being proactive and arranging a ride home with a friend's older sister. By being unforgiving and dumping Max. By being wise and never forgetting the boy who tried to take what wasn't his to take.

The teacher didn't require us to sign our names.
We handed in our confessions anonymously.
She was right, that teacher.
We were young.
We were fanciful.
I was naïve.
Naïve to think a childish party with raging hormones and reckless drinking would be the worst thing to ever happen to me.
Now, four years later, I had a different answer to scribble down.
An answer I wished I knew how to survive.

The worst thing to ever happen to me? Being stolen, sold, and gifted. Being delivered to a man who isn't just a man, but a monster. Being told I now belong to him.

How did I survive it?

I guess I'll have to fight and find out...

Chapter One

"HERE."

My head raised from my knees. My eyes peered into the dank and dismal darkness. A ghostly figure of a blonde girl holding up a bowl danced in front of me.

I was hungry. Thirsty. Hurting. Lonely.

She offered salvation to most of those things, passing me a bowl of nondescript food and a torn piece of bread. My hands shook as I took the bowl from her, bending a little to reach from where I hugged myself on the top bunk.

She flashed me a smile, nodding in approval. "If we don't eat, we don't have enough strength to fight."

I nodded back. I didn't want to talk. The men who'd snatched me from the hostel where my boyfriend and I had been staying promised painful punishment if I talked to the other girls trapped in hell with me.

But this girl…she'd only arrived today.

Her fear made her a little reckless, even though I'd seen her crying.

Men's voices grumbled from outside the door, tearing her gaze worriedly to look. I froze with the bowl in my hands, waiting for a monster to walk in and hurt us.

But the voices faded, and the girl looked back at me. "What's your name?"

Such a simple question.

But a terrifying one because my name was no longer mine. No longer mine to use. Freedom taken from me along with everything.

I licked my lips, testing my throat that still throbbed from screaming so hard when I'd been taken. I'd been in the communal kitchen of the hostel cooking veggie tacos for me and my boyfriend, Scott.

I'd been the only one. The only backpacker in an empty kitchen while Scott hung out in the pool hall with a guy we'd just met from Ireland.

I'd grown bored of the potato and leprechaun jokes and sought refuge in the quietness of the run-down kitchen.

Alone.

Until...I hadn't been.

Until three men arrived with black gloves and sinister smiles.

Until those men noticed me, assessed me...snatched me.

"I'm Tess," the blonde whispered, Australian accent feathering around her words. "I was kidnapped. They hurt my boyfriend."

I shoved back the memories of my own kidnapping. Of hands on my arms, fingernails on my skin, a gag shoved in my mouth. The clang of a pot falling on the tiles, the smash of a plate as I kicked and thrashed.

I hadn't been quiet.

I'd screamed. I'd fought.

But no one heard me over the din of the music in the pool hall.

I shuddered, forcing my voice to stay level and low. "I'm sorry they hurt your boyfriend." I shrugged. "Mine doesn't know where I am."

"I don't know if mine is alive." Her eyes glowed with tears. "He might be dead on the bathroom floor where they beat him."

She had it worse.

At least my boyfriend had been safe. What had happened to hers after she'd been stolen?

It was the unknown that hurt the most. The not knowing if her boyfriend was alive or if mine was looking for me. The total uncertainty of our futures, diverted without our permission from the path we'd chosen.

How could another human do this to us? What gave anyone the right to steal us from a life and trap us in the dark with no answers, no comfort, no sign of this nightmare ever ending?

"I'm sorry," I whispered. "Are you okay? You weren't hurt too badly?"

She sniffed with pain. "I'm fine. Are *you* okay?" She stepped closer to my bunk, her blonde hair dirty and limp. "You don't look so good."

I waved her concern away with a lacklustre smile. "I'm still alive."

She sighed as if I'd said I was broken beyond repair. "Being alive might be something we'll end up regretting."

Other pairs of eyes looked over to us, narrowed with fear and harsh with warning. Silence had been our only companion since I'd been thrown in here two days ago.

This girl had taken that silence and filled it with fight. The food in my hands reminded me that she was right. No matter what they'd done to us, we couldn't just accept it. There had to be a way—some way—to stop this.

Without dying in the process.

Tess sighed again, a huff of anger and a puff of despair. "I just want to go home."

A whisper of agreement filtered around the room.

I nodded. "Me too. All of us do."

My other companions had trickled in over the past forty-eight hours. Two girls had been here before me, but the others were new, just like this brave Australian girl. I'd never been much for talking to strangers and preferred silence over conversation, yet she reminded me of a time when things had been so much simpler.

A girl of a similar age. A young woman just embarking on her life after suffering through adolescence and education. We'd earned our freedom, yet these men had killed it before it'd begun.

"They can't do this." Tess's hands curled by her side, crushing the piece of bread she still held.

I nodded again. I opened my mouth to agree.

But really, they could.

They had.

They'd taken us, and we had no control.

We could scream and curse and crawl around in the dark for a way out, but in the end...we just had to be patient and hope fate was kind to us and ruthless to them. That karma would be on our side.

No one knew what was in store for us but nasty misery held the truth.

We were theirs.

To use.

To sell.

To kill.

We could rebel all we wanted and use energy, wishing it wasn't so…but in the end, the ones who would survive were the ones who waited and watched and learned how to use the monster's weaknesses against him.

"I'm sorry about your boyfriend," I murmured. "I'm sorry they took you." I pulled back into the shadows, curling around the food she'd given me, settling deeper into silence.

"Get up, *putas*."

I opened my eyes.

The oppressive blackness was sliced with a wedge of light, spilling through the open door. Two men barred the exit. One had a jagged scar along his cheek, the other an oily leather jacket.

The one with the leather jacket marched straight toward Tess and snatched her off the bottom bunk. The one with the scar joined in the game, dragging girls off the bottom bunks and yanking legs of the ones on top. Not waiting for the rude alarm clock to hurt me, I leaped off the top bunk and landed on filthy floorboards.

My denim shorts and lemon t-shirt had long since succumbed to dirt and disgust.

The scarred guy sneered at me, then shoved my shoulder and sent me crashing into the framework of the bunk just because he could.

I gritted my teeth as quiet rage slithered through my chest. A rattlesnake of hatred. I was the girl at school who always played by the rules and made friends with everyone. I was the one teachers used as a good example. Not because I was perfect but because I'd learned how to *play* perfect.

I didn't pick fights or argue trivial matters. I held the enviable position of not being tied to one clique. I hung out with the nerds, the cool kids, the druggies, and the jocks.

I was neutral. I was calm.

But beneath that façade, I was pure emotion.

I didn't bother wasting energy on petty and pointless things because I knew life hadn't truly started yet. I'd bided my time. I'd accepted the delay that school delivered before my life could really start.

And now that it had…now that I didn't have to be perfect, well…it was personal.

This situation was too dangerous to ignore, and I wasn't weak enough to accept it.

I wouldn't stay quiet.

I wouldn't obey.

My natural instinct was to lash out. To puncture their chests and rip out—

"Let go of me, you bastard!" The blonde girl, Tess, screeched and wriggled in the man's hold. Her foot kicked his kneecap. I cheered for her. His palm crashed against her cheek. I pitied her.

He dropped her to the floor as if to stomp on her head, but his partner muttered something in Spanish, and he chuckled instead. Hauling her to her feet, he shoved her through the door, stepping out of the way as more men entered to shepherd the rest of us.

Another girl gave in to the urge to rebel, shouting something in Swedish. A man buried a fist in her belly, sending her crashing to the floor.

Backing away, he left her crumpled at his feet and snarled at us to follow.

I lagged behind the tired, shuffling captives, going as close to the punched girl as I could.

She pushed herself upright on wobbling legs, groaning and wrapping her arms around her middle.

Our eyes connected.

Our voices stayed silent.

We nodded in joint sisterhood.

She had the same instinct.

To fight.

To stand up.

To say no to injustice.

But there was a time for violence and a time for patience. Only a few could balance the righteous heat with cold calculation. I shoved that fiery desire to destroy them deep into a heart pumping antifreeze through my blood, granting icy control.

Tess and this other girl didn't have that trick.

They gave in to the wildness being in a cage caused. They stormed ahead with attitude and hands fisted, painting a target on their backs to be hurt.

Up ahead, Tess refused another order.

She earned a heavy cuff to her head.

She stumbled.

A noise of hatred rumbled in my chest.

A swat came for me, but I ducked and kept my eyes on the ground. I didn't let the monster touch me, but I didn't look at him. I didn't goad him into trying again.

Tess tripped but didn't fall, and together, we all marched where the men commanded.

Passing door after door, I nursed my rage as we finally entered a room that looked transplanted from a jailhouse.

Multiple showerheads all in a line with no privacy or seclusion. Cracked white tiles held yesterday's dirt and yellowed soap littered the unsanitary floor.

Tess was jerked forward by the man wearing a leather jacket. He laughed and commanded she strip.

She spat in his face.

A gasp sounded down the line of women.

I smothered a groan of despair and winced as the man ploughed a fist into her cheekbone. Most of the girls looked away as the man muttered something, then stripped her. Ripping off her clothes, destroying any belief that her body was her own.

By the time she stood naked and shivering, her cheek swollen to twice its size and tears trickling unbidden, my control over the lashing, licking fury rattled at its bars.

I wanted to bolt forward and murder the man who'd hurt her.

I wanted a gun to slaughter them all.

I wanted to save these poor women, huddled like little sheep, bleating before the executioner.

I was a swarm of buzzing, pissed-off hornets, and it was so, *so* hard to swallow back the sting of savagery. Instead, I focused on survival and undressed as men poked and prodded us to obey.

The ritual was symbolic.

Yet another play on our distress.

Take away our clothes—the final pieces of our past, and they'd taken everything. Look at our bare skin and perve at our naked breasts and demote us to nothing more than a toy.

A few girls reached their limit as the jailors leered and reached to sample the weight of a breast or the heat between their legs. They crumpled to the tiles only to be kicked until they crawled into the showers.

Outwardly, I didn't move.

My spine stayed straight. My chin held high. My long brown hair kissed above my ass, and my firm breasts belied the racing of my vehemence-filled heartbeat. I didn't look at them as they looked at me. I didn't give them the satisfaction of breaking me just by a stare.

My body was *mine*.

It didn't matter they'd taken my clothes or my freedom. As long as breath existed in my lungs and coolant continued to smother the tempestuous hate in my veins, then I was above them.

The guy with the scar wrapped his hand in my hair and forced me to kneel.

He spat as he shouted violent words in a language I didn't understand.

I kept the glowing hatred far away from showing in my grey eyes. I let him jerk me side to side. I ordered my muscles to go ragdoll with submission and not leap to my feet to destroy him.

Patience was a virtue.

Patience was a gift.

Patience will grant my freedom.

Bored with my aloofness, angry at my non-reaction, the man tossed me into the showers with the other women. Icy rain fell from grimy showerheads, plastering my hair to my shoulders.

My nipples pebbled, and the urge to shiver became unbearable. But shivering was a tell, just like hate was, and I wouldn't let these men see any reaction from me.

None.

Collecting a bar of soap from the feet of a girl sobbing hysterically, I touched her forearm gently. Her dark eyes latched onto mine, frantic and painfully lost. I wanted to shelter and shield her, but instead, all I could do was take her hand, press the soap into her palm, and squeeze her fingers gently.

Turning my back on her, I grabbed another lonely soap and scrubbed away the degradation and dirt from the past few days of living in a black hovel, rinsed out my mouth from the rancid aftertaste of no toothbrush, and ensured I was clinically sterile before the man barked for us to stop.

I was the first to step free from the chilly shower, heading toward the bench where a pile of threadbare towels waited haphazardly. They didn't look laundered. They smelled musky with a whiff of mould. I schooled my features to show no disgust and wrapped one around my nakedness.

I bent to reach for another to cocoon my dripping hair, but a man stepped behind me. A thick twine slipped over my head. A noose yanked tight against my throat.

Down the line of towel-adorned women, some struggled against their new imprisonment as ropes cinched tight. Some cried out. Some begged.

I just breathed.

And hated.

A man with black hair popping out the nostrils of his crooked nose leaned in to lick a droplet from my cheek.

I shivered involuntarily.

I stopped it immediately.

My muscles locked. My eyes focused on a place they could not ruin. My ears rang with his nasty promise.

"You not like the others." Spinning me to face him, jerking the rope so it choked me, he looked me up and down with a leer. "Too good for us, *puta*? Why you don't fight? Why you don't cry? You think you safe? That we don't do pain to you just because you stay quiet?"

The others vanished as I stared deep into his black eyes. He was taller, yet I felt as if I looked down upon him. And in his stare, I said goodbye to everything. I said farewell to the world travel Scott and I had planned—how we'd only just begun our journey by backpacking through America before flying to Mexico.

We'd met five months ago at a local travel show where tour companies and airlines came together and offered one-of-a-kind discounts. We were in the line waiting for a veggie burger from one of the food trucks. Before we'd even covered the basic get-to-know-you questions, we knew enough that we would get on. We were both vegetarians and seeking to explore the planet before forging a career path in whatever would grant us our dreams.

His parents lived in California. My mother lived in London after remarrying an Englishman after my father divorced her for reasons I wasn't privy to seven years ago.

We clicked enough that we agreed to book two tickets on an adventure instead of one.

Funny how I saw all of that in the eyes of a heartless trafficker. I saw my past, I mourned my loss, and I fortified myself for whatever came next.

When I didn't reply, the guy cursed under his breath and yanked the leash around my throat. The other women had already been dragged from the shower block. I followed as if I was a wayward stray, trotting as he jerked me to move quicker to the shuffling crowd up ahead.

The corridor seemed to squeeze around us, giving the sense of being inside a giant snake. We were its prey, cracked and devoured by overwhelming force.

A slur sounded in front. A female shout followed by sharp refusal.

I side-stepped to get a better view just as the guy wearing a leather jacket threw Tess to the ground and relentlessly kicked her. He kicked and kicked until I was sure I witnessed a murder. She couldn't survive such abuse.

It happened so fast. So viciously.

The man bent to grab the rope around her throat, tugging it like he expected her to heel. "Get up."

A feminine groan sounded, barely heard amongst the other cries and moans of the girls who'd witnessed such brutality.

I waited for Tess to stay down. To accept defeat.

But slowly, she stood.

Blood smeared her freshly scrubbed skin, and her eyes blazed with such loathing it licked at my own, encouraging my temper to snarl and claw, desperate to let loose and *fight*.

But now was not the time to choose carnage over careful obedience.

This was no longer a waiting game to see what would happen. We *knew* what was happening. We were being trafficked. We'd been stolen from different lives, stored in darkness, fed by beasts, and now we'd been washed and prepared for sale.

They'd kept us alive this long.

There was a reason.

A reason that came with a fat wallet to buy us and perversions to hurt us.

That was the moment to fear, not this one. That was the time to fight…when the end had finally arrived. These were just the middlemen, and we were worth more to them alive than in pieces.

With my heart pounding beneath the layers of control I clung to, I didn't say a word as a door was opened and a shove between my shoulder blades pushed me into the depths.

Other doors were opened.

Girls disappeared one by one.

We didn't say goodbye, and I doubted we'd ever see each other again.

A lock snapped into place behind me.

A man stood beside a chair that looked like it belonged in a dentist's surgery.

I waited for what came next.

Sullivan

Chapter Two

I STOOD ON THE rocky ledge, overlooking the pristine waters and silky white sand of my beach.

I might as well have been seated on a throne within a seven-story cathedral.

Enter my shores, and I wasn't just the owner of this establishment...

I was god.

And my women were goddesses.

Goddesses to touch and worship and debase to the point of brutality.

But hurt them past our contract, and I took lives as easily as I gave pleasure.

Men came here for what I could offer. For the indulgences I promised.

But not one of them was allowed entry until I agreed.

That was my power.

Piss me off, you're evicted.

Hurt my goddesses, you die.

Simple.

A warm breeze wrapped around me as the helicopter wound down, and the man who hoped he was my next guest climbed gingerly out of it. The helipad was built on a small circle surrounded by basalt rock, signature orchids of my island, and crystal blue water of the sea.

It was a welcoming entry point into paradise.

But it was also the gates of hell if you didn't behave.

I waited with my hands in pinstripe pockets, eyeing him up, assessing who he was.

The investigation into his background showed a financial broker who'd struck it lucky in his early twenties, invested well, and turned one million into five by property developing. Sexual health clean. No physical or mental illnesses. One older brother. Father alive. Mother deceased. Name? Ricky Danrea. For thirty-nine-years old, he'd done okay by success standards but didn't seem to have any luck with a wife.

My staff ushered him up the small bamboo jetty, gave him a welcome drink with yet another orchid, and presented him directly to me.

They all came to me.

No one stayed on my island and played with my women without first being approved.

A piece of paper could only tell you so much about a person.

The eyes were where the truth lay.

Smiling pleasantly, I held out my hand. "Welcome."

"Hello." He shook it, wiping at the sweat already forming on his brow. In pressed taupe shorts and navy polo, he already looked on holiday. Me, on the other hand, looked as if I was headed into a business meeting.

Which was true.

My island was my boardroom.

And this new shmuck?

My latest cash cow.

"Mr. Danrea, how nice of you to request a stay on my humble island."

His blond eyebrow flew up. "Request?" His shoulders braced. "I already paid. There is no request."

I nodded, hiding my patronizing sigh. "I understand. We do have a villa ready for you and are happy to escort you." A staff member appeared with a leather flocked binder and a non-disclosure agreement. "The moment you've signed some paperwork, of course. Along with another minor formality."

"What formality?"

"A trivial affair." I smirked, moving toward him, going too close, popping the bubble of appropriate distance. "Nothing you'll even notice."

He gritted his teeth, standing his ground but pissed off about it. "Tell me, whoever you are, why the fuck am I paying two hundred thousand dollars for a week on this island when your arrival committee is like a pat-down before going to jail?"

My palms itched to do just that.

To tear off his clothes and ensure he wasn't concealing anything that could hurt my goddesses or threaten the private paradise I'd created. Instead, my smirk turned to an icy grin, and I dove deep into his eyes.

Watery blue.

Guarded but weak.

A liar. A coward. A lucky sonuvabitch with no morals.

I didn't like him.

I'd played my role as god for long enough to recognise a bastard.

After all, I was one.

My reflection was a perfect reminder of what not to let onto my shores.

I stepped back, waved the staff member with the NDA away, and clasped my hands behind my back. The helicopter whirred, engines firing, the pilots fully aware they were about to repeat their journey.

"I'll refund you in full, Mr. Danrea. Have a good day."

Turning around, I left my all-powerful ledge, the podium of power, and strolled back down the sandy laneways, through the orchid beds, and beneath the sweeping palm trees.

Serenity fell with birdsong and soft waves lapping at the sand.

I didn't look back as security guards stepped forward, snatched Mr. Danrea, and stuffed him back into the helicopter.

The lost money meant nothing.

I had too much to ever spend.

This wasn't about business anymore.

This was about fantasy.

About freedom.

About fucking.

This was my world, and I was master here.

My island, where I was the law-maker and ruler.

Where I played gods and monsters with goddesses who loved me. Wanted me. Served me.

Who spent their immortality shackled and subservient at my feet.

My office was off-limits to everyone.

No cleaners entered, no staff of any kind. The floors were swept by yours truly. The shelves dusted by a man with untold wealth and severe control issues.

When I'd first found my archipelago, I'd stood on the larger of the forty-four small islands and ushered the real estate agent away. I'd sent him soaring off in his company helicopter, so I could explore the land in peace. I was the only human in the midst of inquisitive parrots and tree frogs, jewelled fish and lethal anemones.

I walked from shore to shore, trading my crisp suit for rolled-up sleeves and dirt-smeared loafers. And in the silence of nature and priceless serenity, I saw a paradise just waiting to be plucked from heaven and tempted deep into sin.

The palm trees rustled with lust, their fronds fondling the warm tropical breeze. The sand whispered about sex and pleasure. The privacy promised any desires would be welcomed.

I hadn't been in the business of flesh peddling. I'd had no intention of using another's assets against them. However, I'd always been shrewd and ruthless, and if I spotted an opportunity…well, I was an opportunist.

As I'd waited for the real estate agent to return, I'd hastily plotted out a business that sprung from debauchery and debasement. I'd always swung toward the darker desires. I'd sampled the underworld of what was on offer in every major city around the world.

And I'd found nothing satisfying.

The clubs where submission and dominance promised titillating desire had been infiltrated by too many wannabes. The hard-core play had become contrived. The truth of no boundaries or borders no longer real.

Subs came with strings.

Clubs came with contracts.

And the permission between legal and illegal became blurred by men who sought to use other's exploitation for their own gain.

And now, I'm one of them.

I smirked at the irony. I shook my head at the inevitability.

Flipping open my laptop, I typed in the thirteen-key password and swiped my fingerprint. The gauzy white curtains fluttered by the open driftwood doors. The squawks of parrots and the squabble of local squirrels fighting over the offerings of fresh fruit

I placed on the intricately carved bird table each morning serenaded me.

I'd bought these islands for me.

To hide. To be free.

After running my parents' pharmaceutical company for a decade, after their yacht sank off the coast of Indonesia, I'd returned to the same area to pay my respects. They had no graves. There were no headstones to confess to. Just clear turquoise water and twinkling islands just waiting to be owned.

Without Sinclair & Sinclair Group, I would never have been able to afford such an impetuous and impromptu purchase. As it was, thanks to my parents' hard work investing in young scientists, along with my own natural inclination toward lab work and ability to cook up new drugs with untried recipes, the company went from private to public to unstoppable.

A billion-dollar behemoth that stole hospital and pharmacy contracts worldwide, undercutting and outperforming so many other household brands of medicine.

Thanks to my tireless work and giving my soul to that company, I had very deep pockets indeed.

So deep, in fact, I'd never reach the bottom or figure out a total number because, each day, that wealth continued to grow. It grew organically, drunk on success, attracting more and more yields, allowing me to buy the secrecy and skills of a very special group of scientists—who I'd personally worked with previously— who ensured my Goddess Isles was more than I'd ever dreamed it could be.

It wasn't just a paradise.

It was a fantasy.

Multiple untold fantasies. Countless whimsical wishes. Endless mythical desires.

In so many fucking delicious ways.

A new email waited to be read, delivered by the secret server and encoded with impenetrable firewalls. Clicking on the message, I skimmed the content.

To: S.Sinclair@goddessisles.com
From: 89082@gmail.com
Subject: New Employee

Dear Mr. Sinclair,

An employee fitting the description you provided us with has just been acquired by our recruiting agency. She has been prepared for her new role. She will arrive for duty at five a.m. local time two days from now.

We appreciate your on-going dealings.

No sign-off. No name. No hint of the traffickers who did the unthinkable.

I re-read the email, seeing the truth behind the lies and the honesty of what I was.

A girl fitting your request has been found and abducted. She has been held for the required time to ensure no police or embassy searches will be a problem. She will be yours by dawn in two days.

Chapter Three

I KEPT THE FLAMES of my hatred hidden as the man forced me into the dentist chair, wrapped the rope around my neck tight to hold me down, and kept my breathing as even as I could as they lashed leather cuffs around my wrists and ankles.

My towel loosened around my body, threatening to reveal things I didn't want to expose, yet I didn't fight as the buckles clinked into place. I didn't let them see the crawling claustrophobia that I struggled to battle from showing.

I'd lasted this long with silence as my weapon; I could last a little more.

The men muttered to each other in Spanish, looking me up and down as the one with surgical gloves sat on a stool and scooted between my legs.

My head fell back onto the sticky leather of my prison. My wet hair chilled me until goosebumps prickled all over. My teeth chattered, but I clenched my jaw, refusing to give them one hint of my rapidly growing fear.

I clamped down on my bottom lip as grotesque fingers entered me. I stared at the mouldy ceiling while he touched places he wasn't welcome. The violation reminded me of the bonfire night. Of the boy who'd tried to feel me up. The night I'd given as an example of bad things to my teacher.

That was nothing, *nothing* compared to this.

Breathe.

Just breathe.

Every molecule that made me *me* crawled.

Every inch of my personality was tested.

My hands wanted to curl into fists, but I prevented them.

My heart wanted to gallop, but I hushed it to stay slow.

The man between my legs looked up the length of my body, his finger driving in and out deliberately, his head cocked as if wary of my reaction. Wary because I wasn't screaming or struggling. Wary because I was totally untouchable.

With a grunt of displeasure, he ripped his touch away, tossed his gloves onto the floor, and scribbled something onto a clipboard. With another grunt to his colleague, he snapped on a fresh pair of gloves and waited until the other man angled my wrist to face upward in its binds.

I kept my eyes on the ceiling.

I stayed unreachable from what they were doing.

I latched onto the knowledge that they weren't worthy of my fear. A chant formed in time with my skipping, hitching pulse.

This is temporary.

Temporary.

Wait until you meet the permanent problem.

The monster who buys you.

Then fight.

Explode.

Never give up.

Until then…temporary,

temporary,

temporary.

I let the word keep my resentment and desire for revenge dormant while the whirr of a tattoo gun sounded, followed by the prick of multiple needles feeding ink into my skin.

I didn't wince.

I didn't object.

I just kept staring at the ceiling, my humanity unbroken and above them.

Temporary.

Temporary.

The tattoo gun finished.

I risked a look as he threw the gun onto the table, then wrapped my newly graffitied wrist with cling-film.

A barcode.

A symbol of sale and merchandise.

My heart skipped.

My breath caught.

It's fine.

Temporary, remember?

Even permanent ink wasn't so permanent.

When I was free, it would be removed by laser.

I would take great pleasure in deleting their marks of arrogant possession.

The men argued in Spanish. One pinched me hard on the thigh. The other jerked at my towel, exposing my breasts. They loomed over me, trying to catch my eye, but I just stared right through them. I didn't give them the satisfaction of acknowledging them.

They were nothing.

Nothing.

They are nothing.

Fire and fury escaped my antifreeze. It whooshed through my blood, heating it to a boil, scalding me from the inside out.

You. Are. NOTHING!

My nostrils flared with repugnance. My throat filled with revulsion. I wanted to shove the tattoo gun down their gullets and scribe curses upon their souls.

I was so close, precariously close, to snapping.

And if I snapped, I would lose it.

I would become wild like that girl Tess.

I would fight and battle and not care if they killed me in my war for freedom.

They smirked and waited for my final break.

They tasted it. They longed for it.

My eyes met theirs, and I released the snarl that'd tainted my tongue for days. "You're worthless scum. No, you're *worse* than scum. You're the insignificant spore on scum. Do whatever you've been told to do and fuck the hell off. You don't deserve my attention."

I trembled with the vicious desire to bite off their noses and slash at their jugulars. I struggled to swallow back the righteous, murderous urges.

In this situation, violence was better than food or water. It was fuel that would sustain me for the trials ahead. And I flatly refused to waste it on them.

With a deep inhale, I forced my muscles to relax, my hands to splay, my lips to drink in oxygen.

Temporary.
Temporary.
They are nothing.

A sharp slap stung my cheek as the gynaecologist turned tattooist let go of his frustration. "You are not better than us. You are a girl about to be sold. You are a fuck toy. A punching bag. A dead woman." He fisted my breast and squeezed painfully, digging his nails into my nipple.

Tears sprang to my eyes, but I endured the pain.

I did not flinch.

I did not cry.

I just kept staring at the ceiling, commanding my blood to calm, my heart to behave, and my will to survive to stay stronger than my call to be feral.

When his abuse earned no reaction, the man let loose a stream of Spanish slurs and grabbed a sterile packet with a syringe.

The packaging crinkled and crackled as he tore through it.

The light glinted off a thick needle.

Nausea clawed through my tight control. I almost broke. I almost thrashed and begged not to be drugged or knocked out, but...I stayed as silent as a tiny mouse. A mouse that could slip through cat's claws because it was wily and quick and nimble.

That was me.

I would be that mouse.

I would slip free...eventually.

One man jerked my neck to the side, while the other happily caused me pain by shoving the needle into my flesh and shooting something inside me.

It burned.

It bruised.

I bit my lip to silence my internal and external reaction.

With faces blackened with hate for me, they scanned my throat with a technological device. Pain blazed as a small beep sounded, and they nodded. "Works. She is tagged." The man tossed the syringe onto his tiny table of horrors, ripped off the gloves, and added them to the pile on the floor, then snapped his fingers. "Take her. *Vamoose.*"

The buckles were unlatched from my wrists and ankles, and the rope around my neck tugged until I collapsed off the chair. The towel slithered off my body. The twine cut off my air supply. I battled with the urge to be above what they'd done to me versus the need to breathe.

Standing, I ignored my nakedness and reached, as regally as I could, to loosen the knot around my throat.

The man with nose hair and bad breath blew putrid kisses at me, grabbing his crotch and promising, "If you not sell tonight, I have you. I'm gonna stick this inside you and find a way to make you scream."

I allowed one act of rebellion.

Two, actually.

One, I gave him the finger.

Two, I strode toward the door without waiting for him, without my towel, and unlocked the handle before storming forward.

My long hair clung damply to my back. My bare skin puckered with cold. The rope snagged tight before he lurched into action and followed me.

The captor following the captive.

He yanked on my leash, signalling to go right instead of left back to the bunkroom. I yielded to his direction. No other girls. No familiar darkness.

I was once again on my own.

One step in front of the other.

Head held high.

Spine braced.

Was Scott looking for me?

Had he alerted the authorities?

Had he been proactive and reported my disappearance or slow to make a decision, thinking I'd gone off on my own?

Our fight a few days before my abduction came to mind.

I'd wanted to travel to Asia next. He'd wanted to go to South America and Mexico. Normally, we could compromise, but I'd found out he'd promised a friend that he'd be in Cancun for a bachelor party next month. I felt cheated out of decision-making, and he was pissed at my unwillingness.

The joys of a new relationship.

The struggles of knowing how to find common ground.

But despite our little domestic, surely he would know I wasn't the type of girl just to walk out after a spat? I was loyal to a fault. I would never cheat or backstab. I would always accept if I was wrong and do my utmost to fix a problem or have the courage to admit it wasn't working.

The trafficker slapped my ass, dragging me back to hell.

I didn't look over my shoulder.

He spat at me.

His horrid saliva trickled down my shoulder blades, sticking in my long hair.

I didn't even shudder.

"*Puta,*" he hissed. "You notice me. You respect me."

I didn't stop walking.

I probably should have stopped walking.

I shouldn't have been so bold in my dismissal of his control. One moment, I was free, the next, a sickening hug enveloped me, his arms coiling tight, squeezing me into him.

His tongue entered my ear.

He ground his erection into my lower back.

His lust was a vile, villainous thing.

I almost snapped.

I almost let out the blood-curdling scream that lived just above my heart. I almost sliced him with every nail I possessed.

But I bit my tongue.

I endured.

He gyrated against me. "Maybe I buy you. Use you for one week and then kill you." He grabbed my hips and pistoned hard into me. My breasts jiggled. My stomach threatened to evict its measly contents.

I just waited for him to stop.

Temporary!

It pissed him off.

It was the last straw on his temper.

Shoving me to the floor, he jerked at the rope around my neck, strangling me from behind. Instinct shot my hands up to link fingers under the twine, pulling at the tightness, seeking air.

Flipping me onto my back, he grunted and snarled in his mother tongue. He punched me in the temple. Lights flashed. Pain swelled.

The sound of his belt clinking open was the universal warning of a man about to take what wasn't his. He tried to shove my legs apart while fumbling at his crotch, reaching for the organ that would never get within an inch of violating me.

I snapped.

Sipping on small amounts of oxygen, I released the rope and rammed my palm up against his nose. After the bonfire, I'd taken self-defence lessons. After understanding that, as a woman, not all men were trustworthy, I traded some of my naivety for preparation.

Blood spurted from his face, raining over my mouth and chin.

He screamed and punched me again, this time in the jaw.

I moaned as pain compounded on top of pain.

He drove his hips into mine. He hadn't pulled his cock out, and he deliberately dry-fucked me with the zipper of his jeans and the metal of his belt.

It hurt.

God, it hurt.

But at least, he wasn't inside me.

I aimed again, using my sharp nails to lacerate the thin flesh behind his ear.

Another yelp followed by a manic filthy curse.

He wrapped both hands around my throat, digging the rope into my skin, strangling me with a demonic look in his weeping eyes. Blood dripped from his broken nose, staining the hair sticking from his nostrils a bright crimson.

Pride had been a helpful tool, wrapping tight around my rapidly fraying outrage. Unfortunately, it had also been my downfall.

A door opened as more instinct overrode my carefully controlled reactions and electrocuted me into fighting. I kicked and fought. I grunted and scratched.

I didn't want to die thanks to this lowly henchman.

I didn't want to be wasted like this.

Stolen and barcoded, tagged and inspected, only to turn into unsaleable produce on the corridor floor.

Legs appeared above me.

Pristine white slacks and polished silver shoes.

Instantly, the man crawled off me, wiping his bleeding nose on the back of his hand and bowing in submission. He spoke in Spanish, but I understood by his gestures that he was begging not to be punished. That he was sorry for his attack.

I let him plead for leniency while I eased myself upright and snatched the twine from around my neck. Throwing it away, I rubbed at the column of bruised muscle and swallowed past the swelling.

"Are you quite well, my dear?"

I hid my surprise at his cultured refinement, standing slowly and blinking past the pain. I turned to face the newcomer but kept my features schooled and silent.

He appraised me like one would judge a filly at a yearling sale. He held no animosity or contempt, just a thin veil of satisfaction that I seemed to be intact and still sellable. Nodding in welcome, he stepped back through the door he'd appeared from. "Come."

Weighing my choices of disobeying and earning more bruises, or following and finding out my fate, I stepped into his office.

The room held a cob-web-covered chandelier, a cluttered desk, and the aura of shattered dreams. He moved to rest his ass on the desk, crossing his arms expectantly.

The man who'd hurt me entered, jabbering in Spanish, pointing at me as if his attack was provoked entirely by my actions. Through his animated speech, the other man never stopped looking at me.

His white skin made him look American, instead of Mexican. A trust fund baby from Florida. His eyebrow rose from whatever lies the trafficker told him before a smile twisted his lips. He could've been called handsome with his white trousers, crisp baby blue shirt, and bright blue eyes.

But he was the head devil in this disgusting den.

The ringleader.

But also…temporary.

Temporary.

He pushed off from the desk, waving at his minion to hush. "You may leave."

The man paused with his mouth open, unfinished with his tale, but with a flash of loathing at me, he nodded and left the room, closing the door behind him.

He left us in silence.

In the gloom behind me sat another man, clad in black and poised in shadow. The American tried to convince me he wasn't a threat, but I tasted the hazardous menace in the air.

He inserted his hands into his slack pockets and eyed me up and down. "So, you're the quiet, silent type." He smiled. "They're the ones who have the farthest to fall."

My chin tipped up. I actually looked into his eyes instead of through him. He was the one exception. "The only one who will fall is you."

He chuckled. "I like your continued confidence that this will all work out for you."

"One day…somehow, someone will come after you and make you wish you'd stayed fiddling with the stock market instead of women's lives."

Licking his bottom lip, he circled around me again.

My skin crawled, but I remained a naked, unfeeling statue.

"Don't you want to beg?" His finger slithered over my shoulder. "Don't you want to know what's in store for you?"

"My questions won't make a difference. My pleas won't make you grow a heart and let me go."

"Wise woman." Chuckling again, he moved to the corner of his office and scooped up a pile of clothing. Throwing them at my feet, he commanded, "Dress. As much as I appreciate your body, I'm not one for sampling my merchandise." His eyes gleamed. "Especially merchandise that has already been sold."

My heart stopped.

Outwardly, I stayed standing and brave.

Inwardly, things crumbled. My stupid hope. My idiotic belief. The quietly ticking clock that promised rescue if I just clung to sanity a little longer.

His smile widened as if he heard my stalled heartbeat.

Tearing my gaze from his, I ducked to collect the offered clothing, wishing I felt as aloof as I did against his band of merry traffickers. With him, I struggled to wrap the cloak of courage around me.

He knew.

He knew my bravery was a cracked and broken shield against the thickening fog of terror inside me. When it shattered for good, I would have nothing left. No weapons to use. No barriers to hide behind. I just had to hope that I would face my final battle before I broke entirely.

Who bought me?

Who would purchase a person?

Fingering the rough cotton, I aired out the largest piece. The clothing was nondescript and meant to fit any body type. A large grey jumper with long sleeves and heavy hem, a pair of white knickers, and two long black socks that reached my knees.

No shoes.

No bra.

No skirt or trousers.

But at least it was protection.

Pulling on the clothes, I tugged my hair from the collar, fanning it out as best I could so the length didn't drench the back of my new wardrobe. I'd always had long hair. As a child, I'd screamed when Mum took me to the hairdresser. I'd gotten in trouble at school if I wore it loose because it was too long. It was more nuisance than privilege, but it was my favourite feature about myself, and I willingly paid the cost.

The American watched me dress. His quiet study erupted goosebumps that refused to obey me and vanish. A shudder also escaped my control as he cocked his head with appreciation. "I can see why he asked for a girl of your description."

I froze.

I did my best not to reveal my curdling panic.

The tattoo on my wrist itched with warning.

"Where are you from, my dear?" He rubbed his jaw as if he couldn't figure it out. "You have English rose skin, yet an American accent. Your hair is dark but not black. Your eyes are light but not coloured. I'm guessing a generous B or small C cup. Your body is lean, so you're aware of the merits of healthy eating and exercise." Without waiting for any confirmation from me, he continued, "How old are you? Twenty? Twenty-two? Definitely no older than late twenties." He smiled. "At least, your body says you're young, yet…your eyes say you're old. That you're already jaded and turned inward. That you think as long as you stay in your mind, you're untouchable."

Stalking across the room, he cupped my cheek, injecting poison into my skin. "You should know that you *are* touchable. Very much so. In every way possible." His hand slid from my cheek to my breast. "Your new owner will make sure of that."

I sucked in a breath as he let me go.

I allowed a moment of weakness as he turned his back, heading to sit behind his desk.

I collapsed into myself, trembling until my bones rattled.

But, by the time he faced me again, my nostrils flared once with air and my proud shoulders smoothed the shivers from debilitating fear.

Pulling out a file, he tapped it importantly. "Inside here are travel documents to fly you to your new master. We know everything we need to know to provide an adequate delivery to him. However…" He smiled as if he had every right to ask a tiny favour. "I would very much like to know your name. Other girls scream at me, some beg at my feet. Many cry. A few bargain. Yet you…you stare at me as if you're above me, even while I hold your bill of sale." His eyes narrowed with barely restrained monstrosity.

He had a talent like mine.

He could hide his true nature behind his gentile conversation, but beneath that lurked a man who got off on the capture and conquest of trading women.

I stepped toward him, steeling myself against his truth. "Why do you think I would share anything that belongs to me?" My voice resembled a tabby cat with unsheathed claws. "My name is mine."

"That's why I asked politely."

I balled my hands, unable to stop myself. "Will you let me go if I ask *politely*?"

He laughed under his breath. "You're smarter than that, and we've already covered that scenario." Sighing with an undercurrent of respect, he said, "I'll tell you what. Give me your name, and I'll give you a tiny trifle in return."

"What trifle?"

"What do you want?"

"My freedom."

"Yes, but that's already been purchased, my dear. You'll have to ask your new owner about your fate. Maybe he'll give you your freedom if you please him. Maybe he'll kill you and grant your freedom that way. Or maybe you'll grow old in service until the end of your sexual days. Either way…tonight you will be delivered to him. This is your one chance to ask for something before all those choices are taken away."

"Will you hurt my family if you tell you who am I?"

He grinned. "Do you have a little sister who looks like you? Because I have another interested party who would look after her very well indeed."

I ignored the desire to vomit at the thought. "I'm an only child."

"Ah, that's disappointing." He smirked. "You have my word then. Your mother is too old. Your father is of no interest. I promise they are safe if you tell me who you are."

"Send them a letter. Tell them what happened to me. Give them the name of the man who bought me. Give them a chance to rescue me."

The man lurking in shadow let out a guffaw. The American snickered, his blue eyes twinkling with mirth. "You have balls, girl. I'll give you that."

"His name for my name."

He cocked his head, studying me deeper than he ever had. The moment stretched uncomfortably before he murmured, "I'll send them a letter and tell them what happened to you. There will be no chance of rescue or details destined to set you free, but at least they will have closure over your disappearance. They will know they will never see you again."

Tears pricked from nowhere, undermining my self-control.

The thought of my mother opening such a letter. The idea of my father learning his daughter was traded into sexual servitude.

No.

It would kill them.

But...if this was my last chance to say goodbye, then at least I could give them some resemblance of peace.

Even if I won't earn any myself.

Bracing myself, I closed the distance between us and held out my hand over his desk. "Send them a letter saying I've eloped and found endless happiness. Tell them I'm happy and safe, and they never have to worry about me again. Tell them I'm selfish and cruel to disappear but I love them. For always."

His stood and slipped his hand into mine. "Done."

We shook.

We sealed the agreement.

I shivered.

I couldn't help it.

The coolant in my bloodstream turned into ice crystals. The cage I'd placed around my heart webbed with thicker wire.

I was bartering with Lucifer...not for my own protection, but for those I would never see again.

His fingers squeezed mine, his eyes flickered to the man who'd moved from his spot in the shadows and loomed behind me.

I felt him there.

I heard him waiting.

My skin prickled.

My instincts cried.

But I completed my end of the bargain.

"My name is Eleanor Grace. And I will—"

A rag smashed over my mouth, stopping my oath. Preventing me from promising that I would win. That I would find a way to murder whatever monster who'd bought me and survive.

Fumes entered my nose, attacking my ability to stand.

My knees gave out as the world turned dizzy.

Bulky arms caught me, and the last thing I heard before everything went black was the American murmuring, "Goodbye, Eleanor Grace. Graceful to the end and elegant to a fault. Mr. Sinclair will enjoy destroying you."

Sullivan

Chapter Four

"SIR, SHE'S ARRIVED IN Java. The crew are ready to collect."

"Send the doctor first. Remove that damn tracker they insist on putting into their stock."

"Yes, sir." My second in command, Calvin Moor, nodded. He wore his typical suit even though the tropical heat made thick fabric unbearable. The humidity level, even at dawn, didn't give any reprieve. "I'll arrange the removal, and then you're happy for final transportation?"

"Yes." I looked back at my laptop and the latest test results from my scientists. Cal got the message that I was done with him and discreetly let himself out.

Only five a.m. and I'd already been for a swim around the island and met with yet another early bird arrival. Instead of sending this latest guest away, he was allowed to stay.

An older gentleman from Texas. Oil flowed in his veins as surely as blue blood from an American founding family. He was ruthless in business and had special perversions, but he could be trusted to play by my rules.

I tried to keep my mind on business, but it kept trickling back to my latest acquisition.

Had they found someone fitting my requirements?

Was she in good repair or damaged while in captivity and transit?

Could I put her to work straight away or would she require a gentler welcome than some of the more experienced employees I'd 'hired'.

Reclining in the expensive ergonomic desk chair that caused back pain rather than cured it, I raked a hand through my sleek, dark hair. Saltwater and sunshine did its best to bleach the ebony, but it never quite managed. The best it could do was decorate the tips with an island bronze that pretended I had a heart somewhere beneath my ruthlessness.

I'd bought enough from this current dealer to know the stock came from all areas of the globe. Their favourite hunting grounds were backpackers and run-down restaurants in Mexico, but they also travelled abroad, taking their prey back to some secret facility where they held them until the noise of media and outrage of loved ones either became too hot to be a viable transaction or proved their selection wouldn't be hugely missed.

Those who ended up on every media channel and lit a fire under police's asses were released. Those who faded into obscurity were devoured by men like me.

Men with cash to purchase such things.

Things like souls.

I didn't mind the ethics behind trafficking as long as the merchandise was humanely treated. In my opinion, the human race couldn't have it both ways.

We couldn't torture, eat, and abuse animals and think ourselves immune.

We couldn't artificially and forcibly breed animals for consummation and not expect us to be above such treatment. A cow was raped, and its calf torn away and most likely slaughtered before it even had proper hide on its foetal body—all for the dairy industry to pump milk to a population who didn't realise it was slowly murdering them with disease. Lambs were butchered when barely weaned for Sunday roasts. And chickens…shit, billions of those unfortunate feathered fiends were locked in cages, had their necks cut off and their carcasses filled with carcinogens to extend shelf life, only to be bought and tossed out after their expiration date without ever being eaten.

Wasteful.

Distasteful.

Gross.

If society allowed such barbarity to other sentient beings, why couldn't I benefit from trading in fellow humans? After all, I provided them with a free-range existence—to a degree. I fed them the best food money could buy. They had medical treatment, pleasure time, freedom within my laws. All they had to do was provide a service.

We *all* had to provide a service.

From the newly born to the elderly. We were all slaves, ensuring the economy stayed afloat and not crumble into dust at our feet.

I was no different.

My goddesses were no different.

Traffickers and slavers and people captured and bound were no different.

The only difference between my girls and the girls working for some hotshot Wall Street exec was I offered free living, food, and healthcare. The poor girls on a pittance of a salary were one medical disaster away from destitution and bankruptcy.

In reality, my islands of temptation were fucking heaven compared to the rest of the fucked-up cesspit of a globe.

My goddesses should be thanking me.

And they did.

Once they get to know me.

Shoving away the anticipation of my latest purchase's arrival, I returned to the facts and findings on a revised elixir my scientists had been working on. All those years I'd slogged in high-tech labs, the connections I'd cultivated, and persistence I'd nursed—it had all been worth it.

The numbers didn't lie.

The potency was stronger than ever.

I hadn't just founded utopia; I'd created ambrosia.

I fed my immortal goddesses the nectar of the gods, all so they could serve to their highest power.

What sort of monster would do that?

What sort of beast would ensure his conquests wanted to serve him?

Begged to serve him?

Who pleaded to stay…even when he set them free?

Chapter Five

THE HELICOPTER SWOOPED FROM azure sky to aquamarine ocean.

My stomach flipped at the sudden weightlessness, the sensation of skipping across air and gliding through invisible gravity.

The islands below scattered like coins spilled from a billionaire's pocket. Some were smaller than a one-bedroom apartment. Others were large enough for a burst of palm trees to stand tall, dusted with rainbow-winged parrots.

Glittering golden, almost crystal sand winked from the bays of the larger atolls, while the tiny dots of land fought with the overwhelming turquoise-ness of the ocean to be seen.

The traveller's blood inside me fizzed with amazement. The wanderer's need to explore unseen places and walk untouched shores where others hadn't gone before made me forget, just for a second, that I'd been brought here against my will.

A buffet of air punched the helicopter, wrenching it to the side as we hovered and continued to descend toward the capital H painted on a bamboo floating dock. Whitecaps appeared on the otherwise deathly calm sea, ferns frolicked in the updraft of the rotor blades and three men in white shorts and polo shirts waited with their hands clasped behind their backs, looking up at us.

Looking up at me.

I sat in the back of the helicopter on my own.

No ropes, no cuffs, no method of imprisonment.

The pilots paid no attention to me, concentrating entirely on delivering me and not falling out of the sky.

After the long journey I'd had—shoved in a coffin-shaped box with basic air holes, a packet of stale crackers, out-of-date fat-riddled salami, two bottles of water, and a bucket for calls of nature, this was an incomparable method of transportation.

I didn't know how long I'd flown in that wooden coffin, but the ringing of my ears and the ice on my skin said it wasn't with a commercial airline. I'd been cargo. Smuggled. Hidden.

I'd faded in and out of consciousness, thanks to whatever drugs they'd given me, and I'd resorted to using the bucket and nibbling on stale crackers, doing my best to stay warm in the useless wardrobe they'd dressed me in. I'd left the salami, despite the hunger pangs growing more and more insistent.

Giving up meat hadn't been a conscious decision, more like a fundamental barrier I could no longer cross. I'd never liked the taste of cooked animal flesh, and one day, just like that, my moral compass and taste buds revolted.

That'd been four years ago.

What would happen to that personal choice now none of my choices belonged to me? Would I be fed a diet of carcass and animal products? Given the option of inedible food or starvation? Or would I be allowed to maintain my regimen?

The questions added to the thousands of others I'd had since I'd woken to the swoop of a Boeing shooting me from earth to sky and taking me to who the hell knew where.

In my wooden box, I'd had nothing to waste the time away with, so I'd latched onto questions instead of regrets. I couldn't think about Scott or the blossoming relationship we'd shared. I couldn't think about my friends I'd left behind or the fact I hadn't called my parents in weeks because international roaming was so expensive.

I tried to stop thinking that my Facebook page would become one of the countless ghost accounts of people who'd died and no one had removed their profiles. I would be there, but gone. Alive, but missing. I would become an unsolved mystery, only causing heartbreak until time obscured even that and my family moved on.

That won't happen.

You'll escape before then.

Escape?

I hugged myself as the helicopter hummed above the bay of the largest island in the sprawling vista we'd flown over. The shores wrapped into the distance, north and south, the sand held deck chairs and beached kayaks, the palm trees hid the thatched roofs of accommodation, and the idyllic paradise that should've graced any glossy travel magazine as an exclusive, expensive vacation, hinted that nestled within the pretty purple orchids and manicured sandy pathways hid people.

One person in particular.

Someone who'd reduced me to a possession he thought he could own.

He's wrong.

But...escaping?

Despite my best intentions and regardless of my resolution not to give up, I didn't see a way free. Wherever we were, gallons and gallons of water stood between me and safety. I could swim, but I wasn't the strongest. I could try to call for help, but would an island this far out to sea have internet and phone lines?

I didn't have a clue where I was.

After the plane had touched down and my coffin with its many tiny holes was unloaded, I'd been driven into an aviation hangar. There, the nails had been pried off and my lid opened, only for two men with black hair and exotic eyes to hoist me unceremoniously from my little nest.

My muscles were stiff.

My body covered in bruises.

My legs useless after being bent for so long.

I'd tripped but forced feeling and fight to course through my blood as they dragged me forward.

I hadn't spoken to them, and they hadn't spoken to me, merely guiding me into a small office inside the hangar where the whiffs of fuel and jet planes were replaced with paper and technology.

No one occupied the space, and the desk was uncluttered from work.

They'd shoved me into a plastic chair, given me another bottle of water and a small muesli bar, allowed me to use the bathroom, then waited for something.

Someone.

When the doctor arrived, I'd expected it to be *him*.

The monster who'd purchased me.

But he'd been young—either straight out of medical training

or still studying. He didn't wear scrubs or have the aura of a medical professional. Instead, his hands shook a little as he pointed at my neck where the tracker had been inserted and my skin still smarted.

His black eyes stated he was from a hot country and not the west. His tanned skin and black hair best suited for long sunshine hours and humidity.

I'd noticed the muggy heat when they'd opened the plane.

I felt it in the heaviness of my hair and the slight tackiness to my skin. At least I wasn't cold anymore. I preferred the tropics. My internal thermostat was better suited for heat than for cold.

Knowing I must be close to the equator didn't help much. I could be in any Asian, Indonesian, or Polynesian country.

No one spoke to give away a language or accent. No one blatantly said, *"Hello, Eleanor. Welcome to such and such. We're sorry about the upheaval of your life. How about we put you on a plane and return you to your boyfriend straight away?"*

Shoving away such stupid thoughts, I'd stayed frozen as he'd rested on his haunches, opened a bag with syringes, scalpels, and other sterilized equipment all wrapped in individual packets, and proceeded to localize an area of my throat, nick my skin with a wicked-looking blade, and pull the tracker free with a pair of tweezers.

I hadn't fought him.

I didn't make his job difficult.

I'd wanted that nasty thing removed, and he'd done it.

I even smiled in thanks as he dropped the rice-shaped deceive onto the floor and crushed it beneath his shiny black shoe.

He didn't stitch my wound closed, just applied some sort of adhesive, pressed a small bandage over it, then turned his attention to the rope burn around my throat and wrists, the bruise on my temple, the freshly oozing tattoo, and raised his eyebrow expectantly, asking universally, even if we didn't speak the same language, if I had any other ails.

I'd wanted to tell him to give me his cell phone. To ask him to free me. But he stood when I didn't point at other injuries and began to pack up his tricks. The salve he'd put on my bruises and the cream he'd put on my tattoo all went back into the depths of his bag and vanished behind its zipper.

The two bodyguards stayed close beside me, removing any hope that I might be able to bolt with this young doctor and hop on the closest plane home.

Home...

Will I ever see it again?

I'd asked that far too many times as I'd been ushered from the hangar, shoved onto the silver helicopter, and endured a stern-faced pilot strapping me into a five-point harness.

Before I could wriggle free, the engine started, the clouds dropped strings from the heavens, tied us tight, and ripped us from the ground in one swift pull. We'd left behind one destination for another, swooping out to sea just as the sky lightened with a new day.

The sunrise had been spectacular.

All tangerines and apricots bathed in golden threads as the sun stretched and yawned.

It was no longer dawn.

The sun had reclaimed its place in the sky and blinded out the stars, giving me the final glittering view of my new home.

How cruel that my imprisonment was prettier than any dream I could imagine. How unfair that my cage was the Garden of Eden. A Shangri-La dripping in promise and protection, hiding the sinister snakes and sin at its core.

My bones rattled as the helicopter finally stopped teasing with descent and landed slightly too hard on the helipad.

I'd arrived.

Sullivan

Chapter Six

I WAS LATE TO my own welcome party.

I was the host and owner, the life-giver and keeper of the new goddess who'd just stepped onto my shores, and I'd missed her touchdown.

Shit.

Slipping my arms into my silk-cashmere blazer, I strode down the sandy lane linking my office to the jetty where every conquest and guest was processed. Unlike my high-paying guests, my inspection would last longer than just a stare into their eyes and quick appraisal of their personality. With guests, I'd already done my research. Background checks and online sleuthing yielded enough to make a calculated guess that I could weed out the behaved from the reckless.

But a new goddess?

I knew nothing.

I want to know everything.

Buttoning a silver engraved button, I smoothed out my graphite suit and stepped into the sunlight just as the girl was unbuckled from the helicopter and given a hand to help her climb the three steps down.

She didn't recoil from the courteous offer of help. She didn't screech or scratch or act stupid in any way. Instead, she held her head high, inserted her hand into the staff member's waiting below, and allowed him to guide her down the jetty bobbing on the gentle waves caused by the landing as he escorted her all the way to me.

I didn't move, studying her every step.

She was taller than some of my other employees. She was willowy, but her legs weren't weak, skinny things. They were toned with flickers of muscle beneath alabaster skin. Even barefoot, she moved with assurance and a liquid type of sensuality.

She didn't stumble or shy away, even when she looked up to my palm tree-surrounded podium and caught my gaze. Her full lips parted as she inhaled—the only sign of nerves—before gritting her teeth and arching her chin higher.

She didn't look like she'd been bought and smuggled here. She seemed as impenetrable as a paying patron. A female looking to indulge in her own devious tastes.

She didn't act like any of my other goddesses. Their reactions ranged from tears to tempers and everything in between. I'd had to duck a swinging fist or pluck a sobbing girl from the sand. I'd cajoled and cursed, laying out my laws to wild-eyed and fury-filled women.

But not this one.

This one moved like she had a crown upon her head. A crown made of dignity and diamonds, heavy on her brow but invaluable to her sense of worth. Her ankles were narrow, her wrists delicate, her collarbones perfect sweeps of femininity leading to the elegant line of a regal throat.

For the first time, I felt a kick of interest.

A brief skip in my familiar cold-hearted heartbeat.

Closer and closer she came.

Harder and harder the kick of intrigue.

Waving my hand, I signalled the staff member to let her go, to step aside, to vanish. He bowed his head immediately, relinquishing her hand and backing away to subtly disappear to complete one of the countless chores he was paid to do.

I waited to see what the girl would choose.

She was technically free.

She could run back to the sea.

She could leap into the salt and try to swim to freedom.

She could attack me.

She could plead with me.

She could self-harm or shutdown or scream until her tongue turned crimson with blood.

Yet she did none of those things.

Her bare feet sank into the crystal sugar sand. Her breakable fingers fluttered once by her sides as if she fought the urge to curl them. Her head tilted, cascading incredibly long, tangled hair over her shoulder.

Knotty and dull, the length was a distraction from the otherwise pleasing features of her face. Pixy chin, high cheekbones, smoky grey eyes, and eyebrows that slashed across her smooth brow with temper and seething refinement.

Fuck, the price I could charge for a night with her.

Even straight out of her abduction, with shadows smudging her beauty from travel, rope burn around her neck, tattooed barcode on her wrist, and bruises marking her otherwise perfect skin from her punishments, she was a fucking natural-born immortal.

Raw and untouched, she bristled with injustice and courage. She could be Artemis's reincarnation or perhaps Aphrodite's twin.

She didn't need to be turned into a goddess, she was one.

One I very much wanted to yank from the stars and slander with every debasing, demeaning, and downright disgusting act I could think of.

The kick of interest turned into a lick of lust.

I'd never sampled my stock. I didn't play with the toys my customers paid for.

But her...fuck, I was tempted.

Sorely, *deliciously* tempted.

Our eyes locked, grey to blue.

My island, my pride and joy and deliverer of fantasies, vanished behind a suffocating void. There was no parrot chatter. No jasmine breeze. No lapping waves.

There was just her.

The dark-haired, coldly judging, queenly, impenetrable girl.

My lust thickened, coiling from my belly to my cock.

I curled my hands, fighting my body's reaction to swell, to heat, to crave this innocent consort.

And then, she moved of her own accord.

Not away from me, but toward me.

My legs locked, my body turned rigid, my heartbeat increased into a steady pound of hunger.

She stopped with a metre between us. The grey jumper she wore hid her body, but it couldn't belie that beneath the fabric was yet more wonder. Shapes and sinew. Curves and caverns. A girl who was grace and elegance.

"Are you him?"

Fuck, her voice.

Low pitched but soft. Husky but feminine.

Shit, her lips.

Naturally peach with a stung bottom fullness and shapely bow. Everything about her mouth was made for sucking a man's cock and granting him every pleasure he requested.

My suit became tight.

My blood hissed into my trousers, adding pressure to my throbbing erection, reminding me it'd been a fucking age since I'd stuck that part of myself into another. Since I'd stopped indulging in my own fantasies to focus on delivering them to others. Since I'd become disillusioned with the idea of fucking an immortal. Since my illusions had skipped the binds of reality and ensured sex with normal could never compete with the soul-quaking fucking of a siren or angel.

Well, hadn't my dreams just been fucking granted?

What was she? *Who* was she? Where in the goddamn hell had she come from?

Those traffickers deserved a raise. A bonus. A place in eternal paradise for delivering her.

She's mine.

Bought and paid for.

I swallowed hard, battling the undeniable black satisfaction that gave me.

I didn't have to rent her for a night.

I didn't have to give her back after I came deep inside her.

She was mine.

All mine.

Her eyes narrowed, glaring grey daggers. "Are you him?" she repeated.

I snapped out of the void. The black silence popped, bringing back the scents of orchids and fresh pineapple, the whisper of ferns and fronds, the squawk of birdlife.

"Depends on who you think I am."

It was her turn to strike stupid.

Her gaze glazed for a moment as if stunned by something painful. Her lips parted. Her body swayed. The energy between us crackled, not with strangers meeting for the first time, but two creatures suddenly ravenous for fucking.

I couldn't help it.

She couldn't help it.

It was natural.

Life's design, and fate's purpose.

Men came here to fuck.

I welcomed them to choose their preferred goddess.

But this one...she'd been tailored for me. Her body already wore my mark. Her heart already stuttered for me to snatch her, mount her, fuck her until we both either entered the Kingdom of Heaven or plummeted to the Gates of Hell.

I was fine with either destination.

As long as I could taste, touch, *own*.

Shaking her head, she blinked and balled her hands. A trace of defiance, a flicker of annoyance, but most of all, no sign that she'd felt the undercurrent of greed that'd sprang from nowhere and still tainted the island heat around us.

"I think you're a man with ludicrous, grandiose ideas that he has some right to buy another."

A smile stretched my lips. "And yet...here you are. Bought and paid for."

"I'm not some shopping list you get to jot down and have slaves collect for you."

"No, that would be *slavers* who caught and delivered you. Not slaves." I looked her up and down. "The only slave here is you."

She jerked back. "So...you don't deny it?"

"Deny what?"

"That you're a monster who buys others."

I leaned toward her, pleasantly surprised and dangerously turned on when she didn't back down. When her nostrils flared as if smelling my sea salt skin and the coconut cologne I religiously used. When her grey gaze turned a rich shadow with things that tempted me beyond belief. "I don't deny it. After all, my money brought you to my shores. Here you are. All mine." My belly twisted with lethal desire.

I pitied her, really.

The other goddesses had it easy. They'd been welcomed to my island, settled into their new home, advised of their strict guidelines, and prepared for their exclusive employment.

Not once did they intrigue me like this one.

Not once were they in danger of charming me like a perfectly prepared appetizer.

Poor, poor thing.

My client's tastes might be varied and vulgar. They might

have rascally needs and wicked fantasies, but they didn't come close to my depraved desires.

I stepped back.

I couldn't.

For all the provocation her majesty enticed me, she was worth far more to me in servitude than in my bed.

The moment the guests saw her, she'd be requested.

Again and again.

I could charge double. Triple. A thousandfold.

And they'd pay it.

Not because of her elegant polish but because such perfection called out wolves to maul. She promised an end to the famine of boredom. She and her invisible crown just begged, fucking *begged*, to be pawed and clawed and fornicated.

She was priceless.

"Come. Let me show you around your new cage." Stepping back, I opened my arm wide, waiting for her to step into my dominion.

Chapter Seven

HE STOOD THERE, SURROUNDED by palm frond shadows, his arm spread, revealing a suit that clung to his rigid, flawless body.

No beer belly. No flabby jowls. No pockmarked skin or terrible body odour.

Why did he have to look like every element of my wanton dreams come to life?

It wasn't fair.

Fate had somehow read my fantasies and stitched together every facet that I found appealing in the male sex, improving on the design, fabricating something inherently faultless, all while hiding the rot deep inside.

I already found his personality appalling.

When he'd spoken, I'd suffered a visceral reaction of loathing.

His cultured, clipped baritone dripped with blackness. It'd reached inside me and left an oily, suffocating residue on my heart. My organs felt like the sticky feathers of dying seabirds, iridescent from grease and entirely unwashable.

I knew what he was.

I wasn't stupid—not when it came to him. I didn't need to be worldly to understand that this was not a man. This was not someone I could ever trust or let my guard down with.

He was an untamed hunter. He was sheathed claws and hidden teeth; a well-groomed pelt hiding the viciousness within.

I forced courage that I didn't have into my snippy voice. "I prefer to skip the tour and, instead, negotiate the terms of my freedom."

"Oh, you would, would you?" His lips twitched into a small smile. His head tilted just slightly, as if tasting my fight and battling his own reaction toward me. It seemed I wasn't the only one hyperaware.

My awareness came from adrenaline and the chemical makeup of my body as it sought a way free. Everything was brighter, sharper, louder. That was why I noticed so much about him.

The *only* reason.

What was his?

Compared to Scott, this man was from a different galaxy. He'd not only been forged from all the best pieces a male could inherit but had somehow improved upon the perfection.

His calculating, unreadable blue eyes had poisonous hooks designed to snag and trap, rendering me breathless. His glossy dark hair fought to remain entirely ebony, but the tips rebelled with a sparkle of sun-given bronze. His nose was straight, his chin strong, his cheekbones refined as any blue-blood. The dark scruff on his face was another hint of rebellion to perfection—darker than a five o'clock shadow but not quite a beard. It acted as the perfect frame for his mouth.

I tore my gaze away from his harsh lips and the flash of a tempestuous tongue.

He gave in to his smile, letting it twist harshness into cruelty. "I'm not in the mood for negotiations."

"And I'm not in the mood to be purchased."

"That's convenient because the transaction has already been completed."

I crossed my arms. "How much?"

He looked me up and down as if wondering who the hell I was. "Excuse me?"

"How much did you pay?"

He narrowed blue eyes that mimicked the sky above. "Too much for you to ever comprehend."

"Tell me a number."

"I don't discuss business with my possessions."

My temper made me quake. I couldn't contain it. My feet sank into sun-warmed sand, my toes curling for purchase. "I'm *not* your possession."

"We'll discuss titles and what you are later." He frowned at the glowing sunshine beaming upon us. "For now, follow me. Discussions are always less fraught in the shade."

Without waiting for me to respond, he turned and stepped in shiny expensive shoes down the sandy path. Once again, I was struck mute at the power emitting from him.

The irreproachable varnish over his every move. The self-possessed carriage and undeniable assurance that everyone obeyed him without question.

I didn't want to obey him.

I wanted to march back to the beach and keep going until the sea claimed me. I wanted to approach a staff member and enquire if this was all a mistake and I was free to go.

Or…you could stop wasting time, quit admiring a monster, and get this over with.

Looking around at paradise, I was more wary of perceived open spaces than I was with subtle guards watching my every move. I'd been given the illusion of free will. But in reality…there was no such thing on this island.

There might not be iron bars or padlocked gates, but this was still a prison. The only difference was nature kept me trapped rather than manmade devices.

The sooner I learned his vulnerabilities and what I could use to my advantage, the better.

With a heavy sigh, I tightened the cape of my courage…and followed him.

He didn't slow his long gait, and I hurried to keep up as he vanished around a corner planted with a spray of colourful flowers. Another corner. A breeze sweet with honeysuckle. Another laneway twist. A dabble of shadow beneath trees. Until, finally, the pathway turned into a small courtyard, trading sand for basalt tile.

My feet froze on the border of yet another paradise.

The courtyard held a fountain of three mermaids tipping water from seashells, the droplets spritzing in the sun and creating hundreds of rainbows. They were naked, and their breasts gleamed with pearlescent scales, the colour cascading down their sides to mystical tails.

The tropical plants bordering the space ranged from light green to dark forest, all lush and glossy, heavy with fruit and flowers. A bird table sat on the wooden deck, big enough for an entire flock of finches to land and take their fill of speared pineapple, juicy watermelon, and a splattering of banana, mango, and sunflower seeds.

The man who thought he owned me strode up the three steps to his deck, tapped his shoes against the side of the villa to remove loose sand, then disappeared past the floaty curtains and through open French doors.

His black voice feathered back to me, disjointed from the beauty of such a place. "Stop wasting my time and come inside."

My eyes skipped over the idyllic space as I skirted around the fountain, earned a few droplets on my skin that leaped from the mermaid's hands, and ducked a low flying parrot as it landed on the bird table. Bracing myself, I traded the overwhelming heat of outside for the relieving cool of inside.

A rattan fan spun lazily in the open rafters of a thatched roof, pushing hot air out and leaving refreshing oxygen behind.

The décor was silver and white with a splash of woven grass. The wood was all silvered driftwood, the walls whitewashed, the furniture light and clean lines. The woven flax on the floor set off the white couch, glass coffee table, and the large driftwood desk perfectly.

Artwork of green-sketched ferns and ghostly silhouettes of half-drawn women hung huge and imposing.

A door in the opposite wall led to a bathroom sparkling with opalescent mosaic tiles from floor to ceiling. Glass replaced the ceiling, drenching the space in sunshine. The basin was one large carved piece of black marble, and the shower big enough for four people.

Two more doors led to rooms that were closed, but the openness and simplicity of the lounge did its best to relax me, even as my instincts stayed on high alert.

What *was* this place?

The entire villa could've been feminine, if it wasn't for the man seated within the centre. A man who could cover himself in pearls and prisms and still not be able to reflect anything than what he was.

Merciless and undeniably masculine.

He flicked a pen over his knuckles, watching me in a silent, lethal way.

My stomach coiled, blending fear with unwanted need.

He didn't need to purchase women to earn every sexual favour he desired. Anyone—single and sane—would struggle not to be entranced by him.

If we'd met under different circumstances, I would've expected him to be untouchable by people like me. People of a middle-class persuasion. He didn't need to buy me to say he had money. It was obvious he had mountains and skyscrapers of the stuff. He bled wealth. He breathed affluence. He was the epitome of abundance—abundant physical assets, monetary riches, and a treasure chest of private islands.

I didn't move.

He didn't speak.

We never looked away from each other.

I stood at the foot of his desk while he reigned on his throne. A lowly servant at court waiting for her liege's command.

I hated the way he made me feel.

I despised the heat creeping through my veins.

But...I had to admit.

I'd hated the traffickers in Mexico.

I'd nursed my hate like a glowing ember, feeding it twigs of injustice to stay aflame, tossing a few dried leaves of righteousness for fuel.

But this man?

This man threatened to turn that flickering coal into a furnace.

One look from him and my heartbeat relocated into every extremity, and my temperature increased a thousand degrees.

I *detested* him.

But I was drawn to him.

There was something...something ruthless and savage about him. Something instinctual that sensed predator from prey and firmly put him in the category of dangerous.

But beneath that savage suaveness, something smoothed the merciless edges, granting a strange kind of enigma.

Cold and hot.

Immune and unprotected.

He wasn't as invincible as he appeared.

Find his weaknesses.

Use them.

Abuse them.

Get free.

"What is your name?" he asked quietly. Too quietly.

I narrowed my eyes, ignoring my aches and bruises. "I already gave my name to them. They didn't pass on that information?"

He let the pen fall from his knuckles. It clattered against the desk, making me jump. "No. We're not in the habit of gossip."

"My name is not gossip."

"Your name is no longer yours."

I stepped closer to his desk, purely because every part of me wanted to run in the opposite direction. "My name is and always will be mine. No matter if you think you can own me. No matter that you paid some bastard his fee. I am a living, breathing creature, and you cannot—"

"Enough." He swiped his hand through the air, silencing me. "I'll go first, shall I? My name is Sully Sinclair. I don't care what you call me inside that overzealous mind of yours, but while you serve on my island, you will address me with respect."

"*While* I serve you?" My lips pulled back in a snarl. "And what does that job entail exactly?"

His lips spread into a sinister smile. "Fucking, of course. Lots and lots of fucking." Dropping his stare, he deliberately undressed me with his eyes. My nipples pebbled as he studied my breasts. My skin goosebumped as he trailed down my belly to my core and beyond.

It didn't matter I wore a sack-shaped jumper. It didn't matter I had underwear on.

I was naked.

Well and truly stripped to my barest of forms, and my hatred reached a whole new level. I was tired, jet-lagged, strung out, and in pain. I missed Scott, my parents, and my carefree, untouched life. To be told that I'd been reduced to a whore—worse than a whore—an unpaid sexual slave…yeah, I reached my shaky threshold.

"I will *never* fuck you. You'll have to kill me."

He laughed under his breath, rich and deep. "Who said anything about fucking *me?*" His eyebrows shaded icy blue eyes. "I'm the proprietor of this paradise. You work for me to entertain my high-paying guests." He stood, moving slowly around his desk toward me.

I wished I hadn't taken off my knee-high socks in the helicopter. I could've used one to strangle him.

"My clients range from young to old, handsome to obese, generous to monstrous. They all come here for one purpose." He stopped within touching distance but kept his hands to himself. "That purpose is to fuck. To let their darker desires come out to play. To do things to you that they would never do to their wives."

I hid my shudder. "Why don't they pay someone, like normal

people?"

"Pay?" His eyebrow shot up. "Oh, they do pay. They pay me very well indeed."

"I mean, why don't they just hire a prostitute? A woman who actually gets to keep what she earns and not someone like you who buys unwilling trafficked women."

He laughed. The sound rolled like thunder with a hint of rain. "If you think prostitutes get to keep what they earn, you're a very naïve little girl."

I bristled at the word. I'd admit when I was young, I was naïve. Just like my teacher said. But...that was before. This was now. I'd grown up since. I'd opened my eyes and matured to the ways of corruption and greed.

I didn't drop eye contact even though his blue gaze resembled the inside of a fire. The hottest part that glowed past orange and yellow. The nucleus where even metal could be melted. "Don't you see how wrong this is? To purchase a woman with the sole intention of using her against her will?" I allowed a thread of vulnerability to enter my voice, seeking some sort of humanity through the intolerance he wielded. "How can you justify stealing my life for your gain? Can't you empathise? Imagine if you were snatched from your partner and beaten, tattooed, and imprisoned by men, then sold to someone who promises a future of fucking until you're no longer of use. You ought to be locked up. You should have your freedom taken and then see—"

"Silence." Grabbing my cheeks, he squeezed until my mouth pursed and words were an impossibility. My skin heated beneath his touch, sickly and desperate to get away.

"So, you had a boyfriend in your previous life." He sneered. "I can assure you, whatever tame boy you were in love with will never see you again."

I didn't bother enlightening him that Scott and I were good travel partners with similar personalities, but as far as love went? I wasn't in love with him. Five months wasn't long enough to know...was it? He might've ended up being the one or...we might've gone our separate ways.

Either way, my relationship was beside the point.

The point was this bastard had *stolen* me.

He thought he was god, and I had to obey.

No.

Just no!

I raised my hands to push him away. I went to tear my face

from his hold.

But he trapped me before I'd even formulated the thought. His hand caught my wrists, hurting my fresh tattoo, shackling them together while his fingers dug harder into my jaw, promising pain if I didn't submit.

"Don't fight. I see it there in your eyes. I feel it in your pulse beneath my touch." Ducking until his nose brushed over my ear, he whispered threateningly, "I wouldn't pick a battle you can't win. I don't want to hurt you any more than you already are. Not because I have compassion, but because you won't be able to work as soon as I require. However, push me...and I won't hesitate to remind you of your new place. With as much force as necessary."

My heart skittered as adrenaline bubbled with fear.

He pulled back, our eyes locking again.

For the longest second, he didn't move. His gaze danced over my face, the blue depths turbulent and unstable. The prey in me froze, recognising the thin ice I kneeled on.

He wasn't entirely human. Wasn't entirely in control.

He made a noise deep in his chest. A noise that hijacked my fight and flight response and weakened my knees. I was in danger. The worst danger I'd faced. Worse than any angry trafficker. Worse than any pissed-off captor. This man might rule over an exclusive island. He might purchase women for men who gave untold fortunes for pleasure, but beneath his pricey clothes and cultured whispers, he hadn't evolved from our ancestors.

He was a primordial beast with primitive black and white views. An archaic brute who still believed women were there to serve...in any capacity men commanded.

My hate reached an entirely new level.

His cologne of coconut and something earthy spiralled up my nose as his lips parted, and he breathed as if tasting me. As if he could sense how alert I was. How full of loathing and injustice. How hard I struggled to contain the restless fury inside me beneath strict calm-headedness.

I was actually afraid of the blustering acrimony within my heart. I'd meant to just nurse it, to let it feed me strength until I got free. But somehow, that rage had mutated, stealing space to sprout scaly wings, pierce wicked talons, and hunger for the blood of everyone who'd stolen me.

I didn't just want to run back to my life. I wanted to leave this man broken and bleeding before I did. I wanted him in jail. I wanted the Mexicans in a grave. I wanted the whole sick and twisted world to die a miserable, poetic death.

His fingers dug extra hard, my teeth pinching against my cheeks. "Stop it."

I narrowed my eyes and shot every vicious, violent thing I could think of in his direction.

A shudder worked up his arm and down his spine. His gaze left the realm of sane and slipped directly into diabolical. "Fuck, you really shouldn't have pushed me."

Shoving me away, he marched to a carved wall unit where hundreds of little drawers waited like an apothecary dispensary, hiding pills and potions, secrets and sins.

Ripping open a drawer in the top row, he fisted something and turned back to face me.

I hadn't moved.

My legs were full of metal that he'd melted and hardened to anchors. My heart flew too fast, making my pulse unsteady and lack of nutrition obvious on my burned-out system.

Straightening his shoulders, as if hauling himself back from whatever edge he'd almost fallen from, he strode back toward me. Slow and meticulous, he held out his palm, revealing a crystal vial.

A vial with a silver cap and a tiny sticker with a purple orchid on the front. "Your first requirement as an owned woman." Taking my hand, he planted it firmly into my grip. "Drink it."

My eyebrows flew up as I opened my fingers and gawked at the tiny bottle. "I won't drink anything if I don't know the contents."

He ran a hand over his mouth, letting it fall away as he struggled to stay normal. "Let's just say…it's plant-based and good for you." Pacing around me, he went to recline against his desk, inserting hands into perfectly pressed slacks. "It won't hurt you; you have my word." His eyes gleamed, hinting it might not hurt me, but it would do *something*.

My hackles rose.

I wanted to throw the bottle to the floor and smash it.

I went to tip if from my palm, but he murmured, "If you damage, destroy, or do anything to that elixir, you will *severely* regret it."

I paused. "Elixir?"

He nodded, holding me prisoner with his stare, just daring me to ruin whatever he'd given me. "An elixir guaranteed to make your life here far more bearable."

Frowning, I studied the miniature bottle. It couldn't have held much. Thirty millilitres at the most. "What does it do?"

He chuckled, far more in control of himself than before. "Take it and find out."

"Elixir means a magical or medical potion. I don't take drugs, and this isn't a storybook. So, I *politely* decline."

His chuckle tapered off into a scowl. "You're forgetting that you no longer have free will." Pushing off from the desk, he ripped his hands from his pockets, snatched the bottle, twisted off the lid, and grabbed my chin. "The first thing you should know about me is...I'm not a patient man. When I tell you to do something, you do it. Immediately."

His eyes pinned me to the floor as he pulled my bottom lip down with his thumb and tipped the bottle into my mouth.

I fought to repel backward, but he just walked with me, dumping the contents onto my tongue. The second the last droplet entered, he tossed the bottle away, grabbed me in a bone-crushing embrace and planted his hand over my mouth and nose. Pinching my nostrils, he took away my air, clutching me close as I wriggled and squirmed.

I begged with my eyes for him to let me breathe.

I kicked at his shins to get away.

But he just held on with unnerving, unyielding strength. "Swallow and I'll release you."

I shook my head, tasting the sweet, rose-infused liquid. Hating the slight numbness on my tongue and the tingle in my cheeks. Already it affected me. What would it do if I let it slide down my throat?

My lungs clawed for air.

My mouth tried to open beneath his large, heavy palm.

I gasped and choked, and still, he didn't let me go. He moved with me when I backed away, patiently allowing me to come to the conclusion that I had no choice.

I do. I do have a choice.

Die or swallow?

That wasn't a choice at all.

We danced a little more. I tripped over the woven flax mat, and he kept me upright, tutting under his breath. "Swallow."

I fought one last time, moaning and trying to get my arms free from his vise-like hold. But blackness feathered my eyesight, and my lungs ached as if they'd filled with poison.

I stumbled again, unable to coordinate my legs.

He showed no signs of mercy. No flicker of indecision or

clemency. Just ruthless behest to win.

The pain of no air became unbearable. The instinct to survive overrode my need not to drink.

I swallowed.

I stumbled.

He let me go.

I fell to my knees, bouncing hard on the hardwood floor. Little grains of sand stuck to my bare legs as I planted my hands into the ground and breathed.

Breathed

And *breathed.*

Gasping and grateful for sweet, sweet oxygen.

The taste from his elixir still lingered on my tongue. Fragrant and subtle. Sugary and potent.

Moving toward me, he slid to his haunches. Stabbing one finger onto the floor for balance and using his other hand to tip my chin to face him, he waited until I stopped panting before he smiled.

The feral glitter in his blue eyes terrified me. "Now listen to me. Pay attention…you don't have much time."

Sullivan

Chapter Eight

I SHOULDN'T HAVE FED her the elixir.

Especially the upgraded version.

Normally, my goddesses didn't receive a dose until the night of their first client. I might expect their servitude and offered no sway in following my strict rules, but I wasn't above humanity—if it suited my purpose.

I wasn't such a monster that I didn't offer a small rehabilitation period. A settling in time, as it were. By now, the girl I'd purchased would have heard my terms, realised I wasn't such a bad guy after all, understood that as far as bastards went to be sold to, I was the best they could've ended up with, and agreed to behave.

They were escorted to their villa.

They were left alone to acclimatise.

They were free...or as free as an owned possession could be.

But no.

This fucking girl had to intrigue me.

She had to stand up against me even though I'd treated her with respect and decorum. She'd turned a simple conversation into a war, and that was something you should *never* do with me.

I didn't lose.

To anyone.

And now…fuck, she'd pay the price.

I didn't let the thought linger that I might've broken her by making her drink. I didn't worry that such a prime, highly sellable product might not make it to the shelf. All I'd cared about was she'd defied me, and the price for that was great.

It was time to ruin that aggravating pride, smudge out that bold elegance, and destroy that goddamn grace by any means necessary—before it became a problem and ruined the obedience upon my island.

She scrambled away, ripping her chin from my knuckles. "What do you mean…I don't have much time?"

Standing, I smirked at her clueless on the floor. "You probably have about ten minutes…fifteen tops."

She crawled to her feet, pushing unsteadily upright to face me. Nervousness painted her beautiful features. "What will happen in ten minutes?"

"You'll find out." Turning my back on her, I returned to my desk, collected my pen, and began the meeting all over again. This time, the girl drifted to stand demurely in front of me. No fire burned in her gaze. No hate tainted the air. She'd turned inward, assessing her reactions, doing her best to guess what her system would do and racking her brain on how to save herself.

There was no saving her.

She would be in a personal hell for quite a few hours.

Swallowing any remaining animosity, she balled her hands. "Is there an antidote?"

I laughed a single bark before I could stop myself.

An antidote?

Ha!

There was an antidote…of a kind.

But she wouldn't be getting it from me.

No matter how much she begged. And, oh, she'd beg. She'd offer me her soul in perpetuity in about nine and a half minutes.

"Normally, I take my time explaining what your future holds. But…seeing as I lost my temper and have done something rather unfortunate, I will have to rush, to ensure you hear what I say before…." I looked her up and down, eyeing her closely for signs that she could no longer coherently follow my voice.

She still stood quietly. Still focused on me.

Her tongue licked her bottom lip just once, her eyes flaring at the sensation. Her chest rose as she inhaled, a lightning shiver shooting down her spine.

Shit, that stuff *was* strong.

Wrenching out a contract, I slapped it onto the desk, the fine-print facing her.

She shivered again as she moved forward, her clothing rubbing on skin that was steadily turning into overly sensitive sandpaper. "What's that?"

"That is binding and already signed by me." Scooting my limited-edition Mont Blanc to her, I added, "Sign it and it's done."

"I won't sign anything that I haven't read—"

"Just like you won't take drugs you don't know or agree to something you haven't analysed to the point of suicide. Yes, I'm beginning to understand that about you."

I already understood more than that.

I'd already deduced that this girl...she wouldn't be allowed near me unsupervised after today. I wasn't so cocky to think there wasn't something about her that tempted me beyond realms that should never be crossed.

If I was honest, I'd been waiting for a purchase to affect me worse than the others.

I'd been dealing in sex for so long now, I secretly wondered if I'd ruined any chance of suffering true lust again. I hadn't expected someone as young as her to entice me, but then again, I'd been a fucking idiot to list all the feminine attributes that *I* found attractive—not just my clients—for my next goddess.

I should've known I'd custom-designed a mail-order fuck slave that I'd have trouble resisting.

After all, I had strong inclinations toward brunettes. And she was most definitely a brunette with her dark, bitter chocolate hair. I liked tall girls with strength in their limbs and a willowy grace that belied feminine power. I liked clear skin and light eyes.

I should never have let her on my fucking shores.

She moaned low under her breath, wrenching my gaze to watch her closely. Her lips had parted, sipping air as if afraid of the creeping, stealthy takeover of her body. Her nipples had hardened beneath whatever shit the traffickers had dressed her in, and her thighs pressed together against her will.

Goddammit, it'd affected her too fast.

Standing, I stormed around my desk, grabbed her hand, and wrapped her fingers around the pen. Pressing her wrist against the paper, I commanded, "Sign. It makes no difference to me if you do or don't. You're here, you're mine, your future is already entirely in my control. This part is for you. For your peace of mind."

She swayed, her eyelashes fluttering as her pupils dilated. "Why…why do you want me to sign then? Why do you care about my peace of mind?" Her voice had slipped from snippy and sharp to sensual and full of sex.

"Because I find a willing employee better than a forced one."

"You should've just hired people then, instead of kidnapping them."

I smiled, pulling her closer, angling her hand so the nib of the pen dug into the paper and bled ink. "But then I wouldn't get the same level of quality, would I? Owning something rather than asking ensures much better results."

She leaned into me, her nose seeking my lapels and inhaling deep. She moaned again, her eyes closing and forehead furrowing as she fought the hostage takeover of her senses. "What…what's happening to me?"

Ignoring her question, I rushed, "I own forty-four islands. I rather like that number. Therefore, your time here will be measured by that amount." Manhandling her, I moved behind, supporting her sudden lethargy while keeping her hand on the contract. "Four years. That's all I ask. I bought you. I could keep you for eternity. I could use you until you're worthless, then kill and feed you to the numerous sharks that stalk my shores. But…I won't. I value commodity. I appreciate hard work. And I reward good behaviour."

She reclined into me, her spine arching and her ass rubbing against parts of me that should stay the fuck away from her at all costs. I went to push her away, but she snapped upright, bashing her hipbones against the desk in her need to get as far away from me as possible.

Huh.

She was strong then.

Strong enough to fight the potency swimming in her veins.

But she wouldn't win against it.

No one could.

That was why I had the best scientists working on the formula. Why the word elixir promised such impossible feats like turning metals into gold, alchemists into immortals, and humans into demigods.

My island wasn't just a fuckfest for the obscenely rich.

It was a wonderland for the men who'd become jaded by life. Who wanted the fantastical. Who believed in the utopia that we'd all been so cruelly denied.

Women.

Willing women.

Animalistic, *X-rated* women.

And this elixir, made from the very same orchids that grew on my archipelago, granted them paradise in the form of an overly-sexed, hyper-sensitive, orgasm-begging creature who no longer knew her own name, who no longer cared about what she looked like naked or had any capacity to lie, cheat, or fake her own desire.

Men came to my island for the joy of not only sleeping with a goddess but being gods themselves. The sole giver of pleasure that women crawled for, cried for, craved over and over and fucking over again.

The hunger, the greed, the all-encompassing need to be fucked ensured both parties were satisfied. Nothing was false about the barbaric, raw sex that happened here. The girls were dripping, and the men fed off their uninhibited eroticism.

My sole purpose was to select women who, once they took my elixir, became slaves...not to me...but their own snarling, starving libido.

And this girl? Fuck, she had a long way to fall. A long way to realise that her pride would soon be stripped, her morals shredded, her priorities up in flames.

Her mind would soon be taken over by more *basic* requirements.

The need for a cock.

The greed for a man—any man, *multiple* men—to fill her up and thrust until that crippling, clawing fervour could be sated.

I felt sorry for her.

Sorry that, unlike the goddesses who received the dose just before their first client, who went to their chosen on their hands and knees, their body wet and carnal, and had the reward of being fucked until they either passed out from delirium or drained their partner from every drop of cum he could give her, this girl would suffer.

Fuck, she would suffer.

Her legs buckled as she ground her hips into my desk. Her skin flushed. Her body heat scorched a thousand degrees.

My own body responded.

My cock, that had never fully calmed down, thickened to the point of excruciation. It would be so easy to unzip and fill her.

She'd let me. Fuck, she'd beg me.

She'd spread and arch, and I'd thrust—

Shit.

The longer I stayed here, the bigger the cracks in my willpower.

She shook her head, falling deeper and deeper into the lecherous lewdness she couldn't control.

I had to get away from her.

I had to lock her away from everyone—male and female if I didn't want her to mount someone to chase relief.

My fingers tightened around hers, digging the pen deeper into the page. "Four years. A tiny cost to have your freedom returned."

She moaned again, louder this time, losing civility under the crippling greed. "Just give me my freedom now. Give me..." Her head fell back as she pressed her pussy against the desk again. "Give me something. God, what did you give me? What's happening to me?"

Deciding to destroy her just because I could, just because she drew out needs I didn't want, I swept her hair away from her nape, and pressed a chaste kiss to the heat-sticky skin, inhaling the flush of a woman in full musky heat. "You're freer than you've ever been in your life."

She did more than shudder. She almost orgasmed from my touch. Her entire body quaked as internal muscles clenched so hard, I almost saw the wave of ecstasy flutter her stomach. "Please...make it stop."

"Can't." I kissed the nodules of her spine, tracing where they disappeared under the thick wave of tangled hair. "Just give in."

"No."

"No?"

I reached around and grabbed her between the legs. "Are you sure? Don't you want to ride my hand? Don't you want to come so bad your teeth ache, your belly aches, your entire soul aches for me to bend you over right here and fucking drive my cock inside you?"

"Oh, *God.*" Her free arm lashed around my neck, clinging to me as her hips rocked into my hand. "Let me go."

"You're holding me." I chuckled, but it came out more like a growl.

"Stop this. God, stop it." Her hips thrust forward. "I don't want this."

A spurt of heat and wetness filled my hand.

I dug the heel of my palm against her clit. "Your body says

otherwise."

The long jumper she wore rode up until I cupped her through her underwear. The material was fucking drenched. The slipperiness went past coy and straight into desperation. I rubbed her, dragging my fingers through the sopping saturation of her cunt. "How badly do you want me to stab my fingers inside you?"

She cried out as she thrust wildly into my hand.

A second later, she tried to push me away, shaking her head, almost sobbing. "No. No. Let me go. I don't want this."

I smirked and let her go. I backed away, leaving her steaming with a slick of wetness glistening on her thigh. "Sign the contract and I'll take you to your villa. You can spend the day getting off until you calm down."

"I can't." She buckled over, clutching her stomach as if she could vomit out the effects.

That wouldn't work. It was in her blood now. It was racing through every vein and artery, swelling her clit, her nipples, her brain with the incessant need to fuck.

Fuck.

And fuck.

"How many men?" the question ripped with torture from her lips. A heady groan followed as her hand pressed against her pussy. Embarrassment flooded her cheeks, fighting the urge to masturbate in front of me, not knowing that in another minute she'd do anything I asked.

She'd insert anything inside herself. She'd have sex with anything in this room if I allowed it. She'd fall to her knees and stick her entire fist inside her if I promised she could have my cock as a reward.

See how I don't like to play games, girl? Don't ever cross me. Don't fight me. You'll never come out on top.

I wiped my hand on my trousers, smearing the leftover residue of her need. "Four men. Sign and give me four years. Four times you'll be given this drug and four times you will be fucked within an inch of your life and love every sordid moment of it."

Her gaze met mine, frenzied and almost demented with lust.

I didn't move.

I let her make the choice.

Suddenly, as if she couldn't bear it any longer, she spun around, snatched my pen, and scrawled her name on my contract. She willingly entered my employment.

With a manic moan, she slithered from standing to her knees, rocking with her arms around her middle at my feet.

Stepping around her yearning puddle, I read the name she'd given.

Eleanor Grace.

I smirked down at the wild creature, fighting the urge not to fuck her own fingers.

Not so graceful now, are you?

Her hand wrapped around my ankle. Her fingernails dug into my flesh. She looked up with far too much determination. *"Please."*

A beg.

A beg oozing with need.

I froze, crippled beneath a wave of my own consuming hunger.

Seeing her like this, knowing she'd let me do anything to her, fuck...I should get far away from her. I should lock her up so no guests could take her. I should keep her far away from the other goddesses.

But...in her thirsty grey eyes, I drank a different version of elixir.

Mine wasn't chemically delivered but entirely designed by my own urges.

I wanted her.

I more than wanted her. I wanted to fucking *destroy* her.

I wanted to fuck her until I killed her. Until we both stop breathing, straining to copulate, brutal and broken until the end.

She'd cursed me.

In a flash, I knew what her goddess name would be.

Jinx.

Eleanor might've been her name when she was a tame, sexually repressed girl dating an equally repressed boy, but while she was mine...she was Jinx.

I shouldn't call her that—what if her arrival wasn't just poorly planned, but the beginning of bad fortune on my islands? What if she lived up to the promise of a jinx? A voodoo? A plague upon my shores?

But her eyes flashed again, stormy and as dark as slate, and I accepted that she'd already put a spell on me. She'd become my nemesis. A female who I didn't know. Who I'd paid handsomely for. A woman who didn't have to say a word to me, and I'd grown insanely hard with the incessant desire to rip her apart, challenge everything about her, and suck her passion dry by any means necessary.

Bending, I removed her claws from my ankle and hoisted her to her feet.

She squeezed her eyes at the sensation of me touching her. She crowded into me, rubbing against my leg like a cat in full season. "Please...help me. I can't take it."

I allowed her closeness.

I permitted one moment where I dabbled with the idea of keeping her as my own personal entertainment.

And then I ensured I'd never have to break my ironclad rule not to indulge in my goddesses. Because I had one last weapon to ensure she might want to fuck any man on this planet, but I'd ensure she'd never want me.

I could remain immune and resist the temptation of killing both of us with undiluted pleasure.

She gasped as I tugged her hair, tipping her head back so I could whisper directly into her ear. She quaked in my hold. Quivered for my touch, any touch.

"I left out a little of the fine-print, Eleanor."

Her head turned; our eyes locked.

"You didn't think I'd only ask you to sleep with four men in four years, did you?" I kissed the tip of her nose, sending another wash of lust to incapacitate her.

I smiled as I let her slither down my body to the floor where, this time, she didn't stop her hand from slipping between her legs.

I watched as she curled into herself, no more embarrassment. No more barriers that society placed on us as people. No more expectations that men and women weren't meant to be animals and enjoy in our baser desires.

We *were* animals.

As surely as any other creature.

But we were the only ones who hid sex behind closed doors and buried our true natures until no one was truthful about what they wanted.

I'd just freed her from that oppressive cage.

I let her be true.

I gave her the privilege of sexual honesty.

But that privilege came with consequences.

And my consequences hadn't been delivered yet.

Ducking to my haunches, I captured her chin again. When her glazed grey gaze met mine, I murmured, "Four men a month, Eleanor Grace. One hundred and ninety two men. And then...you're free."

Chapter Nine

IT TOOK LONGER THAN normal for his dark voice to slip past the lust-fogged haze of my brain. It took another moment for the trick to fully be understood.

I'd signed because one man a year for four years was survivable. I'd signed because I'd rather have a guarantee of an ending, than battle for the unknown escape that may or may not eventuate.

But...four men a *month*?

One a week?

One hundred and ninety two strangers who would touch me, fuck me, make me take this dreadful, heinous, body-stealing, mind-breaking, thought-silencing, rational-killing drug?

No!

No way.

In a flash of coherency, I launched at him.

One moment, I rubbed myself over my knickers in full view of this monster—hating myself, cursing myself, unable to fucking stop—the next, I toppled him backward and straddled his hips.

My coherency faltered, falling beneath the crippling, clawing greed.

God, I *needed*. I craved. I arched and spread my legs, pressing down until our groins connected.

I couldn't control it.

It was as if tiny monsters ran in my bloodstream, turning me against myself, shredding my decency, my common-sense, deleting every ethic and moral I'd ever had.

I *hated* it.

I *hate him*.

I went to slap him, but he grunted, locking possessive hands on my hips.

The second he touched me, it was all over.

I quaked. Any remaining shred of who I was became tinder under a glowing lava of lust. It sparked, caught fire, incinerated me to ash.

My skin blazed. It burned. It *hurt*. It hurt so much to be bruised and bitten.

I couldn't stop it.

My hand fell from the almost-slap, landing on his chest. I undulated on top of him, trying to get off, desperate to dispel the driving, suffocating need to come before he threw me away.

If I came, maybe I could get back in control of myself.

If I gave in for just a second, I might get free.

Please!

For a fraction of a moment, his blue gaze shot black, and he jerked me impossibly hard onto him. The seam of his zipper caught my clit. The violent pressure of being ground onto him made stars supernova in my core.

Yes.

No.

Fuck.

My eyes flared as I screamed at myself to run like a normal person, all while my body rocked against the impressively large steel in his trousers. I was crazy with need. And he was as horny as I was, yet he hadn't taken the drug.

He'd turned me into this animal.

My lack of control turned him on.

His stare trapped me in place. He drove upward with his hips.

Another whip of desire dragged an embarrassing cry from my lips.

My hate coiled with need.

My fury plaited with yearning.

Every synapse and instinct that kept me alive switched from survival to sex.

I trembled under salacious perversion and the unbearable, *unbearable* need to come.

He never stopped glaring as I rocked on him, using him,

stealing something of him because he'd stolen all of me.

I hyperventilated as the coiling, clambering orgasm barrelled from my fingertips to my toes and ricocheted into my pussy.

Yes.

Yes.

Holy...

My head fell back. My mouth opened.

He tried to shove me away—to prevent me from finding release, but I was already too far gone.

For the first time in my twenty-two years of life, I let go.

I allowed the sensations of being fully swept away to snatch me, trap me, wring me dry as my internal muscles squeezed to breaking point then *shattered* outward.

I rode him.

I dug ten fingernails into his chest as I shamelessly screamed, thrust, and stole every droplet of pleasure from him.

I'd never felt anything like this.

Even when in the middle of sex, clutching Scott's warm body, feeling him pump inside me; even mid-orgasm that I'd grown proficient at giving myself in the shower—*nothing* felt as good as this.

As *all* of this.

Nothing.

This was something else.

This wasn't legal.

This would kill me.

Need crackled like electric shocks beneath my skin. The drive to have a cock inside me so cruel and clamorous, it was as violent as hail bouncing off my naked body.

The two elements combined—fire and ice—made me a trembling, ravenous thing.

I waited for exhaustion to kick in—to be sated from the most intense release of my life—but my heart rate never slowed. The electricity didn't stop torturing me. Another greedy command whispered darkly through my core.

There was no reprieve.

No moment when I could be sane and stop being this wanton creature, enslaved by her own perversions.

Come again.

Again.

You need it.

I couldn't think about anything else.

But I *had* to think.

I had to remember what he'd said.

Something about men.

God, yes...a man. I needed a man. I needed what they could give me. I needed to be mounted and ridden. I needed to be filled and consumed.

I cried out as a full-body quake jolted me. The experience was like an all-over orgasm. My skin felt like it'd burst open. My blood boiled with bubbles of potency, and my muscles cramped from the hyper-drive my system revved at.

Closing my eyes, I wanted to die.

I wanted to escape my own body—to put it out of its misery. Slowly, despite all my efforts to stay sensible, I lost myself. The nucleus of who I was grew further and further away, buried in a tomb and covered with sands of this treacherous island.

I forgot about what was so important. I gave in to the undeniable command to come and come because I couldn't do anything else.

I couldn't win.

I couldn't fight.

Vicious hands shoved me to the floor.

I bounced as he clambered to his feet. His bronze-tipped hair was no longer sleek and perfect but tussled and wild. His eyes glowed with viciousness and the same mirroring hunger to fuck.

His hand fell to his cock, squeezing the huge outline in his trousers with white-knuckled fury. "Touch me again and you'll no longer be protected."

"Protected?" I blinked, clutching tight to conversation, using it as a life raft.

Words.

War.

Those were important.

Not sex.

God...*sex.*

Stop it!

"Protected as a goddess. The price I can charge for you is all that's keeping me from destroying you."

The threat echoed with sexual promise, but it also vibrated with truth. It whispered that I needed that protection. I shouldn't throw away my value because, if he took me, I would never be leaving this island.

Four years from now.

Never from now.

He'd kill me.

And with the way my body begged and howled for his, I'd probably scream in ecstasy and let him.

And that was delicious ice water thrown directly on my face. Imaginary ice cubes bounced off my brow with coherency.

I was lucid…just.

Dangerous. Dangerous.

This isn't a game.

Snap out of it!

I tugged on my tangled hair, doing my best to yank sense into my chemically altered brain.

Amazingly, another wisp of sexual fog receded, bringing a homicidal embarrassment that I'd been reduced to nothing more than a rutting creature, demented with need, lowered to a desperate version that I would never *ever* have permitted myself to become.

"You can stay here until you've wrung your system dry." He growled under his breath as he visibly struggled to take his hand away from his cock. "Once again, you've destroyed your own welcome party, Eleanor Grace. You should be out sunbathing on the beach by now, but instead, I have to lock you in my office so you don't fuck one of my valued guests."

I swayed, once again suffering mental images that I *desperately* wanted. The core-clenching deliciousness of the word fuck made wetness trickle down my thigh even though I still wore my underwear. "Isn't that what I'm here to do?" My hand strayed to my breast, squeezing roughly. I tried to stop. It was an impossibility. "Isn't that why you gave me this horrific substance?" I moaned as I pinched my nipple, wishing I was naked. He was naked. Everyone was fucking naked and fucking each other.

"There are rules. Approved locations. This isn't an orgy. This is business."

"How can you think sex is a business when—"

"Sex is the oldest business in the world." He ran a hand through his hair, slipping back into the formidable island mogul I'd met on the beach. "It's the rawest commodity we have."

A flicker of a thought filled my sex-obsessed brain. "If it's so valuable, let me use it to buy my freedom."

"You *will* use it to buy your freedom. Four men a month. I believe that's perfectly fair. I could command you fuck four a day. Four an hour. I could string you up and leave you at anyone's mercy."

I battled away the pictures in my brain. The aphrodisiac that such horrendous acts painted.

Do it.

Let them.

Drain me dry from this horror.

Gritting my teeth, I forced out, "I'm not talking about perverts who pay you to trap and drug unwilling girls." I moaned under my breath as another wave of intoxicating hunger tried to give me an orgasm just from the soft friction of my clothes, from the tightness of my knickers, from being alive in a world that was so erotically charged.

"You're saying you're unwilling?" He chuckled with black venom. "When you humped me without my permission? While you stand there, touching yourself?" He bared his teeth. "Currently, you are the most willing woman alive. You would sleep with anyone, anything. You would do whatever I commanded if I promised you could have my cock."

Oh, God.

I stumbled.

I landed on my hands and knees.

I felt violently, physically ill as the craving inside turned frenzied.

I needed another release. It wasn't just a passing thought. It was a literal life or death requirement.

I went to lie down. To do the unthinkable and make myself come in front of him.

But his voice snapped me upright. "Don't touch yourself."

Lifting my heavy head, shuddering as my hair slipped and licked over my back and shoulders, I stopped fighting to stay human. I was on all fours. My legs were spread like a mare in season. My hips rocked, seeking something he refused to give me.

I was no longer a person.

I was a beast.

"Come here." He moved backward until his legs hit the white couch. "Prove just how willing you are, Eleanor Grace. Before I deliver your final lesson."

Lesson.

What lesson?

I tossed those questions out as irrelevant.

Crawling to him, tears welled and dripped down my cheeks, leaving a wet trail on the floor behind me. I cried for my humiliation. I cried for my pain. I cried with the knowledge that I wanted to kill this man, but if he so much as touched me, I would be his for eternity. I would sell my soul just for one plunge of his cock.

I would debase myself to the point of ruin if it meant he could take this nightmare away.

He sat slowly, watching me crawl to him. Unbuttoning his exquisite suit jacket, he winced as he positioned his erection so it didn't wedge against the material of his trousers but aimed upright.

I caught a glimpse of the tip as he unfastened his belt and let the rest of himself poke out the top of his waistband. Shiny, broad head, oozing pre-cum, angry red flesh.

Just like I could no longer control my thoughts or system, I lost the ability to think in cohesive sentences.

A sledgehammer of sensation made me mute and dumb.

I wanted to go to him. To unzip him. Maul him. Sink deep, deep down on that impressive cock.

No!

I shook my head again, trying to scatter the insanity.

But it was so *hard.*

So insanely hard when I was beyond aroused.

Aroused didn't come close to the jumping, jolting stimulation I suffered.

I was berserk with it. Disturbed and distraught and inflamed with lust, lust, lust.

Stop it!

Breathe!

Fight!

It's just a drug.

It can't control you.

But it could.

It did.

I cried harder, even as my hand drifted to my core.

"You're stronger than I gave you credit for." His voice was thicker, darker, full of sand and storms. "But I suggest you stop fighting and give in. The elixir can either grant you a night of unbelievable pleasure, or…it can bury you in the pits of despair. You don't have a choice, Eleanor Grace. Your body is primed to come over and over and *over* again. Some goddesses can have upward of thirty orgasms in one session. There is nothing you can do about that fact. It's just science, reprograming your nervous system to need sex as much as you need air." He half-smiled, wicked and unrepentant. "Now, stand up. Come here."

It took everything inside, but the sliver of promise that I might be freed from this torment hoisted me to my feet.

He cocked his head, looking at me from head to toe as I stood tear-smudged and wild with demoralizing moisture dripping down my legs. "You really have fallen far from your prim little pride, haven't you?"

I didn't reply.

I couldn't.

I just let my body take over, swaying to the pulses inside my empty core. I fell a little deeper, sucking in a haggard inhale.

"That's it. Let it take over." His voice lowered to a rumble. "There's no shame in reverting to what we all are beneath our lies."

My insides clenched as my clit sparked with another release from his baritone alone.

He let me suffer in silence for a few seconds before he barked, "Come here and show me." He snapped his fingers. "Show me that you've stopped fighting. Let me see what my guests will enjoy."

My eyes flashed wide, struggling to comprehend.

When I didn't move, he murmured, "Remove your underwear."

In any normal situation, I'd tell him to fuck off. I'd spit in his face. I'd run the other way. I'd be reckless with my life, all because propriety said it was better to die trying to escape than protect your existence by obeying.

But...this wasn't a normal situation.

I'd fallen far, far from normal.

I had no free will anymore—a slave entirely to my libido.

I was his puppet. I was anyone's puppet who promised satisfaction.

And so, I hooked my fingers in the elastic of the white, drenched underwear and pulled them down. The grey jumper whispered against my skin, touching my breasts, my belly, my butt.

I shuddered as cool air licked around my over-sensitive flesh. Another full-body clench hinted that in another few minutes, the substance inside me would've taken over so completely, I would be able to come from no stimulation at all.

"Pull up your clothing." He shifted his hips, the tip of his cock blatantly obvious, imprisoned against his stomach. His suit jacket splayed on either side, framing his mirroring greed.

I winced as my fingernails caught my thighs, pulling the heavy hem of the baggy jumper up and up.

I revealed myself to him.

I stood there, baring my pussy, letting him stare at the tidily shaved part of me that only two boys had ever seen, and I felt no self-consciousness. No shame. No anything.

I only felt heavy and hungry and swept up in the heat of it all.

I *liked* him staring.

His eyes made my clit pound and tiny fissures of release coil in my belly. I didn't care about right or wrong. I only cared about how he made me feel.

And fuck...I felt high.

I'd never been so drunk on sex in my entire life.

"I'm going to charge double for you, my dangerous Jinx."

I blinked, narrowing my eyes against the strange address. But he could call me whatever he damn well wanted if he had the antidote to my disease.

Shifting again, he unzipped his trousers and shoved down his black boxer-briefs. The angry veins of his cock pulsed with a similar relentless pursuit to come.

God, he'd fill every inch of me. He'd pulverize me. His thrusts would splinter me apart, fragmentize every thought, and demolish any memory of who I'd been.

But he didn't invite me to replace his hand. He just kept staring, stroking himself with white-knuckled starvation.

Exquisitely slowly, he placed his other hand upright on the arm of the white couch. His fingers splayed upward like blades.

I licked my lips.

My belly flipped.

"Come closer." His voice no longer resembled anything human. We'd both left that realm for dark, dripping places.

I obeyed without question.

I had no more questions. No more guilt or worry. I only had lust and pain.

Pain!

Please...help me.

"You've shown me yours, and I've shown you mine." His gaze tore from my pussy, then landed on his upturned hand. "Now sit."

I didn't need any other commandments.

I wouldn't play coy and ask what he meant.

I couldn't play stupid and blush and deflect like any normal girl in this nightmarish situation.

I merely moved forward, positioned myself over his hand, then sank, of my own desperate volition, onto two of his upturned fingers.

Sullivan

Chapter Ten

THE SECOND HER HEAT sank and sucked my fingers inside her, she detonated.

She jerked and screamed, her hands clutching at my forearm, her legs spread over the arm of the couch, her hips rocking wildly on my hand.

My wrist fucking hurt with her full weight. She ground deeper onto my fingers as ripples of release squeezed her, over and over again.

Her head fell back as another orgasm tore her apart, swift on the heels of the first.

I let her use my fingers.

I watched her transcend from meek, trafficked slave to resplendent, gorgeous goddess.

And I suffered a similar thirst to come.

My fist worked up and down my cock, punishing with a pressure that guaranteed to bruise.

She was beyond drenched. So ready to be fucked; her pussy so swollen and slick that my two fingers weren't enough for her.

She mewled and panted, sounding as desperate as she was.

More tears rained down her pretty cheeks, splashing onto my suit as she rode my fingers, seeking something bigger, brutal—becoming frustrated with the lack of girth and length.

How easy it would be to tell her to get up and sit on my cock.

How grateful she would be for me to bend her over and crash inside her.

How fucking stupid could I be to even entertain the idea?

I gave her my hand so she wouldn't break entirely. My intention wasn't to condemn her to despair and ruin. My goal was to set her free. To show her that here, on my shores, there was no such thing as frigidness. She needed to learn her body. Every woman I'd bought was required to become intimate, *extremely* intimate, with every crevice and hole, accepting their perfections and flaws as one exquisite package because the form they had was the gift that would grant their freedom, along with a thousand orgasms as payment.

She would learn to beg for another dose of elixir. She would drop to her knees and crawl for a single drop.

I grew harder at the image. My thighs trembled with an impending release.

This new girl needed to get the fuck out of my office.

I needed her gone.

I jerked as I fisted myself too hard.

"Get up," I snarled, masturbating myself while she chased another detonation.

Her feral eyes met mine. She went to shake her head, but I dug my thumb into her clit with command. "Do it. Do it now."

With a pitiful cry, she forced strength that she didn't have into wobbly legs and gave me enough room to roll out the pain in my wrist. My fingers held threads of her musky desire. The slippery cords of her release sticky and damning.

With obscene willpower that'd taken my entire thirty-three years to master, I stood and faced her.

We both breathed hard, our exhales raspy and shallow. Her hand reached out to grab my cock. Her tongue wet her lips as she stood transfixed, hypnotised by the sight of my erection and the blatant invitation dazzling in her eyes.

It would be so fucking easy.

Too fucking easy to spin her, shove her, fuck her…hurt her beyond redemption. Beyond resale or profit.

I grabbed her wrist, stopping her short from touching me. "Don't."

She writhed on the spot, tearing her hand from my hold to rub against her over-sensitive flesh.

I'd achieved what I'd achieved by not giving in to my diabolical thirsts. I wouldn't fail now. No matter that I couldn't remember ever being this fucking turned on.

However, I wasn't above torturing her as I splayed my fingers covered in her slimy cum and ensured she saw it glittering like cobwebs in the sunshine.

She moaned under her breath as I wrapped those fingers around myself, smearing her wetness all over me.

The pressure to come hinted I could give in right there. The tingle and sharpness just begged for permission—for one lapse of concentration to ejaculate. Every instinct bellowed to command this girl to her knees and come on her goddamn face.

I was tempted.

Sorely, fucking tempted.

I stepped toward her with the order on the tip of my tongue.

Her gaze forcibly left my fist-wrapped cock, crawling to my eyes and locking there. With trembling hands, she grabbed the hem of her jumper again, bringing it up over her hips, revealing her pussy.

Her clit was so swollen it glistened through the manicured hair—hair that could stay, as men who visited my island liked women, not little girls. The insides of her thighs were powdery with dried moisture where the flesh around her cunt was drenched.

She kept pulling her jumper up and up, exposing her perfectly formed breasts and tight, pink nipples. Her face disappeared for a second as she tugged the clothing over her head.

Her hair crackled as her eyes sought mine again, standing there stark fucking naked. Her ribs were visible as she panted. Her tallness gave her an ethereal quality even while muscle definition said she didn't rely on false gifts such as good genes. She wasn't lazy. She used her body for activities and adventures…and now she wanted me to use it in every dirty and demeaning way possible.

I grunted as the first spurt of my orgasm hit me by surprise.

She gasped as the pearly droplet shot from my cock and splashed against the floor.

On the precipice of giving in and milking every delicious clench, something flashed in her gaze.

A ripple of disgust.

A coil of abhorrence.

She still hadn't given in entirely.

She still hadn't accepted her fate.

With meticulous slowness, I pressed my rock-hard cock, still pulsing with cum, against my stomach and winced as I struggled with my zipper. Tugging my shirt over the tip still visible above the waistband, I let my belt hang on either side, casually buttoning up my blazer while she stood weaving before me.

It was the hardest fucking thing I'd ever done.

My teeth cracked with self-control and denial of my climax.

Her cheeks blazed as I continued to study her nakedness.

Once again, it'd seemed my ego had come to bite me in the ass. I should never have used my own fantasies as a shopping list. Her body was flawless. Prim but limber. Lean but curvy. Her skin held bruises, rope burn, and ink from her time with the traffickers and the bandage on her neck hinted she'd end up with a little scar from her ordeal.

If she could drive me this close to breaking my infallible rules while dirty, injured, unwashed, and exhausted…what the fuck would she be like after my staff had taken care of her?

She wouldn't require time to get into shape. She wouldn't need special meal plans or exercise regimes like some of my other 'recruits.' She was perfect in every fucking way and the stormy grey depths of her gaze, still battling lust and loathing, made rage overshadow my hunger.

I wanted to break her into goddamn pieces.

I wanted her to know just who her life belonged to.

Four years wouldn't be enough.

Cursing those black-coated thoughts, I yanked my cell from my pocket and dialled without ever looking away from Ms Eleanor Grace.

She dragged fingertips down her waist, shivering as goosebumps sprang over her skin. I didn't know if she was aware that she constantly touched herself, seeking, seeking, always seeking a release.

"Yes?" Cal, my manservant, for all intents and purposes, answered on the second ring. "Need something?"

"Come and collect our newest goddess from my office. Take her to her villa. Ensure no one goes near her, do you understand?"

Eleanor shivered again, her nipples peaking to an all-new tightness just from my voice.

Fuck.

All it would take was one tiny command, and I could be inside her. I could break her apart. I could ensure she learned her lesson that I owned her. Breath, heart, and fucking soul.

With my fingers clutching my cell so tight, the casing cracked a little, I added, "She's high on elixir. If you let her near any of the guests, I'll castrate you, got it?"

Cal chuckled in my ear, nonplussed by my threat. He'd heard worse. And he knew what the girls were like when they were drugged.

Watching them in their heat always made me hard to partake in what they so violently wanted and also pity them in their desperation.

However, today, I felt no pity for this girl.

This Jinx...this purchased mistake.

"I'll ensure she's kept well away from anything she can fuck." Cal snickered.

I hung up.

I cupped Eleanor's cheek.

She immediately turned her head, trying to bury herself in my touch. Her lips met my fingers, and she recoiled, only to suffocate under another wash of elixir and lick my thumb.

"Please." Her throaty beg made my imprisoned cock ooze another drop of cum. "Please...I need to be filled. I need..." She swallowed hard. "You."

My stomach knotted itself into an agonising mess.

My balls throbbed with excruciation to shoot the remainder of my pleasure into her.

My entire body could no longer fight the blend of wanting to destroy her, coupled with the hunger of consuming her.

But she wasn't worth ruining myself over.

She was nothing.

Merely an acquisition to make me richer than I already was.

And fuck, she'd make me rich.

Grabbing her chin, I murmured harshly, "Fuck anything without my permission and the sharks will enjoy a snack, after all." Tearing my hand from her cheek, I walked around her, stiff, hard, and achy. "Now get out of my fucking office."

Chapter Eleven

I LOST COUNT OF my orgasms after I hit ten.

Hours blended into each other.

My system revved at a million miles a minute, keeping me alert, alive, and entirely too reactive to any stimuli, yet beneath that thirsting drive for more and more pleasure, I was *exhausted*.

My limbs had turned into useless noodles. Any sensation against my skin sent me into a full shudder that almost crippled me. The only serenity I'd found was in the lapping ocean outside my villa.

My fingers and toes had wrinkled from staying in liquid for too long, but the thought of dragging my aching, wrung-out form from the weightlessness of salty sea was too much.

I can't.

I'm...I'm done.

More tears squeezed from my eyes as I floated on my back, mingling with the ocean that kissed and soothed my traitorous body.

Sunset slashes of mauve and mandarin Picassoed the sky above me.

The air temperature had fallen from unbearable to temperate, and the ocean continued its non-judgemental embrace. It cocooned me gently, washed away my abominable behaviour, and rinsed away the finally fading dregs of debilitating need.

I didn't have a bikini on.

I didn't care I was naked.

I'd blindingly run into the sea after my fifteenth or fiftieth orgasm, sobbing in fatigue and unable to stand another touch. Even though it was *my* touch. My fingers that wrung bliss after bliss from my bruised and throbbing body. My hands that couldn't stop even though I begged for a rest.

I'd put my jumper back on, trying to prevent myself from torture.

I'd tried tying my wrists together with a towel.

Nothing worked.

Unable to take it another minute, I'd bolted from the villa, past the security guard posted so I couldn't enlist some despicable paying guest to rape me, and over the glittering crystal sand. The beach undulated beneath my bare feet in erotic ways. The splash of cool water on my legs threatened to become sexual, but I threw myself headfirst into the wetness, staying under until my breath grew thin and my heart pounded for another requirement other than drugged desire.

My grey jumper had become waterlogged, dragging me to the shallow bottom where sand glittered through turquoise clarity, and sparkly, metallic fish darted suspiciously around me.

By the time I'd come up for oxygen, I was able to take a breath that didn't hunger for yet more pleasure and, in utmost relief, threw off the sodden jumper, watched it sink, then gave everything I was to the sea.

That'd been at least two hours ago, and I still hadn't moved.

After a man in another suit had carted me from Sinclair's office and dragged me down yet another sandy pathway, I'd ached with a need so painful I'd almost fallen to my knees when his fingers locked around my elbow.

Sinclair hadn't looked at me as I was unceremoniously removed from his picture-perfect office. Even after everything that'd happened between us, he looked unruffled and entirely unmoved. No sweat on his brow, no dampness crinkling his clothes.

How cold-blooded must he be to not feel the humid heat or show any signs of the lust scalding his veins? And I knew he *had* felt lust because he'd almost come. He'd stopped himself. He'd tucked himself away mid-release as if I was an abomination and didn't deserve whatever consummation we could've shared.

My back had slicked with as much moisture as my pussy. My temples and hair were damp from sweat—perspiration from desire as much as the tropical mugginess.

He was the most callous and cruel person I had ever met, and, floating weightless in the sea surrounding his island, my hate returned a thousandfold. Lust didn't overshadow my every thought anymore. The boundaries and borders that allowed civilisations to evolve from rutting beasts to intelligent humans were well and truly back in place.

What an absolute asshole.

What a *monster* to drag me here against my will, feed me a drug—also against my will—and then watch me flounder for something I abhorrently didn't want yet couldn't stop begging for.

He could've had me.

I would've done anything in that moment to have him enter me and give me what I was so empty for.

But now...

Now?

God, now I was prepared to murder him with my bare hands. I wanted to slash his jugular with that condemning pen I'd used to sign his awful contract. I wanted to swim and swim until some fisherman scooped me from the sea in his net and tell the police about this sick and twisted island that he'd trapped me on.

What would Scott think?

I blushed a deep crimson. Even though my behaviour wasn't my fault, and I'd fought it at every step, I still suffered guilt so thick it made me nauseous.

How would I ever look him in the eyes again, knowing how I'd acted?

My guilt turned to homesickness.

Had he enlisted the authorities to look for me yet? Did my parents know I'd gone missing?

My eyes burned as another cascade of tears began.

I hiccupped and swallowed them down. I honestly didn't have the strength to cry. I'd reached the end of my limit. I needed to sleep, to rest, to forget.

Allowing my legs to sink beneath the surface, I hovered vertically instead of horizontal. My eyes met those of the guard who'd never left the sand, even in the beating sunshine. He'd kicked off his loafers and hovered around on the edges of the lazily lapping waves, ready to launch after me if I did make a swim for it but content for me to bob if that was my only intention.

He was young. Probably only mid-twenties, yet he willingly worked for a monster like Sully Sinclair.

My fists curled in the water.

Don't think about that bastard.

He was yet another topic I had no energy for.

For the first time in hours, my thoughts were my own again, and my throbbing body licked its wounds rather than drove me to do unspeakable things.

I could no longer ignore my wrung-out tiredness.

I hadn't slept since I'd been corralled from the room I'd been held in with Tess, forced to shower, been tattooed, tagged, and knocked unconscious to fly halfway across the world.

After today and what Sinclair did to me, I had no energy left for escape.

Tomorrow.

Tomorrow...I'll get free.

With a groan and a thousand pounds pressing on my shoulders, I stood in the waist-deep water and made the agonising trek from the cushioning ocean back to harsh gravity.

The guard watched my every naked move, but he didn't approach me; he didn't give me any signal that I was in danger of him molesting me. Instead, he allowed me to inch my battered and lust-broken body up the beach to the private villa I'd been tossed into.

I didn't know what part of the island I was on or if I even had neighbours. The way the villa had been constructed made it seem as if I existed entirely on my own. No hint of cages or locks. No obvious imprisonment or signs of co-inhabitation.

My feet ached. My back ached. My core ached. Even my fingers ached from making myself come over and over again.

All I wanted to do was to sit down in a sprawl and never move again.

But...I also wanted to shower away the last week of my life. I wanted to be clean when I finally succumbed to sleep.

Dripping saltwater over the white sandstone tile, I cut through the lounge with its matching silver driftwood furniture, gauzy curtains, and high thatched roof and rafters like Sinclair's office. Unlike his office, though, this one had an annex with a huge king bed, crisp white sheets, mosquito net slung over the carved bamboo headboard, and a bathroom off an alcove where a kitchenette waited with a fridge stocked full of water and icy beverages.

In my exhaustion, I didn't even care I was held there as his prisoner.

In another world, this was a beautiful hotel. In a previous existence, long travels equalled jet lag, and I couldn't keep my eyes open much longer.

Stepping into the bathroom, I tried not to marvel at the exquisite vanity carved like a wave with the bowl curved and sensuous along the entire wall or the glass door leading to an outdoor shower surrounded by palm fronds and a rock wall for privacy.

Sluicing off salt and shampooing my hair, I barely managed to dry off and face plant onto the inviting bed before I passed out cold.

A phone.

The first thing I saw when I opened my eyes was a phone.

My heart rate spiked from exhausted dreams to manic hope. Jack-knifing off the bed, I launched at the innocuous phone waiting on the simple side table holding a lamp with a rattan lampshade and a box of tissues.

Grabbing the receiver, I checked for a dial tone before punching the emergency number.

Nothing.

Clearing the call, I tried again, only to hear a click and a pleasant feminine voice, "Good afternoon, Jinx. Are you ready for something to eat? We can have room service delivered, or you're welcome to come to the goddesses' private dining villa."

I froze.

My fingers latched tighter around the phone as my manic hope deflated to dejected desolation. Of course, they wouldn't allow outside numbers. Of course, my freedom wouldn't be that easily obtained.

"Hello? You there, Jinx?"

Pinching the bridge of my nose, I tried to squeeze away exhaustion and a headache caused by dehydration. Had I truly slept since twilight yesterday to lunchtime? No wonder my stomach was hollow and my body desperate for a drink.

"If you're still listening, I'll send lunch to your villa—"

"No." I snapped out of my fugue. "I'd like to go to the dining room. How do I find it?"

A smile sounded down the line. "Great, I'll send a staff

member to escort you. Do you have any food intolerances, Jinx?"

Jinx.

What the hell was with this Jinx business? Vaguely, I remembered Sinclair calling me that. A strange name with no relation whatsoever to me.

Ignoring her question, I asked one of my own. "Why are you calling me that? My name is Eleanor."

A pause before she said, "Jinx is the name you'll be known as while you're employed here. It's a nom de plume, if you were. For your own protection from the guests and a way of distancing yourself from your time here when you return home in four years."

My heart seized.

A name for a goddess.

A name for a whore.

A whore who wasn't employed but trapped, lost…stolen.

Nausea rushed up my gullet, bringing bile and the full ramifications of my new life into brutal effect.

I hung up.

I barely made it to the bathroom before dry-retching into the silver-lidded toilet.

Sullivan

Chapter Twelve

I KEPT MY ATTENTION on the three guests below me.

Sitting on the deck of the central villa that housed all the conveniences of a five-star resort, including three restaurants, a gin bar, small movie theatre, gym, spa, and a few retail shops that specialised in the most expensive, exclusive diamonds anyone could buy, I studied them closely.

At least one of the gentlemen had purchased a diamond—it glinted on a tie pin, stabbed into his floral shirt. I couldn't blame him wearing the flawless stone even without a suit and tie or a boardroom to notice.

No one else in the world had the right to sell Hawk diamonds, but I personally knew Jethro Hawk who ruled over his own estate and inheritance of priceless gemstones.

We'd met under strange circumstances. He had a condition that required behavioural drugs. I had a talent at taking natural ingredients and blending with science to create newer, better drugs. Far more potent drugs.

We'd met when he'd reached his wit's end and needed something new—to continue existing in his painful personal world. I'd given him something. We'd stayed in touch. He no longer used my drug, and instead, he'd found that love conquered his condition without the use of chemicals.

However, a business deal had struck up from our

acquaintance, and it'd been mutually benefiting. He had power in his own right, just like the guests below me. Drinking a noonday cocktail, they relaxed on the sprawling deck that meandered around koi carp ponds, palm trees, and were home to a few very fat white herons, who were used to being hand-fed.

One man was a politician, hiding from the nasty world of bullshit and over-promises, spending the next three days with us while indulging in some very intriguing fantasies. Another was the heir of a supermarket chain. I'd personally gifted one night on top of the five he'd paid for because he was the first to eradicate all pesticides on the produce his chain sold and had vowed to only provide plant-based meat to his consumers. And the third was a B-grade actor who'd spent a very enlightening time with a goddess called Jupiter.

He'd treated her with respect.

They'd had a mutually satisfying time together.

Today was his last afternoon on my shores.

I oversaw everyone's departure as well as their arrival to ensure their needs had been met, any outstanding bills were paid, and their feedback on any pillow talk a goddess might've divulged was delivered straight to me.

A few had tried to escape by asking their patron to help smuggle them off the island. Another few had agreed to be bought by the guest, if I agreed to sell.

Neither of those things would ever happen.

"Sir?"

I looked up through piercing sunshine to raise an eyebrow at Calvin. "What is it?"

He stood with a smirk that he hadn't eradicated from his face ever since Eleanor Grace had been unceremoniously dragged out of my office...naked.

It pissed me off.

It made me aware I'd stepped over lines I'd promised I'd never cross. She'd gotten under my skin, and that was yet another thing that should never have fucking happened.

Cal squinted his gaze against the bright tropics. "She's left her room. She's being escorted to the Divinity Dining Room."

I instantly lost all interest in the men beneath me on the lower deck. "Bring her here."

He nodded. "Right away." With another annoying little smile, he left to bring a disgraced and fallen angel to worship at my feet.

Chapter Thirteen

I HADN'T SAID A word when the personal minion for Sully Sinclair appeared from nowhere, blocking the sandy laneway and waving my silent guard away. His shiny brown hair showed style and attention, yet his green eyes held mirth at my expense.

I didn't like him.

Just as I didn't like his master.

My throat still stung from retched-up acid. My stomach still roiled against the snare I'd been caught in. And my hunger and dehydration set my teeth on edge, which meant my temper was so, so close to snapping.

I had no patience.

No tolerance.

If I opened my mouth and graced him with a word, it would be filled with profanity and probably get me in a hell of a lot of trouble.

So…instead, I chose wisdom and zipped up my lips with fiery control and merely glowered at him as he said, "Your company has been requested at the main villa. Follow me please." With a sweeping gesture, he turned and strolled up the pathway, expecting me to fall in step with him.

And I did.

I didn't really have much choice. I wanted to know this island. The sooner I knew where each path led, which villas were safe, which were not, and just how big this place was, the sooner I could formulate a plan to leave.

We didn't meet anyone else as he led me in polished shoes over white-golden sand until the shadowy tunnels caused by palm fronds gave way to a large oasis of sunshine. No natural shade granted the large area that'd been cleared for a huge open-aired, beautifully styled cabana.

Black umbrellas towered over private dining tables on the bottom deck, sparkling ponds with pink and white lilies broke up the large expanse of teak flooring, graceful herons picked their way daintily between two tables which held three men drinking cocktails.

Within the shade of the large villa, a restaurant gleamed with cream napkins and fine dining. It made me feel woefully underdressed in the white tennis-style dress I'd found hanging in the wardrobe. Barefoot, hair washed and brushed but wavy with humidity, and no energy to move after the catastrophe I'd been put through yesterday, I was terribly insignificant and left hating the sensation of being small, meek, and totally at the owner of this establishment's mercy.

I sighed, feeling more drained and lonely than ever as I followed the architecture to the second tier. Another wraparound deck with a carved banister that kept the natural contours of branches, bound together with vines, creating a treehouse persona. Something not quite manmade but of a Mother Nature creation.

Big black sails strapped from the centre point of the structure fanned out to attach to links on the deck, drenching the second level with much-needed shadow from the cooking midday sun.

I froze as I locked gazes with my nemesis.

Him.

Sully Sinclair sat like a royal dictator, a coffee cup in one hand and a pair of sunglasses in the other which he put slowly, regally on his nose.

My temper cut through my aches and bruises. My fury curdled any tiredness and hunger.

Digging my bare feet into the sand, I went to spin and leave.

I couldn't see him.

I didn't have the control not to say something that would assuredly get me into a heap of trouble.

But fingers latched around my elbow, keeping me in place. "Running away isn't polite."

"Kidnapping isn't either," I snapped, ripping my arm from the man's hold and breathing hard.

I hadn't meant to say that.

I vibrated with the urge to say more.

To scream at him. Scratch him. To give him a slur-slandered message to hand deliver to his diabolical master.

He smirked, his gaze flashing between me and the man he served. "It'll be interesting to see how long he permits your disobedience."

I bit my tongue so hard, it bled.

He waited as if he wanted me to retaliate. When I didn't, he seemed disappointed but not entirely surprised. "You're not the first to rebel, you know. And I'm sure you won't be the last." The man stepped toward me, conspiratorially, threateningly. "They all give in, in the end. They all realise how good they've got it here." He smiled as he studied me. "You'll learn too, I promise."

We stood dappled by sunlight, and I despised that he was handsome, just like Sully Sinclair.

Why was it that beauty always graced the wicked?

I didn't like his promise.

I refused to reply to his radical concepts that a kidnapped and *stolen* woman would be happy here. Just because the sun sparkled on pristine sand and jewelled birds flew unhindered through lush greenery didn't mean this wasn't the Garden of Eden with a dark secret to tell. And just like the Garden of Eden, it all dissolved into death and decay the moment that apple was tasted.

I would never fall into the trap of eating a poisoned apple. I wasn't Eve, and I wasn't Snow White. I was Eleanor Grace—not ~~Jinx~~—and I didn't need someone to rip back the curtain on the truth of this place.

I knew the truth of it.

This is Hell.

And Sully Sinclair and his minions were hobgoblins of the underworld.

I crossed my arms, accepting the challenge of his servant. It was rash and stupid to stand up to him, but I had a good guess that captive women here might be fed a drug and used against their will, but I doubted abuse—that wasn't paid for and within the strict terms that Sinclair agreed to—was allowed.

What was the point in beating up the merchandise? Who would pay top dollar for a slave when she had a broken arm and a black eye?

Bracing my spine, I clipped, "Finish your task and take me to whoever requested my company. I can guess who that is, by the way, and somehow, I don't think your master likes to be kept waiting." I spread my lips into a thin, brittle smile, looking past him to Sully Sinclair who'd abandoned his nonchalant sprawl in his chair and now stood with hands throttling the banister, coiled like a black panther above us, ready to slay. "He's not happy that you're detaining me, and I'm not happy with this conversation."

The man's face drained of colour, his eyes turned hard, all while his mouth quirked into a condescending smile. "Wow…you really are destined for pain."

In one heartbeat, I feared I'd made a colossal mistake and braced for a punch. In another, I shivered with the simplicity of what he'd said. The utmost assuredness that I would be in pain and lots of it.

I wanted to jump back in the ocean and never step foot on dry land again.

I'd somehow grow a tail, covered in pretty scales and powerful fins, and vanish into the depths where nothing and no one could hurt me.

Turning and unblocking the path, he spread his arm for me to step in front of him. "After you, Goddess Jinx." He bowed mockingly. "I must say, I'm going to enjoy watching your employment."

He chuckled, sending a wash of goosebumps down my back as I marched past him and locked eyes with Sully Sinclair again, glowering from the clear blue sky above.

Behind me, the man whispered, "You know…you've already fucked up worse than any girl who arrived before you." He laughed again, low and a little too full of anticipation of what my future held.

I once again ignored him, focusing on stepping on the shadowy sand rather than the golden grains in full sunlight, unwilling to burn the soles of my bare feet.

The hair on my nape stood up as the man added, "It's not the men who pay for the privilege of fucking you that you have to be afraid of, Jinx." His arm appeared by my head, his finger pointing at Sully. "It's that man. And you've gone and made him pay attention." He clucked his tongue like an old busybody. "Probably shouldn't have done that, but it's too late now."

As my feet reached the deck and I climbed the three steps from the sand to smooth wood, his words licked down my spine. "Four years was a small price to pay for your freedom, but now that Sinclair's interested in you? Well, you might as well make yourself at home because I doubt you'll be going anywhere."

I slammed to a halt as he skirted past me and smirked. "Come along. Like you said...don't want to keep your god and ruler waiting."

Sullivan

Chapter Fourteen

SHE ARRIVED AS IF gracing *me* with her presence, not the other way around.

I'd been right to be wary of my intense reaction to her yesterday when she'd been dirty and exhausted from her arrival. Watching her stalk toward me with her spine regal and head wearing its invisible crown of dignity and diamonds, I hexed her all over again for the way my cock swelled and sat up in full attention.

Her hair had been washed, and the bitter chocolate glowed like molten cocoa. Fine strands of red burned like fire, glittering in the sun. The length was longer than I'd assumed, now the tangles and knots had been smoothed, allowing the thick curtain to frame her face and hang intoxicatingly down her back.

Her bare feet revealed tiny breakable bones that undulated with every angry step. Her ankles were the perfect size for a man's hand to snap around and wrench open perfect porcelain thighs.

Her eyes narrowed like a lynx, partly from the sun's brightness and partly from pure hate, retaining their rare shade of silver and fog, and her skin held a dusting of colour from spending most of her afternoon in the ocean yesterday.

I'd had reports on what she'd indulged in.

I could guess how many times she had to get herself off.

I was pissed that I hadn't been there to watch…or participate.

I hated that I had any reaction toward her whatsoever.

It didn't take a guy with a hard-on to admit that this girl was beyond fucking gorgeous. Her ethereal quality alone made her glow with refinement, and the temper that she couldn't quite hide gave her the aura of untouchable.

Which made her all the more fucking delicious because she *was* touchable.

Very, *very* touchable.

She was *buyable*.

A scrape of a chair leg on the deck below wrenched my attention to the three guests who'd gone silent. One stood, gawking at Eleanor as she marched toward me. Another held his cocktail to his lips but sat transfixed, drinking her in instead of the alcohol. And the third gulped then threw me a very obvious eyebrow, a silent demand that he wanted her.

Form a queue, asshole.

I already knew there'd be a bidding war for this girl. All it'd taken was one appearance and already the guests had decided they'd be the one sticking his cock in her tonight.

I peered at her closely.

The shadows under her eyes had receded—still there but not nearly as dark. The bruises on her legs and arms were less prominent. The bandage on her neck was gone, revealing the small incision where the tracker had been removed. The rope burn around her throat was less angry and the idiotic barcode tattoo on her wrist—that matched a few of my previous goddesses—not as fresh. Overall, with her sun-kissed island look, glossy hair begging for a man's fist, and impertinence dripping from her pores, she could be ready to work tonight...if the price was right.

My cock pounded harder.

Possession licked through my veins at the thought of anyone spreading her legs and taking what I'd had dripping on my fingers yesterday.

She might sell for the highest profit margin I'd ever commanded.

But it didn't mean I could control the rage that simmered inside.

"Finally dragged yourself out of bed then?" I smirked, keeping my voice hard and condescending. "Spent quite a few hours 'entertaining' yourself?"

Her nostrils flared with indignation.

She didn't respond even though her body vibrated with every silent shout she swallowed back.

I deliberately sat back down, hiding the rock-hard erection I sported.

She might've had countless orgasms yesterday, but I hadn't had a single one. I'd buried myself in work. I'd conference-called my scientists to give them the good news on the revised elixir. I'd swam around my island four times to resist the urge to masturbate.

I wasn't a prude. I relieved myself often. I dabbled in fantasies while my hand pumped out pleasures, but I always kept the girls I fucked faceless, nameless, unknown.

If I'd come last night, I knew whose face I would've pictured and that would not have been good for me, Eleanor, or business.

"How tired are your fingers from fucking yourself? Or did you use things around your villa to get off?"

Her jaw ticked as she clenched her teeth. She swayed before me, standing like a statue carved from granite but quickly cracking under immense pressure. Her chin rose and her gaze shot past me to focus on the aching expanse of treetops and turquoise ocean. The only landmark on the horizon, blotting out the perfection of endless sea, was another island.

Another island I owned.

And past that one was another and another and so on.

That was why I could be liberal with my boundaries. I didn't lock the girls in their villa. I didn't have bars and gates around my shores. They could try to swim. They might even outswim one of their guards, but if they made land, it was most likely *my* land they sought solace on, only to find themselves kindly escorted back.

Not one had gotten past a third island.

Most of them didn't even try, knowing how futile such an attempt would be.

I cocked my head. Would this girl try? Would Jinx be the one who got away? After all, I'd named her for the bad luck she'd brought upon me. Perhaps, she had yet more to deliver before our time was through.

"You know...if you're just going to be silent, I can ensure that's a permanent situation for you. I'll command Calvin to remove your tongue for good." I sipped the final dregs of my coffee, shrugging. "Speaking is a privilege. Speaking to me is the biggest privilege of all. But if you don't want that ability, then—"

"Fuck. *You*." The moment the ugly curse fell from her pretty mouth, she gasped. Her hands opened and folded by her sides as if she tried to scramble her temper back into its cage, but it was too late.

Her eyes sought mine.

They locked and held, and she let loose everything she'd been hiding with a vicious hiss. "How *dare* you give me that drug yesterday. How *dare* you make me do such humiliating, *disgusting* things. How fucking *dare* you take away power over my *own* body, laughing at my misery, making me degrade myself in every possible way a woman can."

She swooped toward me, fury painting her cheeks bright red, her hair whipping in a sudden balmy breeze. She looked like Medusa with a nest of snakes crawling over her shoulders, ready to sink venom into my neck from a thousand tiny fangs. "I've never hated anyone as much as I hate you. I hate that you saw me like that. I hate that you made me like that. You think you can sit there, smirking at my distress? Laughing to yourself that you made me willingly sit on your vile fingers. Don't think for a moment that I held *any* attraction for you. Don't kid yourself into thinking I wanted *any* of what happened."

Her nose wrinkled in absolute disgust. "Seeing you touching yourself, getting off on my pain, proved what a sick and diabolical person you are. There is *nothing* redeeming about you. At least the traffickers were honest about who they were. You…you think you're a lenient pimp with girls who actually *want* to be near him. Newsflash: *no one* wants to be near you. *No one.*"

She laughed wildly, totally drunk on her anger. "To say speaking to you is a privilege? Fuck that. Speaking to you is the most revolting thing I could *ever* do. I wish I'd been sold to anyone else. Literally anyone."

Sucking in a shallow breath, she snarled, "And in answer to your sickening question if my fingers are tired? Yes, you *fucking* bastard. Every part of me is tired. Every part of me aches. I've never been so sore or disappointed in myself in my entire life. I passed out cold once those god-awful effects wore off. I wished I'd never woken up and died right there in my sleep. Don't you get that I'd been *stolen*? I didn't answer some stupid job advertisement to be here. I didn't ask to be part of a cult where you initiate your groupies by making them become some sex-starving creature. *I was taken*, you creep! I'm here against my will! In case you aren't aware, trafficking a person means everything they held dear is snatched away and leaves them more lost and alone than ever before. I arrived to you running on barely any sleep, very little food, and a hell of a lot of fear, yet you sit there, all puffed up on your pride, wearing that ridiculous suit in this sort of weather, while patting yourself on the back for my humane treatment, when really, you're the worst of the lot!"

She slapped a hand on the table, making my coffee cup rattle in its saucer. "There. I've spoken to you. I've once again gone against my will. Now, kill me, for all I care, for raising my voice to you. Beat me within an inch of my life for cursing you. But don't you ever, *ever* think you're better than me just because of what you made me become yesterday. Don't you *ever* feel superior just because you stole everything that made me *me*. I curse the very ground you walk upon, Sully Sinclair, and I promise you, right here, right now, that I *will* find a way to make you pay for what you did. That I promise with every bone in my bruised and battered body."

Snapping upright, she held up her middle finger, swearing at me in silent language as well as the sewage she'd just uttered, addressing me with no respect whatsoever in front of guests who viewed me as a god with his harem of goddesses. "Fuck you, *Sully*. Just, fuck you."

Fuck.

She really, really shouldn't have fucking done that.

I was livid.

Beyond livid.

I was wrath itself.

For the longest moment, I let her tirade fade from ringing in my ears, replacing her shrill distress with calming twitters of birds and rustles of palms.

Then, I stood achingly slowly.

I smoothed my suit, I checked my tie knot, I glanced down at the guests blatantly rubbernecking at the carnage above them, and then I pinned her to the spot with every rampage and roar percolating in my chest.

Slowly—so as not to snap my restraint—I moved around the table toward her.

She didn't move.

Her chest pumped with breath. Her breasts strained against the white fabric of her dress, her lips glistened from her violent speech, and her skin flushed with fear not just fury.

But she didn't run as I reached out and grabbed her wrist.

She didn't flinch as I squeezed her breakable bones with every vibrating ounce of rage inside. And she didn't argue when I pulled her away from the banister and goggling guests.

She'd said her piece.

She'd resigned herself to the consequences.

Wise girl.

Stupid girl.

My fingers hurt from squeezing her so hard. Her pulse pounded in my grip. We kept a sedate and gentile pace, leaving behind sunshine and entering the main villa where a coffee house served all-day beverages and café items, sitting above the Michelin star restaurant below.

The pastry chef looked up from kneading dough, went to smile, saw my thunderous expression, and darted his gaze back to his task. A server appeared with a tray of fresh coffee cups, only to turn on her heel and scurry back into the kitchen.

Everywhere, inconspicuous staff scattered.

Eleanor remained as silent and as damning as her savage outburst but she didn't once try to run. She allowed me to cut off her blood flow to fingers that had already turned a vague tinge of blue. She followed almost at my side, not behind me or beneath me, jinxing the very air between us.

She might not fight or flee, but she wasn't meek.

Nothing was fucking meek about this girl.

I'd gotten her wrong.

I thought she was a young, fanciful idiot who'd barely lived and definitely didn't have such reckless abandon for her survival. But really...beneath that false mask, she had a temperament to rival mine. A spirit that just begged to be goddamn broken. A tendency to bury what she truly wanted to say until...she couldn't stop it anymore.

My palm smashed against the door leading toward the wooden walkway linking this villa with yet another building, allowing us to travel two stories up. We walked in the treetops, brushed past heavy coconuts, and ignored the inquisitive parrots that fluttered around us.

I never released the pressure around her wrist, and with every step, my mood darkened until all I could see was black. Black as night. Black as endless death.

I didn't look at her.

I couldn't.

I'd snap.

Reaching the next villa that housed a conference room for those guests who couldn't turn off from work completely, a high-end safety-deposit room for any valuables, and an in-house doctor who could perform almost every surgery with his highly trained team right here in paradise, I snatched open the door, jerked Eleanor into the empty conference room with its bare architecture, polished hexagonal table, and entire bank of screens ready to link any bigwig to his underlings, then threw her against the wall, slammed the door, and locked it.

But I didn't turn around.

Instead, I cricked my neck from the overwhelming tension.

I removed my sunglasses and studied the grain of the redwood door.

Inhaling and exhaling, calm and slow, I did my best to rein in my temper…so I didn't fucking destroy her.

Chapter Fifteen

I'D NEVER BEEN A trapped gazelle in a cage with a lion before. I'd never been a gerbil fed to a snake, just waiting for it to pounce. But I knew exactly how those poor critters would have felt as I stood waiting for Sully Sinclair to snap.

His back strained beneath his immaculate suit. His fists never uncurled by his sides as he kept his gaze trained on the door, as if it could somehow be stripped from its hinges and used as a weapon against me.

Neither of us said a word. The silence between us became sharper and more deadly than any knife or blade.

My heart no longer pumped but whirred like a broken apparatus, racing toward its final beat, confused about its purpose. The adrenaline drenching my system told it to race and race until it finally popped from exertion, so at least I would die a quick death. But the poor thing struggled against the sickening palpitations, fighting to find a life-giving rhythm, destining me to Sully's fury.

I swallowed hard as he finally turned around.

Slowly.

Ever, ever so slowly.

He moved as if a sudden noise or motion would snap his hard-fought control. He acted as if he was afraid of his own wrath, which in turn made me petrified.

I wished I could go back in time and never open my mouth. I wished I'd been strong enough to withstand his taunts and torments. Why had I let him get under my skin so badly? Why had I let loose even while I'd desperately tried to shut myself up?

I blushed all over again, reliving the horror of what I'd snarled. The truth of it was undeniable. The righteousness of it utterly deserved. But I didn't want to die, no matter how reckless I'd been. I didn't want to suffer a punishment that would leave me bedbound and unable to find an escape.

Stupid.

So, so stupid, Eleanor.

He stood facing me. His dark hair stayed swept off his face with its bronze-tips glinting like treasure in the strands. His eyes seemed to glow with the depths of the sea. Not just blue—not just aquamarine or turquoise, but a blend of every pigment: sunshine and shadow, depths and shallows, turmoil and debilitating temper.

His jaw worked as he ground his teeth. His powerful throat corded with muscle, and a vein pumped visibly as he continued to hold himself in check.

I'd meant what I'd said that I found him diabolical and vile. But I'd lied when I called him grotesque. *Had* I called him that, or had I managed to keep that one accusation swallowed?

Either way, he wasn't grotesque—not in the physical way at least.

He was probably the most stunning man I'd ever get close to in my entire life. His tall height was perfect for my leggy length. His features were symmetrical and masculine. His hands fit my body. His fingers knew how to draw pleasure. His cock was every girl's wet dream.

Yet…funny how his physical attributes did nothing for me.

His soul was putrid, and because of that, I found him utterly unattractive.

The tense standoff between us lasted for far too long. My knees started to shake, and the power at telling him off quickly faded for jittery nausea. Not that I'd let him see that. Not that I'd back down—not when I was the one to pick this fight.

Finally, he cracked his neck again, forced his hands to spread as if draining a few drops of his temper through his fingertips, then slowly, he came toward me.

Last time, I'd held my ground. I was too foggy with yelling at him and high on my own disregard for my life.

This time, I'd had too long to cool down, and I was far, *far* too aware of what he could do to me.

He could kill me.

He could honestly, truly kill me, and no one would care.

But that wasn't the worst he could do.

First, he could do an untold number of things to me until I *begged* for him to kill me.

He'd proven he had no morals. He'd shown he had no regard for my health.

Shit.

I bolted away.

I scrambled around the huge angular table, hoping to put the large expanse between us, so I could at least debate my life before he stole it.

But...my sudden reaction unleashed him.

The temper he'd been trying to swallow into the pits of his belly snapped, and he launched after me.

His shoes slapped on the sandstone tiles, pushing him into speed.

My bare feet gripped on the floor, but it was no use.

I ran.

He caught me.

In one second flat, he grabbed my hair with one unforgiving fist, marched me toward the table, then folded me forward until my belly and breasts squished against the cool wood, and his rock-hard thighs and cock pressed me into submission.

He shuddered.

I arched up, trying to remove his hold.

The pressure on my nape restrained me. My hair spilled from his hold while the messy strands cascaded over my cheek and onto the table.

He didn't speak for a second, breathing deliberately, the puff of his hard exhalations tickling my exposed skin.

"You're new. You're young. You're afraid." His voice sounded as if a decade had gone by. A decade where he'd been drinking saltwater and smoking endlessly. He sounded gruff and rough and entirely slipped from his throne of decorum. "For those reasons alone, I'm doing my best not to ruin you."

His free hand skated over my side, caressing my contours, touching the globes of my breasts flattened on the table. "I'm also reminding myself that thanks to your little 'outburst', the amount men will pay has just quadrupled."

He chuckled blackly. "Men are all the same, you see. We pretend we want amiable and capable. We tell poised and powerful women that we are proud and find their independence such a fucking turn-on. But really…we want a fight. We want claws and disobedience because then it gives us the right to retaliate." He grabbed a handful of my ass, squeezing brutally hard.

I'd have bruises. I'd remember his possessive grip for all time.

"You've had a chance to tell me your truth, now…allow me to return the favour." His hand slipped to my crack, tracing the sensitive, personal area and making me squirm uncomfortably. "Because you are new here, you lack appreciation of how rare it was for me to request the company of a girl. I never bother myself with a goddess once they've arrived. I leave their initiation and training to the highly qualified and obscenely paid staff who ensure my girls are content and my guests are sated and well catered to."

"You're not god, you know. Let me go."

"Hush. Your time of talking is over." He dipped a finger into my crack, pressing my underwear tight against my flesh. "It's time to listen, rebellious Jinx."

Not allowing me any leeway, he shoved his free hand up my dress and found the waistband of my lacy peach knickers that I'd found in the wardrobe in my villa. Without any request or hesitation, he yanked them down.

I clamped my thighs together.

It made no difference.

He kept pulling until air licked my exposed skin and the horrid sensation of having pieces of me stripped away once again made angry tears burn my eyes.

"You act as if I'm the worst human alive. You paint me as the villain, even if your life wasn't as perfect as you make it out to be before you were stolen. You detest me." Keeping his one hand clutching my nape and pinning me down, he bent as much as he could and jerked my knickers to the floor.

They locked around my ankles as he kicked my legs apart, acting as shackles, reminding me I was his prisoner, whether I wanted it or not.

His hand clamped on my hipbone. "Do you know my goddesses would be insanely jealous if they saw you? If they saw *us.*" He rocked his groin into me, hinting only his clothing stopped him from taking anything he wanted. "I have eavesdroppers. They report on what my girls discuss." His voice lowered to a whisper, sharing a secret with me. "They plot for ways to seduce me. To trick me into falling in love with them."

Bending over me fully, his suit brought stagnant heat and unbearable weight against my back. "Want to know why? Why bought and sold women no longer hate me but devise ways to make me keep them?" He bit the shell of my ear. "Because, little Jinx, they want access, not just to my fortunes, but to this very island they call home. They never want to leave. They don't want to stop being free in their pleasure. They want to fuck and orgasm for the rest of their godforsaken lives. And they think by fucking me, they'll get their wish."

I moaned against my will as his hand trailed between my legs, stopping dangerously high on the inside of my thigh. "Are you wet?"

His question was short and sharp, unlike his lulling storybook of lies from before.

I bared my teeth with rage. I struggled to look into his eyes, unable to turn my head with his unyielding hold. "No, I am not wet, you cretin. You didn't force-feed me that drug, so hell no, I'm not wet. I will *never* get wet for you."

He chuckled low and vain. "Never is a challenge."

"Never is the truth."

His eyebrow cocked. "I think I'll find a different truth." He laid more weight on me, making it hard to breathe. His mouth found my ear again, but this time, he didn't speak.

He kissed.

His lips were soft and coaxing, gentle and confiding. His tongue traced the shape of my lobe, trailing down my throat, pausing over my pounding pulse.

"Get off me!"

He made a guttural noise as I bucked beneath him, hating, hating, *hating* that heat swarmed outward; an intoxicating melting in my core that had nothing to do with this perverse punishment and everything to do with hardwiring of skin and synapses and the unbreakable connection of touch and want.

It was as debilitating as taking a drug to hijack my brain's pathways. Yesterday, he'd used my mental desire against me. Today, he conjured entirely physical. Both I had no control over, even though I hated him to the point of tears. Even though I would willingly stab a dagger into his black-crippled heart. "Stop."

"Not until I prove a point."

"There is no point."

"There is if you're wet." A smile tainted his vibrating timbre. "Wouldn't that just topple you further from your self-imposed grace?"

"Don't mistake a bodily function for anything other than

what it is."

"So, you're saying I should just fuck you and not hold myself back because it's just a bodily function?"

I tried to hide my fearful quake. I didn't succeed. "You can do anything you want to me. You've proven that over and over again. You could fuck me. You could kill me. There is no one to stop you. But you're lying to yourself if you think I want you just because my body might do something against my will."

"So you don't deny I'm making you wet."

"You have nothing to do with it. It's—"

"I have *everything* to do with it." His lips skated over my throat again, making me shudder. "You're flushed. In another few minutes, I guarantee when I insert a finger inside you, you'll want it."

"I'll never want it," I growled as much as I could with him stopping my ribcage from expanding for air. "A man gets hard because of blood flow to the area. A woman gets wet because of the same thing. It's just biology."

"It's stimulation." He unsheathed his teeth, scraping sharp canines along the path he'd just kissed.

"It's manipulation." I bucked again, wedging my hands under me against the table, trying to push up.

He pulled back a fraction, giving me space to inhale a large suck of oxygen. The life-giving air made my head swim, and for the first time since waking after the most horrendous day of my life yesterday, I noticed how weak I was.

How my biceps wobbled without much strength. How my stomach fluttered around emptiness. How my entire body started to shake, almost uncontrollably—not because of Sully's nasty experiment, but because my blood sugar levels had finally crashed.

Whatever leftover energy I had vanished in a single breath, leaving me woozy, nauseous, and feeble.

I'd never let myself get to this level of starvation before. I was a smart traveller and always had muesli bars, trail mix, or a sugary drink in my bag, just in case we were exploring too far from a food source.

But here, I hadn't eaten since arriving. All I'd had was some stale crackers in a plane crate. God, how long ago was that? This monster thought he looked after his possessions. He gloated about his girls wanting to seduce him so they became his for eternity when he couldn't even stop torturing me long enough to ensure I wouldn't die from malnutrition.

It took every shred of pride I had left, but I let my arms buckle, surrendering to his control. "I'm not feeling very well."

Any ordinary man would back off immediately. He'd ask questions, figure out my malady, and do his utmost to ensure I felt better.

This man...he just chuckled in my ear and trailed his fingers to brush against the lips of my sex. "Lies won't get you free." He sucked in a breath as he teased the tip of one finger inside me. "Just like lies about your wetness are bullshit."

God, the pain.

I tensed against the sore, swollen muscles of my million orgasms yesterday. I flinched against the agonising oversensitivity. Every part of me had been brutalised, thanks to his elixir, and just the tiniest touch today was a talon, a claw, a machete.

"Sore, Eleanor?" he murmured, easing the entire length of his finger inside. "Were you a bit rough with yourself yesterday?"

I squeezed my eyes shut as he stroked me.

He didn't drive his finger deep and ruthless. Instead, he feathered his touch as if fully aware of how excruciating it was for me.

His hand around my nape let me go, brushing aside my hair to press a kiss directly on the beads of my spine. His gentleness was totally unexpected after his unleashed fury from before.

My lack of food left me with no reserves, and tears bled from my eyes, splashing on the table.

"Do you concede that I was right?"

I didn't reply. I kept my eyes closed. I tried not to focus on the spinning room.

His finger dived in and out, revealing, in very explicit terms, that there was lubrication. That I was wet—not drenched like I was yesterday, but definitely not dry.

I'd known the second he'd kissed my ear that I didn't stand a chance. All women knew when they were wet, and I couldn't deny he'd won.

But I couldn't *let* him win.

Lying prone on the table with his hand between my legs, I hissed, "I'm glad I'm wet."

His breath caught, his voice layered with black suspicion. "You are?"

I nodded, catching my hair on the lacquered wood. "At least my body has protected me from the pain of your touch. At least you can't hurt me, no matter how hard you try. You could fuck me and call it punishment, but because my body anticipated something so heinous from you, I won't have any lasting effects. No tearing because I'm too dry. No blood because I'm not ready. You would just be yet another bastard who took what wasn't his to take, and I would forget about you the moment it was over. My wetness ensures you are *nothing*. Just a temporary nightmare that will be over soon. The moment you finish, I would never think about you again. I would never—"

"Fuck, you have no self-preservation." His one finger became two in one deep, dangerous thrust.

I winced and cried out.

"Believe me, Eleanor Grace, if I ever fucked you, I'd be highly fucking *memorable*. I'd erase all other lovers. You'd never want anyone else. You *couldn't* have anyone else." His teeth snapped by my ear. "You'd be mine the moment I took you."

He arched his wrist, diving deep.

I cried out again as my hipbones smashed against the table.

His hand drove between my legs, proving what I'd just said. He could stretch me, claim me, use me…but he couldn't hurt me—not in ways past the pain of overuse yesterday. However, he could try. He could bruise and break and ultimately kill, but if he thought he could make me want him?

He was fucking delusional.

Natural biology ensured my body would be his plaything, but it allowed my mind to turn off. After all, this was good training. If I didn't find a way off this island soon, I would no doubt be forced to sleep with one of his horrid guests.

Sex is just sex, Ellie.

Think of it as walking and running. It's just an activity.

A start and a finish and then you're done.

Sully yanked his touch away, ripped me from the table, then spun me around to face him. "Who are you?" He shook me, his fingers digging into my shoulders. "Who the fuck are you?"

The sudden motion of horizontal to vertical and spinning in a circle was the final straw on my already incapacitated nervous system.

No reserves.

No strength.

I wobbled as he grabbed my chin with the same fingers that'd been inside me, leaving a musky slippery brand upon my skin. "I should kill you right now…put us both out of our misery."

I repelled away from him.

The room swam.
And I did something I'd never done before.
No...
No...
Too late.
I fainted.
Right there at his feet.

Sullivan

Chapter Sixteen

"HER LEVELS ARE DANGEROUSLY low. Her iron, glucose, sodium…they're all way below what is required for a woman of her height and weight." Dr Campbell snapped off his gloves and turned to swivel his chair to face me.

The vial holding Eleanor's blood lay abandoned in the centrifuge machine. The droplets he'd tested all glowed in different stages of experiment in test tubes and on microscope slides.

"What has she had to eat since her arrival?" Without waiting for me to reply, he added, "I don't think she's sick or suffering a long-term illness. However, I'll have questions when she wakes. It is worrying that she fainted, though. Her blood pressure is extremely low—that will be the cause of her blacking out, and the wounds left over from her relocation could also have drained her of energy."

He paused, looking at me expectantly over his half-moon reading glasses. Pushing sixty, Dr Campbell came highly recommended and exceedingly expensive. But he was the best consultant and surgeon for my populated islands.

Leaning against the shelving on the other side of the small medical room, I kept my arms crossed. I didn't glower at Eleanor as she lay prone and lifeless on the gurney. I didn't relive the moment of triumph when I'd found her wet, then the frustrating annoyance of her crumpling at my feet.

At first, I thought it was a trick. A way out of our fierce debate.

But when I'd nudged her with my shoe and she hadn't moved, I'd hauled her into my arms, stormed to the doctor, and demanded he figure out what the hell was wrong.

I didn't like weak things.

I didn't like feeling as if I'd caused her to collapse, all because I'd pushed her too far. I'd been pushing her since she fucking arrived. I'd hounded her and tortured her, and this was my penance.

"Sinclair...are you listening? What has she eaten since arriving? Maybe she's intolerant to something? Perhaps she requires medicine that she hasn't received? The sooner I know—"

"I don't know her medical history, but I don't think it's anything to do with what she's eaten...more like what she hasn't."

He stood, glancing at Eleanor. Her long hair cascaded off the gurney, a waterfall of gleaming chocolate. Her lips were slightly parted, her forehead smooth in slumber, her eyelashes feathering shadows on colourless cheeks.

She no longer looked like an avenging immortal but a hapless human who'd gone to war with a god and failed.

"You don't think she's eaten a thing since landing yesterday morning?" His white eyebrow rose in shock. "She arrived early. That was over"— he checked his wristwatch —"twenty-nine hours ago."

I shrugged, cursing him for making me responsible for her passing out, all while I wished I could blame someone else. But really, the problem was entirely my fault. She'd arrived, I'd force-fed the elixir so her only concern for the rest of the day had been sexual hunger rather than bodily starvation, and then exhaustion sucked her deep with no reprieve.

I should've ensured she'd eaten, or at the very least had something to drink the moment she stepped out of her room. Instead, she'd picked a fight with me, ensured my guests witnessed our unsightly domestic, and then had the audacity to keep standing up to me when all I wanted was some space to think. Some understanding of why I found this woman so goddamn enticing.

She wasn't special.

Sure, she was gorgeous but so were my other goddesses.

Why did she have the power to make my blood boil and cock pound?

Why did she make me struggle to remain human when all I

wanted to do was ravage the fuck out of her?

"She needs nutrition, Sinclair. Urgently." He moved toward a cupboard holding countless drawers. Each drawer hid something barbaric: needles, scalpels, and other tricks of the medical trade.

Withdrawing a syringe, he said, "I can give her something intravenously. At least it will kick-start her system." His eyes hardened. "But you need to feed this woman if you want her to be strong enough to serve you."

Nodding once, I let him busy himself with fluids and medicine. Turning away, I swiped on my phone and called Calvin.

Like always, he answered by the second ring. Punctual, polite, ready to please. "Hey. What do you need?"

"A smoothie. Get the kitchen to make something with as many vitamins and minerals as they can stuff inside a liquid lunch. Bring it to the surgery immediately. Then get them to cook a meal with every vegetable and fruit we have on this damn island. Take it to Jinx's room in thirty minutes. Got it?"

"Got it." He hung up.

I swiped a hand through my hair, tucking my phone back into my pocket. My eyes drifted once again to Eleanor, expecting to see her out cold, only to lock eyes with the condemning grey gaze of a woman who survived entirely on hate and fury.

"Ah, you're awake." Dr Campbell smiled down at her, the needle he'd been about to puncture her with poised like a tiny harpoon. "How are you feeling?"

Her gaze snapped from mine, to the doctor, around the room, then locked onto the syringe. She jack-knifed up so fast, her forehead hit the doctor's chin, causing both of them to recoil with a groan.

The gurney creaked, and her hair fell around her face, hiding her from me as she pressed shaking hands to her eyes and weaved weakly on the raised platform.

The doctor recovered before her, ensuring the needle was still sterile and hadn't touched anything. Placing it delicately into the stainless-steel tray on the bedside table, he waited until she swallowed, shook her head, and dropped her hands before saying gently, "You fainted. You're okay. I'm Jim Campbell, and I've been taking care of you while you were unconscious." He smiled with his perfect patient manner. "Your blood pressure is very low, but I hope, once you eat, you should feel right as rain."

Eleanor swallowed again, throwing me a filthy look before looking gratefully at the doctor. "I agree. I know I'm dehydrated and overly hungry. I wanted to eat hours ago, but…" She snorted, glowering at me. "*Things* delayed me."

"Yes, well. You can't be ignoring meals again. It's a detriment to your health." He stared pointedly at the syringe. "I can give you something to replace the minerals that you're lacking, a boost as it were. Would you like it?"

She shook her head so fast, she almost passed out again. "No. No more drugs against my will."

"It's not a drug, but I understand." He moved the needle away. "Are there any underlying conditions you have? Any medicines you should be taking that perhaps you don't have access to in your new…eh, employment?"

She once again glared at me, the grey of her gaze crackling with lightning in raging storm clouds. "No. I'm fine. I'm normally perfectly healthy." She turned to look at the doctor again, saying harshly, "However, being stolen, sold, and then tormented by that man lurking in the corner hasn't exactly been productive to my mental or physical well-being."

I hid a cold chuckle behind a cough. "If you think Dr Campbell isn't aware of what goes on in this place, think again."

Campbell flushed. "Just because I know doesn't mean—"

"You're compensated accordingly." I pushed off from the cupboards. "Now that Jinx is awake, let's discuss her health check and birth control."

"I think the exam can wait, don't you?" He sniffed with as much attitude he dare give me. "Let the poor girl eat and rest. We can book in the examination in a couple of days."

A couple of days?

Well, there went the scenario of putting her straight to work.

I could already taste the disappointment of my guests.

"Stop talking about me as if I'm not sitting right here," Eleanor snapped. "And for your information, I don't need an exam. I had a sexual health update five months ago before…before I began a relationship with my boyfriend." Her eyes narrowed to daggers, hiding her grief. "I was clean. And as far as birth control goes, I opted for the IUD that lasts five years. With travelling around the world, I didn't want to bother with popping pills and struggling to find the same brand in different cities, so don't you dare get pumping me with things I don't need. Don't overdose me when I've swallowed my pride and told you everything you need to know. And don't you dare stick anything inside me. I've already been subjected to that by the traffickers who sent me to you."

My hands balled at the thought of her treatment before becoming mine. I never asked what the men did to the women I purchased, and hearing it from Eleanor, I didn't like it. I didn't like knowing she'd been violated.

You violated her, you bastard.

Yeah, but that was different. I might torment her, but I had boundaries…even if they were flexible and threatening to break around her.

At least, she was clean and immune to the nasty disease of pregnancy. Once she fortified her system with food, she could be capable of working tonight.

No reason I should delay cashing in on her bottomless value.

But did I trust her word? *Should* I rent her out tonight? Or should I allow her at least a few days to acclimatise before giving her to someone else?

A stab of white-hot jealousy caught me completely unaware.

That emotion was foreign to me. I hadn't felt the thorns of green-eyed covetousness since I was a fucking teenager losing my virginity to my older brother's ex. Even as I'd filled her, I'd been jealous knowing other men had fucked her.

The envy had only lasted two weeks before I'd realised that there was nothing to be jealous of. That girls weren't important enough to pine over. That I had much better things to concern myself with.

I scowled and killed any shred of possessiveness I felt toward this inconvenience and highly fucking dangerous goddess. Just because of my reaction to her, I would make her work. Shit, I'd work her harder than any of my other girls.

Four men a month?

Perhaps it *should* be four a week. Farming her out often would ensure any interest I had would evaporate. Thanks to hearing the praises from the guests who'd had her, seeing their smirking satisfaction, reading their gushing feedback on her talents, I'd be firmly put in my place and her in hers.

Fuck.

The doctor nodded professionally. "Sounds as if you're fully aware of your body and what you put inside it."

"I am." The withering look she gave me could've peeled paint off walls. I physically felt it. A lash of acid and acrimony. "I don't let junk food or unhealthy things get anywhere near me."

I smiled sadistically, wanting very much to say she'd inserted two of my fingers inside her voluntarily yesterday. I should remind her of her performance begging for my cock. I wanted to shove my hand under her nose and make her sniff her dried desire from before.

She'd had *something* unhealthy inside her.

She'd had me.

And if I couldn't break this unnatural fucking fascination toward her, she'd be suffering a lot more.

I'd fuck her.

I'd tie her to my bed and ride her whenever the mood struck.

Screw lucrative contracts and eager guests.

It was my turn to enjoy a goddess. After all, this was my Elysium, not hers.

Christ, I'd gone bipolar. One second, I'd confirmed my intention to use her value for my gain, and the next, I squandered away her potential all so I could have a taste.

Back the fuck off, Sully.

She is what she is.

Nothing more.

A quiet knock sounded. The door opened without waiting for admittance, and Cal strolled in. His navy suit was as pristine as if he'd been working in a high-rise with a low-set thermostat. It didn't matter it was pushing thirty-four degrees centigrade outside with a humidity factor of ninety percent; we were running a business, not enjoying a vacation, and business deserved the correct attire.

Not because of the stupid image but because a suit was power. A suit made other suits bow in respect. A suit kept the unruly men who paid to fuck my girls tight under my iron thumb.

Eleanor couldn't keep her dislike off her face as Cal marched to her with a dewy-icy glass full of delicious looking smoothie. A twizzle stick and straw sat up in the thick pink liquid. Seeds from berries and glossy glow from almond milk ensured her system would be drenched in everything it needed.

Cal eyed me, then the doctor, before finally pinning his green gaze on Eleanor.

They didn't speak but raging animosity filled the room between them. He passed her the smoothie soundlessly. She accepted wordlessly. He backed away, gave me a slight nod, then headed toward the door. "Her lunch will be in her room in thirty minutes, as you requested."

I nodded as he sniffed in annoyance and exited the surgery,

closing the door behind him, leaving a dirty trail of accusation and curiosity.

I got his wondering about my behaviour. I'd never stepped out of my role as law-maker and island-god before. But I wouldn't tolerate his judgement.

Dr Campbell cleared his throat, all too aware of the tension between my new goddess and me.

Eleanor pointedly ignored me and attacked the smoothie as if she'd hunted it, killed it, and couldn't wait for the first splash of berry-blood on her tongue.

I lurked by the wall, doing my best to stop yet another bolt of lust as her lips encircled the paper straw.

I wanted my cock to be that motherfucking straw.

I wanted it so bad my balls cramped with cum.

I wanted her more than the mountains of money she'd give me.

And that was the worst confession I could ever utter.

Chapter Seventeen

NOT ONLY HAD I been whisked away from Scott and normalcy, dumped on an island that could've been heaven on earth if it wasn't for the deranged proprietor, but I'd also somehow ended up in an alternate dimension.

A paradox universe.

That was the only explanation for how I'd been bent over a boardroom table with Sully's fingers inside me as a punishment this morning, to now staring at him over a table laden with plates, bowls, and every deliciousness on the planet this afternoon.

I hadn't moved since he'd escorted me to my room, waved silently at the groaning fare displayed on a table that'd been elegantly dressed on the small deck outside my villa, then stalked behind me until we both sat awkwardly. Every move made us hyperaware of each other as if this was a very, *very* bad date.

I couldn't help the way I ogled the food. The smoothie had granted some energy but hadn't begun to fill the emptiness inside. My stomach snarled to devour every tasty morsel in sight, but I didn't reach for a fork. I didn't make any sudden moves around him…not after last time. Not after his temper had snapped the moment I'd tried to run.

It seemed we both had a gift at controlling our impulses. I'd managed to stay silent in Mexico, for the most part. I'd done okay swallowing down what I truly wanted to say—until Sully gave me no choice but to be swept away on an avalanche of insinuations and complaints.

And he'd almost gotten his anger under control after my outburst. He'd used tricks and familiar methods to dampen his rage, so he never broke the suave character of unruffled businessman he portrayed.

Yet all it'd taken to break him was for me to bolt.

A knee-jerk reaction to get away from him had bulldozed past his walls and ensured he was as much a slave to his outbursts as I was to mine.

I glared at him across the table, cursing the feathering scents coming off each dish. Paprika and garlic and smoky notes all shot up my nose with coaxing appeal.

Three-tier plates held selections and temptations of every exotic meal imaginable. However, there was no Western food. If I guessed, I'd say most of the menu was Indonesian.

Is that where we are?

My breath caught. I hadn't had time to think how adrift I felt, not knowing where in the world I was currently residing. But with one hint of a location, my heart galloped to know more.

I didn't want to be the first to speak. I didn't want to seem as if I'd accepted his presence or was in any way grateful for his help. The embarrassment I'd already suffered from him driving me to such filthy acts yesterday was layered with yet more chagrin now that I'd fainted in front of him.

Two things I would never have done in front of *anyone*, let alone *him*.

I'd never fainted in my entire life.

I positively *despised* that he'd seen me that weak—even though it was *his* fault. Just like yesterday was his fault. Just like all of this *is his fault!*

My anger sprang from nowhere, breaking any hesitation in reaching for the food. Screw him if I moved too quickly. Fuck him for making me afraid.

Snatching a small noodle dish with crispy shallots and a fried egg on top, I snapped, "Where in Indonesia are we?"

Sully froze in his black canvas chair. His blue eyes mimicked the sparkling ocean behind him; the sun painted him in golden graces. Just like in his office, his skin didn't shine from sweat, his heavy five o'clock shadow was immaculate, his suit without a wrinkle.

He might have a volcano for a heart, silent and seething, puffing the occasional threat of smoke, but when provoked he overflowed. His temper was magma, his lust red-hot lava, the power of his rage spilled out over everything, burning, mutilating, until finally cooling to suffocating ash.

"Clever." He moved gracefully, cricking his neck like he did in the boardroom and placing his arms on the chair rests. "What makes you think you're in Indonesia?"

I chewed a mouthful of the best tasting noodles in my life. I didn't rush. Not for him. I savoured every bite, and when I swallowed, I blotted my mouth daintily with a napkin.

Finally, I pinned him with a stare. "This is Mie Goreng. It's an Indo dish."

"And you know that how?"

"I might be young, but I'm not stupid." I dug deeper into the nest of noodles, peering at the ingredients, ready to take another bite.

Huh.

No prawn.

No chicken.

Normally, I had to shove aside meat in dishes people gave me without asking if I was a meatasaurus. In this dish, however, only fresh veggies and saturated flavours waited for my fork.

His nostrils flared as he tipped his head in a half-mocking bow. "So, you're clever at deducing information from your surroundings."

"Don't mock me."

His eyebrow arched. "Mock you?"

"You sound totally shocked that I might have a brain."

He ran a hand over his mouth, never taking his piercing sea gaze off me. "Oh, I know you have a brain, Eleanor Grace. And a wicked sharp tongue to match."

I vibrated with words clambering up my throat. I'd put my wicked tongue to use by flaying him alive with yet more harsh truths of his treatment, but…I'd just said I wasn't stupid.

And picking yet another fight before I'd eaten would be stupid.

Antagonising him before I had a chance to stuff as much of this delicious fare into my mouth as possible would be the epitome of stupid.

It would also be horribly wasteful.

Ignoring him, I reached for another bowl holding chargrilled aubergine drizzled with peanut sauce. Stabbing the perfectly cooked vegetable, I couldn't hold back my moan as a perfect blend of ginger, peanut, and rich eggplant exploded on my tongue.

Wow.

He chuckled under his breath. "You didn't like my elixir, but you like my food."

"Your elixir is an abomination."

"Yet my food is a blessing."

"It is when you starved me."

He nodded and fanned his fingers out in surrender. "Touché."

Leaning back in my chair, I refused to study him. To try and read what he kept hidden. I just let basic survival be my shield. "Why are you still here? I don't need babysitting and I thought you didn't demean yourself by spending any more time than necessary with your *'goddesses'*."

"You say that word like it's filthy."

"It is."

"They don't think so."

"They're trapped and brainwashed girls. Wait until I remind them of what a gilded cage you've ensnared them in."

He laughed again, cold and calculating but with a thread of heat. "Go ahead. Tell them. They'll soon put you in your place." He leaned forward, stabbing his elbows into the table and steepling his hands. "Let me remind you that my girls crave me. They want me, not just for the term of our contract, but forever." His voice lowered, as if one could be hiding in the bushes watching us. "If they saw this...saw us, you'd probably not be well-liked. They'd be..." He smiled slow and wolf-like. "Jealous."

"Jealous because I've somehow caught the attention of a monster? What poor, delusional souls."

His smile turned sharper with white canines. "Jealous because you've only been here one night and already you've enjoyed more of my company than any of their days combined."

I rolled my eyes. "Lucky me."

His gaze tightened, the blue of his irises darkening with warning. "I'm keeping myself on a tight leash, Goddess Jinx, but just because I'm allowing you liberties, don't think for a fucking moment that I can't take them away."

Goosebumps darted over my skin.

How did he do that?

How did he change his voice from plush velveteen to deadly dagger?

Shuddering in my chair, I didn't back down. No matter how

reckless I'd been, I still couldn't control my suicidal rage toward this man. I had a physical reaction to his presence. I itched with overwhelming hate. "Well, please tell your *jealous* goddesses that I'll happily trade places. I'd be overjoyed to be inconsequential to you, rather than some puzzle you're trying to solve."

"Why do you think you're a puzzle?" He watched me like a hunter.

I stabbed a fork in his direction. "Because of the way you're looking at me right now."

"Like how?" He scowled, wrinkling his roguish face.

"Like you can't understand why you want me. As if you're debating if you should drag me into the sea and drown me or..." I bit my lip, shutting myself up.

Stop it.

Just eat.

Ignore him.

I speared a caramelized carrot, dripping in sweet and spicy sauce. Biting it in two, I chewed with utmost concentration, replacing the tingling heat of our conversation with the numerous dishes waiting for my belly.

"Or what?" he murmured, his voice licking like island air—heavy, hot, and entirely too decadent.

I ate another carrot, hating the knots in my stomach caused by his stare, cursing the pebbling of nipples that were chaffed and sore from my over-sexed ministrations yesterday.

"Tell me, Eleanor, should I drown you or..."

I shivered, stabbing a piece of garlic-infused morning glory. Crispy fried tofu rested on top of the green veggies and its pretty yellow flowers.

He sighed, arching his hips as if making room for yet another hard-on. "We both know what you don't want to say. And..." He wiped his mouth again as one hand disappeared beneath the table. His bicep flexed as he fisted himself. "You're right."

"I didn't say anything."

"It doesn't mean you're not thinking it. That I'm not thinking it. That every second I sit here, pretending to be a gentleman, entertaining you as if you were my guest and not my property, that it's not there...in the background, tainting everything."

My hands shook as I selected a dish with pumpkin and coconut cream. "You're ruining my appetite."

"Our conversation is ruining your appetite, or the knowledge that I'm fighting every fucking instinct not to drag you into that villa and fuck you until you pass out again?"

My fork clattered to the table, spraying the white linen with coconut cream. I braced my spine and stared him dead in the eyes. "Why don't you then? You've threatened me enough. Just get it over with."

He groaned as he forced his hand off his erection and back onto the armrest. "If I did, I doubt I'd stop even if you did pass out."

"Is that meant to scare me?"

"Does it?"

"Of course, it does." I sneered. "I could sit here and tell you that you're never going to touch me. That I won't allow it. But we both know that's a lie. It's a lie because you're ten times stronger and twice as big." Brandishing a butter knife, I added, "To be honest, I'm tired of all of this. I'm tired of you. I'm tired of this place. I'm tired of being afraid. I'd rather you just did whatever you're going to do then left me the hell alone."

Tears pricked but not from grief. They were made up of pure liquid rage. I'd hoped I might avoid being this bastard's plaything. I'd hoped that whatever strange and undeniable hum existed between us would die before he touched me again.

But…sitting there, with the pretence of lunch between us and the lapping ocean creeping higher up his shores, I couldn't be naïve any longer.

This was an island of sex.

The chances of escaping before I had to provide such a service were slim to non-existent, but it didn't mean I'd ever stop trying. Man after man, night after night, I would submit to this asshole's commands because I had no choice, but I would *never* stop trying to reclaim my freedom.

But how could I vanish when he never stopped watching me?

How could I slip away undetected if Sully Sinclair gave in to the burning, sickening violence between us?

The truth was, I wouldn't be able to.

If he kept taunting me like a panther with giant claws, batting me from paw to paw, constantly trying to decide if he should use me or dispatch me, I didn't stand a chance.

One or the other had to happen.

Sex or murder.

And sooner rather than later.

He reclined in his chair, smoothing his grey tie. "An outburst like that is normally severely reprimanded."

"How? By fucking the poor girl into submission?"

"No, by reminding her that all the luxuries and pleasantries she enjoys can be taken away, just like that." He snapped his fingers. "Her villa, her food, her clothing, her very value. They can vanish in one argument, leaving her naked and alone on some forgotten part of my archipelago, dying of sun exposure and dehydration."

"And that's why you think you're god, I suppose. Because you can snuff out anyone's life so easily."

"Precisely." He buffed his fingernails on his blazer. His eyes flashed as if he didn't want to admit something but was going to anyway. "I could send you out there for a day or two for a much-needed lesson. Your skin would crack from sunburn. You'd drink saltwater for a reprieve. You'd become delusional and be only too happy to fuck me when you realised how your existence is a mere speck within my hand, but…where is the revenue in that? Sunburn takes a while to heal. There are long-lasting effects of chronic dehydration. The only path for you, my wicked-tongued Jinx, is fucking me or fucking a guest. One I don't get paid for and the other I do. I still haven't decided which is more valuable to me yet."

I swallowed hard.

I'd stood up to this prick. I'd talked to him without a wobble in my voice or tears in my eyes, but whatever energy the smoothie had given me was suddenly evaporated all over again. I quaked with hunger and horror. I no longer had an appetite, but I was starving.

More starving than I'd ever been in my life.

For help, for hope, for kindness.

My back remained straight as a sword, but my shoulders deflated in defeat. He'd won. He'd *always* win. All I had left was his generosity and continued restraint. Without another argument, I reached for a dish of bean sprouts and tempeh all stir-fried with baby mushrooms.

I stopped with a forkful of juicy mushroom on its way to being eaten. I peered at the table. At every dish and delicacy. And my hatred threaded with a tiny cord of confusion.

No meat.

Anywhere.

No roast duck or barbecued pig.

No fish or crustacean or condemned creature with a heartbeat.

I looked up and caught his blazing stare. And instead of responding to his own internal debate. Instead of giving reasons why he should continue to hold my value higher for another to use rather than himself, I asked an insanely important question. "All these dishes are vegetarian." I gulped. "How...how did you know?"

I hadn't told the traffickers my dietary preferences.

I hadn't told him.

Had he researched my name and tracked me down? Had he stalked my profiles and social media? But if he had...*how* did he know? I wasn't vocal about my lifestyle. Even Scott remained quiet on his vegetarianism because most of his friends were jocks and mocked him for choosing plants over beasts.

This man who put such little worth on a human life had served me a lunch where nothing had to die.

Why?

Sully continued to sit silently. His body seethed with temper all while thoughts and secrets battled in his eyes. Finally, slowly, he stood.

He moved toward me until he towered over my chair. He didn't speak a word as he bent and cupped my chin, holding me firm. "You're a vegetarian?" he asked in a clipped, cold voice, but beneath that was the brittleness of agitation.

I nodded, or as much as I could in his control.

His eyes snapped shut. His nostrils flared. He visibly shook before he shoved away whatever anger surged in his veins and dug his fingers painfully into my cheeks. "Nothing alive will end up on your plate while you serve me. Everything you eat on this island is grown by my own cultivators. My gardens and greenhouses are located one island over. My eggs are laid by free-range hens. My cheese is made from hand-milked cows and goats. Every morsel I feed you has come from the land that I rule."

My eyes bugged.

That was...that was enlightened. That was the habit and choice of someone who either cared about his footprint on this earth or had too much empathy to slaughter or cause suffering.

That didn't fit with the bastard who took great pleasure from *my* suffering. It didn't compute with what I knew about him.

What do you know about him?

Nothing.

I flinched as he bowed closer and pulled me nearer at the same time. Our noses brushed, our eyes locked, and for a terrifying second, I thought he'd kiss me.

But then the moment passed, and he tossed me away as if he couldn't tolerate touching me any longer. Rebuttoning his blazer and smoothing down his dishevelled edges, he backed away, ready to leave.

And once again, I did something I'd never in a million years thought I'd do. I held up a hand, asking him to stay, needing to ask a question.

A question he'd asked me.

A question I wasn't entirely sure I'd like the answer to.

"Who *are* you?" I squinted in the bright afternoon sun. "What man can be so empathic toward animals yet be so callous toward humans?"

He mulled over my query as if it were an astringent wine. His lips thinned, his eyebrows tugged to shadow vibrant blue eyes, and he finally murmured, "I'm empathetic to those creatures born into horror and mutilation. I am not empathetic to the creatures who caused it. I'm using the rules to my own advantage. We slaughter and maim others. Therefore, we are not above slaughter and torture ourselves."

"So...I'm a chicken to you. A cow destined to—"

"You're human. But humans are disposable. Men, women...we're all the same. We think cages are beneath us. We think forced rape is beyond us. We think death is unthinkable because we're *special*." He swiped a hand through his dark, bronze-tipped hair. "We're not special." His lips curved into an icy, heartless smile. "We're just monsters with the ability to speak. Monsters who pay any price to be free."

Turning around, he stalked toward the villa. I sank deep into depressed realisation as he left me on the deck, surrounded by delicious, untouched food that had grown in his soils and blossomed under his care.

Sully operated within his own laws. The laws that humans had devised for livestock.

That was all I was.

Livestock.

With no voice.

No choice.

His dark, seductive timbre sliced over his shoulder. "Enjoy your evening alone, Eleanor. Because tomorrow...you'll have company to entertain."

Sullivan

Chapter Eighteen

"SINCLAIR, A WORD?"

I didn't stop, prowling down the main pathway linking the restaurant villa to the beach housing water sports and loungers.

I'd stalked away from Eleanor's accommodation with only one thing in mind: getting the farthest distance away from her.

She dare be a fucking vegetarian? She dare look at me like I'd looked at her? She dare ask me who *I* was?

Who the fuck was *she*?

What possessed me to purchase her?

I wanted a refund.

I wanted her gone.

No matter the wealth she would bring me, her disruption to my carefully structured world wasn't worth it.

"Sinclair. Hold up."

I swore under my breath and slowed my gait, looking over my shoulder. Markus Grammer held up his hand in a hail, an obnoxious smile on his face and lustful hope in his eyes.

Goddammit.

Stopping, I turned to face him fully, crossing my arms with expectation of his request. If I spoke without clearing my throat, I'd snarl at him to back the fuck off from the goddess he was about to ask for.

But that would be bad for business.

That wasn't my idea of control.

Markus slowed to a stop, breathing hard from the minor chase. He had the fitness level that I expected of a desk-bound politician. He wasn't fat, but he wasn't fit, and it showed in his lack of swimming strength, stamina, and overall activities that he didn't indulge in on my shores.

Raking a hand through my hair, I tugged my tie knot and shook off the residual hunger and fury that seemed to infect me whenever I was in Eleanor's company.

I had no idea what possessed me to stay with her while she ate. Why I didn't just leave her at the surgery and let Dr Campbell or any other staff escort her back to her villa.

I wasn't a chaperone. And I wasn't some lust-struck fool.

I didn't know what I was, and that was what made me fucking rage.

Markus looked at me for the first time; his eager smile dropped with hesitation. "Eh, if this is a bad time...I can—"

"It's fine." Just as I feared, my voice resembled some sex-obsessed Neanderthal. I cleared my throat, coughing for good measure. By the time I smiled and placed my mask of helpful hotelier and exclusive renter of women back on my face, my voice was normal, smooth, gentile. "What can I help you with? Everything okay with your stay so far?" I smiled wider. "If you require anything, anything at all, be sure to have your private butler attend to you."

"I know." Markus nodded gratefully, his floppy blond hair hanging over one eye. Pushing the mess out of his sight, he looked at the sand sticking to his flip-flops before catching my eye again, and rushing, "That goddess we saw in the dining villa. The one who...yelled at you."

I kept my smile strictly in place. "The one who only arrived yesterday and is still yet to learn my laws?"

"Oh, she's new?"

"Very."

"Is she...available?"

I ignored the urge to rip his fucking head off. Since when did I want to maim my guests? Normally, I enjoyed the tease, the negotiation, the power of granting them what they wanted or denying them until they gave better terms.

My animosity toward him didn't come from wanting to negotiate. It came from not wanting to share.

"That depends. I'm fully aware of the value she'll command,

even being as new as she is."

"So…she hasn't been in Euphoria yet? She hasn't been with any other guest?"

I crossed my arms so I didn't tear his motherfucking throat out. "No, she has not."

His eyes lit up with a million candles, his eagerness switching to desperation. "How much?"

And that was the kicker. I'd already milked this man out of a few hundred k. The cost to stay on my shores commanded a steep deposit. Normally, the rate included a single night in Euphoria with a girl I deemed a good match. One night was usually all a man could handle, and the rest of his stay was recuperation from the best fucking night of his life.

However…just like any hotel, there were add-ons and extra activities that weren't covered in the original price…additional pleasure that could be bartered.

"How much do you feel she's worth?" I looked over his shoulder, catching the eye of yet another lust-driven guest as he walked by.

Ah, shit.

The supermarket owner noticed me, changed his direction, and closed the distance between us.

So, the bidding war had officially begun.

Markus heard the soft crunch of sand and slap of flip-flops, turning to face his competition.

Jordon Wordworth gave Markus a tight smile, entirely aware he'd interrupted a negotiation and wasn't too happy about not having a chance to put his own bid forward. I had no doubt he was used to auctions and buying produce quickly, stocking his shelves before the other chains could grab a bargain.

There would be no bargain here.

Only extortion and my still undecided schizophrenia on whether I should sell Eleanor or keep her for myself.

Jinx.

Her name is Jinx.

She is not a person anymore. She is a possession. She is no different than any other girl who provides a service. Don't mistake her for more; otherwise, the only curse she'll cause will be you, you fucking idiot.

"Are you discussing that enchanting creature who had the balls to argue with you, Sinclair?" Jordon smirked. His dark hair held streaks of silver, painting him as older than his thirty-nine years. Despite his salt and pepper mop, his body was in better shape than Markus. He'd be athletic behind closed doors. He'd have the stamina to fuck a girl who wouldn't stop begging for it the moment elixir was slipped down her throat.

"We are." I nodded regally, hiding my sudden black animosity.

"Have you decided on a price?" Jordon asked, his tone unable to hide his craving of her.

"We were just about to discuss that." I narrowed my gaze at Markus. "Weren't we, Mr. Grammer?"

Markus swallowed and raked a hand through his floppy hair. "For the entire night? Not just a few hours?"

I shoved hands into my pants pockets so I didn't dig my thumbs into his eye sockets and bash their heads together. "If you think you can last that long." My smirk was thick and condescending. "As you saw, gentlemen, she has spirit."

Jordon groaned under his breath. "I want her every night of my stay. I'll pay an extra twenty-thousand a session with her."

Twenty fucking thousand?

My temper increased a thousand degrees. "Are you trying to insult me, Mr. Wordworth? Twenty wouldn't even buy an *hour* with her." I couldn't swallow back fresh fury. "And as you're aware, I've already been overly generous to you. I've gifted you one night. That's *free*, Mr. Wordworth. And now you insult me by offering—"

"Fifty thousand," Markus rushed. "Fifty k for five hours."

I pinned him with a feral scowl. "You've just offered me less than Wordworth. Fifty for five hours? That's ten an hour. I already said twenty would be too low."

"Fine." Markus wiped his mouth. "Seventy."

I bowed politely. "Good day, gentlemen. I'm highly confident you'll enjoy the talents of Neptune and Calico. They're both exceedingly proficient at delivering a session guaranteed to leave you—"

"One hundred thousand, Sinclair. For however long you want."

I paused.

My heart crashed and clawed to hold out my hand for such a sum, only to shred it into confetti and throw it in the sea. Normally, that figure would sway me. I'd pat myself on the back for a well-orchestrated deal and snap my fingers to ensure a staff member scurried off to prepare the goddess in question.

But now…now there was hesitation.

A pause, a reluctance—that motherfucking envy that filled me with resentment and rivalry, acting as if I had to compete with these bastards, stewing with malice at the very thought of one of them tasting what I hadn't.

My hands slipped from my pockets and curled tightly into fists.

I very, *very* much wanted to punch him. Punch both of them.

Once they were broken and bleeding, I'd be fully within my right to claim my prize. To return to Jinx as the victor and push her to the sand, strip her clothes, spread her legs, and fucking thrust over and—

"Sinclair, glad I found you." Dr Campbell appeared from the sandy side path that led to his surgery. His forehead furrowed as he noticed the three of us, testosterone ripe in the air, aggression a distinct purr beneath it.

Nodding at the guests, he cleared his throat and pulled a white bottle of pills from his cargo shorts. For a doctor, he kept his uniform lax, adopting the tropical relaxation instead of retaining strict professionalism.

I'd have a word with him about that.

I'd remind him he wasn't retired…yet.

"Here. Jinx needs to take these for the next week at least. It's just a comprehensive vitamin and a few other bits and bobs to boost her system—from your own pharmaceutical company." Pushing the bottle into my palm, he had the audacity to cup my elbow and guide me away from the panting men already enjoying fantasies of fucking a girl who'd fainted at my feet.

"Are you forgetting your place, Campbell?" I snarled, ripping my elbow from his control the moment we were far enough away.

His eyes flashed, nonplussed by my temper. "If you're renting out Jinx, it's with strict medical advisement that she be given a minimum of five days to adjust."

We stood toe to toe. He was shorter, but he used his skills as a medical practitioner to stand on a proverbial box and tower over me.

"She's perfectly recovered," I seethed. "No ill effects of her fainting episode. I personally checked she was eating before leaving her to her own devices."

He shook his head. "One afternoon of food won't be enough." He lowered his voice to ensure the impatient guests didn't overhear. "Her system has no reserves. It will take time to replace what she's lost, not just one meal. If you put her in

Euphoria; if you make her take the elixir"—his eyes narrowed—
"for the second time in as many days, I'm afraid she might suffer
worse than low blood pressure and mineral deficiency."

I crossed my arms. "I appreciate your concern, but dabbling
in my business affairs is not permitted. Jinx is here to work. I
won't have a freeloader on my shores."

"So, you'd rather have a dead goddess, is that it?"

I laughed quietly, icily. "She won't die from a night of
fucking, Campbell."

"No, she'll die from that damn elixir." He squeezed the back
of his neck. "It's too potent, Sinclair. It wreaks havoc on
hormones and imbalances the natural cycle of just about every
system in a human being. They forget to drink, eat. They can't
sleep or rest until it's run its course. The adrenaline alone that
feeds the inflated libido causes hyperawareness, rapid blood flow,
and drenches the brain in—"

"I don't need a science lesson. I'm fully aware of what the
body undergoes."

"Do you?" He scowled. "Have you personally sampled the
drug you expect others to take?"

I barked a chuckle. A chuckle that vibrated with ridicule and
disbelief.

Me?

Take elixir?

Fuck, the world wasn't ready for that.

Any girl in my radius wouldn't be ready for that horror.

I struggled to contain myself on a good day.

If I took one droplet of that substance?

Fuck me, it would be a shit-show.

An endless, BDSM, no-holds-barred, black-listed
pornography where the girl most likely ended up in pieces.

An image of Eleanor with bite marks all over her pristine
skin, sprays of cum all over her face, rope burns on her ankles,
cuff bruises on her wrists…dead from my lust, suddenly swamped
my mind.

Immediately, my chuckle turned to a choke, and I coughed.

The reminder of what I would be capable of was better than
any argument or negotiation.

Eleanor—*Jinx*—had to be kept as far away from me as
fucking possible.

I'd retained my humanity by refusing to partake in what I
sold. I didn't cripple beneath my urges. I wouldn't start now.

Rattling the bottle with the pills inside, I levelled an arctic look at Dr Campbell. "She gets three days." Raising my head and my voice, so the two impatient guests could hear, I added, "The first man to pay one-hundred-and-fifty thousand wins four hours with the spirited, wicked-tongued Jinx."

Both men agreed at the same time.

I didn't know who spoke first, and I didn't care.

I needed a swim.

I needed the ocean where the salt could put out any fire and the coolness could temper any rage.

I needed to sink deep, deep to the reef below and swim with my fellow finned monsters, curbing my urges as surely as they curbed theirs, doing our best not to take advantage of our place on the top of the food chain.

I'd learned from them the art of sheathing sharp teeth and gliding elegantly past our prey—hiding a predator's privilege, fighting the need to eradicate every morsel in our path, pretending we weren't a weapon naturally designed to kill.

Chapter Nineteen

AFTER THE MANIA OF the past thirty-six hours or so, Sully left me alone and peace reigned.

I didn't budge from that table laden with food all afternoon, taking my time to eat what I could out of each dish. When I grew full, I paused and curled up my legs to watch the golden sun glitter on turquoise water, spangling diamonds into my eyes.

When I grew thirsty, I sipped from the ice-cold carafe of mint and mango-infused water I found in the kitchenette. And when I grew peckish again, I returned to sampling, moaning often at the explosion of flavours and appreciating the culinary masterpieces of cuisine.

Even at island temperature and exposed to humidity, nothing could ruin the subtle and spicy tastes of so many exotic dishes, and I became obsessed with clearing each meal, so the chef wouldn't think I didn't love their creations when it was the best food I'd ever tasted.

Better than any food truck Scott and I had sampled. Better than any of his shoestring budget cooking or my ill-fated attempts at baking. Definitely better than the slop the Mexicans had fed me in the dark.

What had happened to the other girls imprisoned with me? Where had Tess ended up? Did she have such a difficult introduction to her new 'master' as I did? What about Scott? Was he desperately trying to find me, or had he moved on and left me as an unanswered mystery?

My questions mellowed in my mind as I continued grazing. Occasionally, my gaze would catch on the chair Sully had vacated, and I worried all over again.

Why me?

If what he said was true—about not being interested in his other goddesses but for some inexplicable reason was intrigued by me...*why?*

Why did I puzzle him?

Why had he made it a personal vendetta to destroy me in every way he could?

Alone, at last, the silence gave me far too much space to analyse and deduce. It allowed quietness to be honest, and I didn't like the confessions that honesty brought.

Sully might be intrigued by me, but...I was intrigued by him.

I hated him—of that there was no doubt or question.

But...he also confused me.

He conjured terror beyond measure but also a heat that couldn't be denied. His attractiveness was just as deadly as those plants that lured frogs and insects to their untimely death, killing them with beauty.

He was that plant, seemingly innocuous when his temper wasn't spiked, carefully calm when he had his own way, yet...utterly ruthless when it came to its prey.

No, he's not a plant.

He's a shark.

Satin and silky, hidden by deep water, camouflaged by sunlight and ocean.

He might be the most attractive male I'd ever seen. He might have made me come. I might've sat on his hand and suffered the most debilitating bliss I'd ever had. He might've been kind enough to take me to a doctor. He might've been brutally honest that there was something we couldn't understand linking us in this war.

But at the end of the day, he still paid money for my *life*.

He still believed he owned me.

He would still rent me out for his gain.

My hands curled.

My hate returned.

He's a monster.

He was supremely dangerous, and I could never, *ever* forget that.

This island was dangerous. This food was dangerous.

Everything about this place was perfectly orchestrated to lull me into acceptance, to cushion me with an existence I could accept, and nullify the fact that I had to pay for this luxury with my body.

No.

My mind turned to thoughts of escape. Without realising it, Sully had given me a blueprint to his empire. He'd told me that all the islands around us were his. Therefore, I couldn't find help on land. He'd told me a farm cultivated his food close by. Therefore, there would be workers and staff who would turn me in.

The only way to freedom would be to either build a raft and sail away without anyone noticing or somehow learn to swim great distances. Both those options sounded as if I was castaway, shipwrecked, and fighting to survive.

In a way, I was.

I'd crashed from my normal world. I'd lost all those I cared about. I was as alone in this paradise as I'd ever been, and I constantly fought the urge to break down and cry. To give in to my grief. To beg someone, anyone, to rescue me. To keep from acknowledging that the only person who could save me...was me.

Because if I admitted that—if I fully accepted my situation—I might as well wade into the shallows and give up because the thought of fighting against Sully every day, of letting strangers enter my body, of going to battle every time that bastard appeared...it was too much.

I wouldn't have the strength.

I wouldn't trust that whatever storm brewed between us wouldn't evolve into a full electrical hurricane, sparking fire, annihilating souls, breaking me apart bone by bone.

My hands shook as I reached for a banana leaf wrapped around jasmine rice and edamame beans.

Enough.

Relax.

Rest.

Recuperate.

By the time dusk fell, I'd done the best I could. Most dishes were empty and those that weren't attracted a few finches and sparrows to partake with me. I placed a few pieces of pumpkin and pineapple on a napkin and left it on the sand, staying silent and still as hermit crabs inched close, sliced off pieces with their pinchers, and scurried back to the undergrowth to eat.

With peace came awareness, and the longer I sat on the deck, watching the golden glow transform to peach twilight, the more I reflected on myself and how strong I would have to be to endure this new fate.

If I never found a way free, could I withstand four years at his mercy?

If I stopped fighting, would I turn into the brainwashed victims that Sully took such great mockery in?

Either way, I had to persevere.

I had to stay ready.

Had to remain true to me.

To *Eleanor.*

Not Jinx.

Not his.

Never his.

I stayed in my villa for twenty-four hours.

Unmolested, untaunted—totally, utterly, blissfully alone.

I slept well, considering the events. I showered in the outdoor shower, serenaded by an inquisitive parrot and sharing water droplets with gleaming green tree frogs. They sat on the fern fronds, ribbiting as the sun warmed the world and the humidity level steadily rose with each minute.

Instead of welcoming more disaster into my life, I avoided going to the dining villa. Using the in-room phone, I requested breakfast, lunch, and dinner to be brought to me, slowly growing accustomed and stupidly thinking I was safe in my private villa where even Sully hadn't knocked on my door.

A pretty staff member delivered a tray full of fluffy eggs, a mountain of tropical fruit salad, and still-warm croissants. Next to the freshly squeezed apple juice rested a bottle of pills with a small note in sharp, masculine handwriting to take one with each meal, doctor's orders.

Between meals, I gradually grew stronger. My body was no longer woozy if I turned too fast, and my vision didn't black out if I stood too quickly. Growing restless, I went for a walk along the beach, spying more villas in the lush foliage, tucked away with privacy, none of their inhabitants noticeable.

Did they house other goddesses?

Guests?

Staff?

As the sun completed its arc overhead, promising morning, then delivering afternoon, before finally condemning us back to the cloak of darkness, my heart worried more and more as evening settled.

He'd said I'd be entertaining tonight.

He'd threatened that I'd be used against my will.

Not wanting to return to my villa, but afraid of what would happen if I was found blatantly searching for methods of escape, I returned to my parcel of crystal sand, shed my summer dress, and slipped naked into the tide.

There, I waited.

My eyes trained on the deck leading into my villa.

My ears pricked.

My heart kicking.

My hands curled and ready to fight.

Sullivan

Chapter Twenty

SWIMMING WASN'T MY ONLY form of exercise.

I had weights in my villa. I ran in the soft sand ringing my shores. I regularly used the landscape of rugged hillside and rock face, splashing up the waterfall and scaling slippery crevices to sculpt and hone muscles that might get lax without use.

But none of those activities could wash away the mess inside my mind like the ocean could.

Yesterday, I swam until I could barely drag my carcass from the tide.

Tonight, I swam without getting winded or waterlogged.

My energy was through the fucking roof.

My sexual hunger past the realm of controllable.

I'd avoided harassing Ele—Jinx all day. I'd woken to find the bottle of pills the doctor gave her mocking me on my nightstand. I'd snatched them with the full intention of marching to her door, using them as an excuse of why I meddled in her life, and demanding her to get on all fours.

My morning wood was more than just blood trapped after sleeping, my entire belly coiled and roiled to fuck. My balls were tight and trapped against my body, begging for a release.

I'd suffocated the bottle of pills in one hand and throttled my cock with the other, fully aware I stood on the edge of a full-on goddamn meltdown. If I went to her, I wouldn't be able to stop myself. I'd be on her, in her, all over her the second she opened the door.

But then the phone rang, and Cal announced that the winning bidder to initiate Jinx into Euphoria was Markus Grammer. He'd already paid the full one-hundred-and-fifty k. He'd extended his stay thanks to Jinx needing three days to recover from her weak spell, and he'd willingly given me whatever budget he'd had for expensive toys and indulgences…all for the pleasure of touching what was mine.

And that's good.

That's what she's here to do.

I liked money.

But I didn't need it.

His cash wasn't wanted because *I* wanted to be the one to fuck her.

Ah, for fuck's sake, Sully.

Digging my arms into the sea, I increased my speed, trying to outswim such persistent urges. All I wanted to do was rewind a couple of days to the email when the traffickers announced they'd found the perfect girl and reply that they could keep her. Kill her. Sell her to someone else far, far away, so I never had to lay eyes on the one person to make me feel anything less than in complete control.

Perhaps, I'd caused this predicament, not her. Maybe I'd bottled up my lust for too long while living on a tropical paradise with extremely willing women. After all, a man could only go so long without sex.

When I'd opened this playground, I'd promised myself not to shit where I ate, so to speak. The girls were commodities, and as long as I treated them as assets destined to benefit someone else, they couldn't turn into liabilities.

When each one arrived, I'd been cordial to them, kind even. I'd welcomed their shyness and stark fear, knowing that eventually, they'd be all too happy to trade four years of their life for an existence that took away every stress ever invented. They didn't have to cook, clean, pay bills, raise spawn, or fawn over useless lovers.

All they had to do was relax on the beach, ring for cocktails, and, once a week, take a liquid that ensured every touch was a pure aphrodisiac.

Their plight could be a hell of a lot worse.

I dived under, welcoming the oppressive blackness found

beneath the surface. As the sun had set hours ago, the flickering torches around the island had been lit, and the lanterns decorating the sandy shores were beacons to any wayward traveller or nymph washed up from Trident's city.

Tiny pinpricks of light from the exquisite galaxy above glittered through the surface, painting the reef beneath me with silver spires. Lazy fish meandered past. An eel undulated in the current. A manta ray blotted out the tiny pinpricks of silver, dappling its oily body with starlight.

It truly was a magical world down here.

Simple.

Accepted.

The meek bowed to the powerful.

The prey avoided the predator.

Everyone had their place, and nature ensured everything behaved within the boundaries of their species.

But not her.

Not that fucking woman who spoke to me as though a queen, glowered as if I was her underling, and even in her fear refused to acknowledge my rule over her.

My lungs burned for oxygen.

Kicking to the surface, I broke the sea without a ripple, sucking in air and tasting salt on my lips. A feminine chuckle skipped over the wetness and licked down my back.

Three goddesses stood silhouetted by moonlight on the beach. Two held cocktails, adorned in scraps of bikinis, and one pranced around like she governed my empire, wearing a see-through gauzy dressing gown with nothing on underneath, open and fluttering in the slight balmy breeze.

I grew instantly hard.

Not that I wasn't constantly hard these days, thanks to that hexing witch.

I should've sent her away the moment I laid eyes on her and felt that warning kick of intrigue.

That had never happened before.

I'd heard other men boast how they'd met the one, and they just knew...instantly. But I wasn't a romantic fool, and I didn't believe in destiny or soul mates. I believed in logic and explanation, and it made me fucking rage not to have an answer as to why every part of me locked onto Eleanor and hummed at high attention. Why I found her more beautiful than any girl on my island. Why I suffered such fury at the thought of renting her out.

Why I couldn't stop fucking thinking about her.

Goddammit.

Lying on my back, I let the drifting current carry me toward the shore.

Tonight, I would send another email. I would request a different girl. Someone to be delivered quickly. Someone who was the exact opposite of my most recent curse. And that new acquisition wouldn't join my stable of goddesses; she'd be my own personal toy.

I'd use her nightly.

I wouldn't be intrigued by her.

It would be purely basic, brutal sex.

That was all I needed. Just like exercise cleared my head, a good fuck would clear my system from its inconvenient obsession with Eleanor Grace.

Letting my legs sink to the bottom, I shivered as my toes threaded into warm sand. Relief came from deciding, but my cock remained hard as a fucking palm tree. I couldn't walk out of the sea with it sticking out the top of my shorts—not with three tipsy goddesses giggling and having far too much fun.

I wasn't kidding when I told Eleanor that the women who'd been here long enough to know the good thing they had all wanted into my bed. They'd grown spoilt and lazy and enjoyed the hierarchy of being adored and lavished with gifts and luxuries.

They didn't want to go home.

And I couldn't fucking blame them.

Goddess Calico was the latest to try to seduce me. She'd picked the lock on my villa and slipped into my bed a month ago. She'd served three-and-a-half years. She was due to return to her humdrum life in six months.

She'd reached for me. I'd stopped her.

She'd tried to kiss me. I'd pushed her away.

She'd made mistake after mistake, trying to make me keep her.

That was why I had the four-year contract—signed by me and them. There was an ending, for both of us. A timeline of togetherness before going our separate ways. Because, in reality, I didn't want to have to be responsible for them as they grew older and less likely to perform.

Just like thoroughbred horses were bred, bloodlines were favoured, and hundreds of thousands of foals were destroyed if they didn't prove they could race, I kept my goddesses in the best possible care for as long as they were useful.

Four years was the optimum time for their sexual use.

After that...they weren't valuable to me anymore, and why should I pay for the best upkeep, care, and nutrition if they were no longer a worthwhile investment?

How was I any different to any other consumer?

I used a product from prime to retirement and then sent it to pasture. At least I didn't kill them when they stopped being of use. I paid them the four hundred thousand dollars that I hid in the fine-print of their contract—paying them for their time, and ensuring their servitude had been mutually beneficial.

It also provided an alibi that they'd been well compensated for their 'employment' if they ever went to the police. A signed and sealed contract, blatantly advertising what they willingly did. All they had to do was take the money and stay quiet, or give it back and fight to survive in a world that wasn't paradise.

Too bad Eleanor Grace, the stubborn twenty-something with silver embers in her eyes, couldn't be as grateful as her predecessors. If she knew how desired I was, she might understand how honoured she was to enjoy my company. How goddamn privileged she'd been that I'd dared let her ride my fingers.

She'd had more of me than any of these willing girls, yet she acted as if I was the devil.

Well, luckily, I'd reined myself in, and from now on, I wouldn't be touching any of them.

Especially that spirited hellcat who I couldn't leave the hell alone.

The soft current pushed me forward and back as the waves lapped noiselessly against the icing sugar sand. I debated swimming to the other side of the island to avoid the women, but in truth, I wanted to write that email. I wanted to get it over with so I could stick with my plan and not do something psychotic when it came time for Jinx to be handed over in two days.

But...I also knew what I'd face the second I stepped onto shore and the goddesses noticed me.

Fuck it.

Yanking my black swimming shorts down with one hand, I fisted the aching heat of my long-suffering erection. This was purely medicinal. Nothing more.

Keeping my eyes on the gossiping girls, lulled into the fantasy that they were untamed creatures there to ravish, I stroked harder, faster, creating ripples around my body.

I didn't need long.

I'd been on the razor edge of coming since I'd poured elixir down Jinx's throat. The halted orgasm I'd almost had in her presence lurked in every cell. The pain it promised hinted this wouldn't be a typical release. This would fucking rip me in two with pleasure.

Biting my bottom lip, staying as silent as I could, I gave in to the brutalising pace to make myself come. The girls didn't see me, surrounded by dark ocean. No one knew I masturbated in full view.

My head tipped back as a lacerating lightning bolt shot from my heart to my belly, dragging claws around my balls.

Ah, shit.

Shit.

A guttural groan couldn't be contained as liquid fire built to a furnace, scorching blood and bone, crippling me in ways I hadn't felt in a very long fucking time.

On the cusp of letting go—on the blinding, blistering precipice of spurting seed into the sea, I opened my eyes.

I didn't know what made me look.

Why my attention searched, found, and snarled as I found the one person I shouldn't associate with pleasure.

Eleanor stood in the shadows of ferns and palms, hiding in the pockets of blackness, eavesdropping on my goddesses.

She didn't see me.

But fuck, I saw her.

I saw everything about her.

I drank in the floaty purple dress she wore, scooped low to show pert cleavage and tied at the waist to reveal her willowy frame. Her hair draped over one shoulder, hanging with weight that begged for my fist, gleaming long and rich with starlight, casting it more quicksilver than chocolate.

Her gaze flashed like a cat's as the girls laughed as a trio.

She scowled and shook her head as if she pitied them, then rolled her eyes as if she couldn't understand them.

They laughed again.

She sighed and looked out to sea.

She looked through me to the horizon cast in midnight velvet.

She cupped her throat and dropped her touch to her heart as if the life-giving organ inside her was failing.

She looked fragile.

She looked lost.

She was the most intoxicating, provocative thing I'd ever seen, and I couldn't stop myself.

I came.

I jerked and shuddered as cords of agony exploded from my balls and out my tip, spilling into the sea in thick white spurts.

Wave after wave of savage pleasure tortured me.

And still, she kept staring out to sea, wishing for a way free, totally unaware that she'd just sealed her fate.

She. Was. *Mine.*

The still pulsing cock I held in my hand would one day plunge inside her.

It was an inevitability.

A promise.

A decree written in the stars.

Chapter Twenty-One

I'D FOUND THE HAREM.

After no one came to claim me, and I grew bored of bobbing in the ocean, I returned to my villa, showered, dressed from the copious choices of summery things in the wardrobe, and then went for a stroll.

The island was a different dimension once the sun had set.

The sandy pathways were arteries leading to some slumbering black beast. The palm trees were sinister umbrellas blotting out the stars, and the roosting of birds was replaced with the steady buzz of cicadas and courting ribbits of frogs.

Without the flickering tiki torches, finding my way would've been impossible. Each puddle of light beckoned me forward, leading me in a direction I hadn't been before. At each bend in the path, I braced myself to meet someone. To bump into a guest, to argue with Sully's minion, or even battle with Sully himself.

However, I hadn't come across anyone, and I'd continued my paint by numbers, padding in bare feet, travelling from torch to torch, lantern to lantern until the dense jungle of the gardens thinned out to the humid breeze of the shore.

I'd slammed to a stop.

Stunned and stupefied by awe.

This place...it was dazzling.

Every adjective to describe something that far exceeded extraordinary paled in the view before me. Of the way the sea sparkled with mirroring stars. Of the way far-off lights from other islands winked. Of the way my gaze soared skyward, making me sway at the endless infinity of it all. The sky wasn't just black with night; it was alive with so many *wondrous* delights.

Stars and planets, milky ways and flickering clusters.

I'd never been a stargazer, but in one second, I went from confident in my worth as a human, aware that I existed and breathed air and ate food to survive, to not having a *clue* what I was.

How could I matter when faced with such vastness?

What inconsequential little thing was I when witnessing the untold magnitude of worlds outside our world? The solar system where we bounced around like a Ping-Pong ball, thinking we were absolutely important and special and *real*, when really...we were utterly insignificant.

I stood transfixed.

My neck ached from looking up. My feet sank deeper into still-warm sand. And tears came unbidden and trickled down my cheeks. Was Scott looking at this vista? Were my mum or dad? Had that guy in Mexico given them my note? Did they hate me for abandoning them or were they happy I'd left them for true love?

My heart hurt.

True love?

More like rotten hate.

Sully had trapped me here; he'd shown me the cosmos and surrounded me with Eden...all for one purpose.

To use, abuse, and ultimately destroy me.

I cried silently for a while.

I let the liquid tracks dry into sticky salt, and then I heard a female laugh.

For the first time since arriving, I was in the presence of women.

Normally, I'd run to them. I'd find solace in my sex and spill my entire tale. I'd ask them to help me escape, to band together and kill the men who thought they were boss, but these weren't just any women.

They were goddesses.

They were *his*.

So I'd faded into the undergrowth and waited.

I watched as three stunning girls appeared with a bottle of champagne, cocktails, and the intention of indulging in a private party on the beach.

They moved with grace and freedom, totally content with their place in this strange paradise. They laughed and joked, their voices low and sensual. No shyness or body issues as one danced naked in her see-through dressing gown, and two stood sumptuously in tiny bikinis.

All were about my age or slightly older. One had dark hair, one fair, and the other skin so dark she blended into the night. They might never have met if they didn't have one thing in common.

Ownership.

To Sully.

As they clinked glasses and swirled in the moonlight, I deliberated on what I should do.

Leave?

Stay?

Watch or grant them privacy?

I couldn't decide, so I inched deeper into the undergrowth, turning into a spy. A spy who hoped by doing something dirty like eavesdropping, she might find a key to escape.

For a while, I couldn't make out what they said. Their voices pitched low and interspersed with laughter. They seemed so carefree and loose. As if they'd never suffered stress or pain. As if they'd grown so accustomed to this life that they couldn't imagine anything else remotely acceptable.

Slowly, the alcohol added volume to their conversation, and sex inevitably became a subject. Goosebumps scattered down my arms as the dark one muttered, "I've only got six months left. When I first arrived, I would've put a bullet in my brain to be free. Now..." She sighed dramatically. "Now, I'd give anything to have that man put something else inside me."

The two pealed into knowing giggles.

The blonde one fanned her face as if she suffered heatstroke all of a sudden. "When I'm in Euphoria, I pretend it's him. I mean...it could be. You never know."

"Oh, yes." The brunette swooned. "I've often pictured him. I don't want to leave without knowing what it would be like...just once."

The ebony girl tapped her on the shoulder. "Imagine slipping him elixir." Her lips spread into a Cheshire cat grin. "All three of us could have him. There'd be more than enough to go around."

The blonde spun in a circle, sloshing her fourth cocktail onto the sand. "Oh, can you picture it? He's so suave and cool toward us. So tightly controlled. I bet you that's not how he'd be with elixir running in his veins."

"He'd be an animal."

"Worse," the brunette said seriously. "He'd be a demon."

"A demon who can curse me any day."

The trio laughed again, but their mirth was tinged with want. Sully told the truth.

He'd been blatantly honest about these women wanting to bed him, all because they flourished in his captivity rather than suffocated.

I didn't understand.

How did any of this make sense?

Sure, he was good looking, but come on, have some damn respect!

Unable to listen to any more of their nonsense, I looked out to sea once again. I rubbed at my throat when I found it hard to swallow their gossip, then massaged my chest as my heart pounded with fear that one day I might be like them.

I might drink from the poisoned well and somehow have my morals and self-worth stripped, leaving me a horny, helpless woman, who daydreamed about a monster who ought to be shot.

No.

That won't happen.

I won't let it.

My gaze danced over the sapphire stars bouncing off the tide. A blot of darkness just out of sight hinted something broke the surface and prevented mirroring galaxies.

A boat perhaps?

No, too small.

A buoy?

What does it matter?

The night had turned late, and no one had commanded I 'entertain'. I didn't have to hide anymore. All I wanted to do was return to my villa, lock the door, and hope that sleep could take me far, far away from here.

Closing my eyes, I sent a fervent plea to continue having strength and never forget who I was—so I didn't turn into a clone of the girls teasing each other on the beach—then searched for a quiet way out of the bushes.

Ferns traced soft fronds along my naked arms as I backtracked. My feet welcomed the cushiony sand as I left the shadows and—

"Hey, Neptune...*look*." The quick command of a tipsy goddess wrenched my head up. She sounded so eager, so awed.

"Is that....Ooh, my God. It *is*." The brunette who I assumed was called Neptune shuddered dramatically. "Do you think he heard us?"

The dark-skinned girl smirked. "Doubt it. Unless he has sonar like a whale."

"He spends enough time in the sea, who knows what talents he has."

Neptune giggled. "With his flair for science, I wouldn't put it past him to formulate a pill to give him gills or fins or—"

"The ability to fuck one of us on the ocean floor?"

"Calico, seriously." The blonde flicked her a stern look. "Must you always be so crude?"

I raised an eyebrow at her sudden propriety, only to sigh in disgust as her stern look gave way to a lewd grin. "I bag the first sea sex!" She stabbed her forehead with her thumb, staking her claim. "I've never been with a merman."

"And you won't...because those don't exist." Neptune laughed.

"Hey, Sullivan is a myth all by himself, so he could be. I like mythical creatures."

"God, you're so annoying, Jupiter. I bag first with the man-mermaid!" Calico launched at her, spilling a glass of champagne and barely noticing a staff member as she dashed forward to refill.

"You know...if he can breathe underwater and we can't, he'll have to keep us alive while fucking us." Jupiter swooned dramatically, ducking out of Calico's reach. "His kiss wouldn't just be erotic...it would be the only thing keeping us from dying."

"God, you're such a dreamer." Calico smirked.

"Hush, both of you. He's almost onshore." Neptune pressed her finger to her lips. "Let's not embarrass ourselves, ladies."

The harem all nodded importantly.

Their giggles faded, but the lusty glow on their cheeks didn't. As one, they turned to watch the figure silently prowling from the ocean. If eagerness could claim ownership over another and staring could force someone to do their bidding, Sully Sinclair would've been a slave to his very possessions the moment he appeared from his swim.

Lucky for him, the girls had no way of making him follow through with their fantasies and could only watch as water sluiced down a flawlessly masculine body, hunger for the impressive bulge between his legs, hidden demurely in black board-shorts, and lick their lips at the effortless power of flexing muscles, strong sinew, and the impressive aura of a man who knew he was above anyone.

Who was used to absolute control.

Goosebumps shot down my spine as he narrowed his eyes and stepped onto the shore, the sea reluctantly letting him go.

His beauty wasn't fair.

It made a mockery of every other beautiful thing because it turned perfection into a sin. Prettiness was a weapon and a curse. In a woman's case, it was mainly a curse. In Sully's case, it was most definitely a weapon.

An annihilation.

Raking a hand through his sun bleach-tipped dark hair, he scattered another rainfall of droplets on his shoulders. He had no towel to wrap around his waist, no way of hiding how supremely toned his physique was.

The girls practically drooled in the sand, never ripping their eyes off him.

Sighing heavily, he stalked toward the treeline, nodding courteously at the goddesses. He didn't speak, almost as if he had no tolerance or desire to torment.

However, that didn't stop them.

The ebony girl, Calico, purred, "Well, if it isn't the Emperor of Sin himself."

Sully didn't pause. His smile was polite but cool. "Goodnight, girls." His long legs ate up sand, prowling closer toward me and the undergrowth.

A flickering tiki torch bathed him in golden flames, highlighting ridges and valleys of his chiselled belly.

"Sullivan...we were just talking about you." Neptune sidled in front of him, stopping his journey, cocking her hip suggestively and licking her bottom lip. "Care to join us? We're a few drinks ahead of you...but you could catch up."

The sexual invitation was so rife in the humid air, I almost choked on it.

Sully shook his head warningly. "Maybe another time."

"Maybe in Euphoria?" Jupiter fluttered her eyelashes, moving closer to him. "Is it true you've never sampled your own creation?"

His jaw worked as if he chewed on his temper. His eyes flickered to the darkness where I hid, almost as if he knew I was there.

He couldn't, though…could he?

Tension rippled down his back as he diplomatically replied, "This business demands all work and no play from me. Euphoria is for you and our guests."

"It could be for you too," Neptune murmured. "All of us. Tonight."

"That won't happen."

"Tomorrow?"

His eyebrows came down sharply, shadowing intense blue eyes. "Ever."

Calico visibly deflated, then moved to his side with sinuous grace. "But don't you want to know what it's like?"

Sully paused for a moment, tasting her question and teasing a reply. Finally, he whispered harshly, "It's best for everyone that I don't."

"Why?"

"Because I don't fuck my staff."

Calico bristled. "We're not just staff. We're—"

His hand lashed out, locking around her chin. "Don't mistake our relationship, Goddess Calico. You are mine to do with as I please. What I please is for you to obey me, to satisfy our guests, and to stop fantasising that I will one day fuck you." Jerking her close to him, he bit out, "That will never happen. I have been perfectly clear about that from the start, so stop this charade and save your lust for someone who wants it."

Pushing her away, he bowed with all the elegance and sovereignty of a paladin. "Now, goodnight. Nep, you're in Euphoria tomorrow. I expect you to be well-rested and not hungover."

Neptune lowered her head, staring into the dregs of her cocktail. "Yes, Sullivan."

"Good." With a harsh nod, he skirted around them and continued his stalk to the treeline.

Time to go.

Scurrying from my hiding spot, I broke into a tiptoeing jog down the sandy pathway. I got to the first turn, but before I could disappear, his voice lassoed around my waist.

"Stop."

I skidded in the sand, partly from shock at his command and partly in horror that he'd known I was there all along.

"Turn around."

I didn't.

I might've behaved and halted, but I wouldn't turn around. Not while he was mostly naked and dressed in liquid salt. Not while my heart still raced after listening to his stupid goddesses. Not when my insides no longer knew what was up or down, right or wrong, real or myth.

The soft footfalls of his steps sent chills down my back.

The next time he spoke, a gust of his breath tickled my nape. "Looking for something?"

I swivelled around, hating the sensation of him behind me. The vulnerability of it. The submissiveness of being open for an attack.

Our eyes locked. Grey to blue. His skin shimmered with dampness in the dancing fiery torches. His jaw clenched as a breeze swept down the pathway, catching my hair and making it whip over my shoulder.

His lips thinned, his powerful throat rippled as he swallowed, and his thick five o'clock shadow twinkled like tinsel, trapping ocean droplets with tiny prisms.

I straightened my spine, forcing myself to hold his stare even though it felt as if he reached both hands inside me and squeezed all the air out of my lungs with his fists. Even though it reminded me of my abominable behaviour, the fact that he'd seen me naked and unhinged...that I'd seen him equally naked and raw.

No matter how much I wanted to deny it, something linked us.

The unwanted aftermath of need. The unhealthy challenge of hate.

His nostrils flared as our stare became an eternity, creating a painful bond, a strange understanding, a terrifying future. "Well?" he growled, his voice gruff and gravelly.

"Well?" I trembled in the sand. My knuckles ached from clenching my hands so hard. What would he do if I hit him? If I let go of all the snapping, howling fury with physical violence instead of just verbal?

"Did you find what you were looking for?"

Why?

Did you?

His question lingered for far longer than a typical query, almost as if it held far more weight than first heard. Almost as if the hidden message was beyond his or my control.

Did you find what you were looking for?

Is it you?

Is it me?

Who are you?

Despite the tropical heat, my blood cast with snowflakes, and I hugged myself. Raising my chin, I replied, "No, as a matter of fact, I didn't."

No, it's not you.

It would never be you.

Scott was my boyfriend. Scott was family and home.

This man...he was my *enemy.*

We were polar opposites, destined to clash, foreordained to doom the other.

"Oh?" His voice darkened. "And what is it you wanted to find?"

"A way off this nightmare."

He froze for a second before his lips twisted into a fox-like smile. "I will personally escort you off my shores. I will be glad to see you gone...in four years."

Shadows of the retreating goddesses flickered behind him. Two dashed away, obviously heeding his warning not to drink anymore and get their beauty sleep. The last one paused, watching us braced against each other, undoubtedly seeing the blistering tension and intense dislike, hearing the flame next to us crackle with the toxic energy that formed whenever Sully and I duelled.

"How about we save each other a lot of nonsense and agree to go our separate ways now?"

He chuckled under his breath. "Your naivety would be funny if you weren't such a pain in my ass."

"I can be a pain in your ass for four years or..." I shrugged. "You can cut your losses and let me go tonight."

He crossed his arms over his naked, sea-gleaming chest. "The fact that you're trying to tell me how to run my business is mindboggling."

I scowled. "Why? You don't think I know how to run a—"

"I know you don't."

"You don't know anything about me."

"I know you're young and have no experience with a company like mine."

"Your company is just like any other. Some investments are a loss and best removed before they cause even more issues."

"You're saying you're a loss?"

"I'm saying I'll cause you untold problems if you keep me here." I narrowed my eyes. "I'm not afraid of you."

He stepped toward me quickly, crowding me, bringing naked, masculine flesh and scorching body heat.

I backpedalled, losing ground, hating myself the second I tripped.

He laughed coldly. "Not afraid? I think you're fucking petrified."

Digging my toes into the sand, I cocked my chin. "I meant what I said, Sully Sinclair. Keep me trapped against my consent and I will make you pay. I'll find some way to curse—"

"Curse me?" His arm shot up, his hand sinking into my hair. In a single heartbeat, we went from apart to linked. His fingers curled tight around the strands, tugging my scalp, sending more chills scattering. "You've already cursed me. You cursed me the second you arrived."

I tried to pull away, but his hold turned aggressive.

"Let me go."

His eyes flashed navy in the darkness as his tongue ran over his bottom lip. "Let you go? I should, shouldn't I?" His stare landed on my mouth, and lust became a sapphire fire in his gaze. "Too bad I'm not going to."

I squirmed in his hold. "I don't want to be here." I scratched fingernails over his wrist, doing my best to loosen his fingers in my hair.

He didn't even flinch.

So many swear words littered my mind. So many angry promises and violent vows varnished my tongue, but I needed air to transform thought into voice. I needed sound to switch silence into shout, and unfortunately, Sully Sinclair had successfully sucked me dry of everything.

"I don't want you here either." He narrowed his gaze. "But we're both going to have to deal with it." His other hand dived into my hair, cupping my head, holding fistfuls of length and keeping me trapped. "Whatever this is…whatever exists between us…it will die soon enough."

His gaze locked onto my mouth, his lips parting. "Maybe if I kissed you…we'd both figure out that this addicting connection is nothing more than—"

"Kiss me and your tongue will be in pieces."

He jerked me forward, pressing his forehead to mine. "Bite me and I'll bite you back. I'll bite so fucking hard…you'll bleed."

I gasped, lightheaded and furious.

"Let me go." I fought harder, not caring I caused myself pain, tearing a few strands in my struggles.

He just held on, his face steadily growing more dangerous, his features more stark, his hunger more acute. "I wouldn't keep moving if I were you." His whisper was so quiet it barely registered above the cicadas, but it was the most malignant thing I'd ever heard. "I'm a moment away from fucking you...right here."

I froze.

The only thing that moved were our chests, pumping hearts and lungs failing to administer oxygen. I swallowed hard a few times, searching for retaliation, trying to understand why his touch was as viperous as a tattoo. His fingers were the gun, his heat the ink, his possession the permanence that ensured I'd always have a mortal mark.

"Go fuck one of your other girls," I snarled. "You're right. They're extremely willing and would welcome you to do anything—"

"I don't want them." He pulled me closer; our hips collided. His hardness against my softness. My purple dress didn't protect me from the scorching dampness of his skin.

My cheeks flushed. My stomach knotted. I couldn't breathe as his head bowed, bringing his lips to hover over mine.

If he kissed me...*God, please don't kiss me.*

I couldn't let him.

Not here with galaxies reminding me how insignificant I was, he was, all of this was. Not here in paradise that had an uncanny way of removing any other reality.

I gulped and shook my head, trying to prevent his mouth from claiming mine. "Why me? Why not them?"

"That's a question I keep asking myself," he muttered, brushing his nose on mine. His eyes bored deep into me, so close, so vivid. "Why you?" Jerking me nearer, until our entire bodies pressed tight, his lips skated on mine.

I held my breath, locked in place for a savage kiss.

But instead of plundering my mouth, instead of crippling beneath the skin-crawling intensity between us, he shoved me away.

My hair tangled around his fingers as I stumbled in the sand, leaving sheets of length strewn from me to him, tethering us together even though he'd let me go.

He looked down at his hands, still stained with my hair, and his face clouded with terrible dark things, then, with gallant grace, he arched his wrists and sliced his fingers free from my clinging strands.

Once the final length tumbled from him, returning to me and breaking us apart, he rolled his shoulders, readjusted his impressive erection, then stalked around me to disappear down the pathway and into the night.

Sullivan

Chapter Twenty-Two

TO: 89082@GMAIL.COM
From: S.Sinclair@goddessisles.com
Subject: An alternative

Hello,

*The recent employee you sent is not suitable. Please send the exact opposite...***so I can stop making such a goddamn fool out of myself—***

Nope.

I punched the delete button over and over until all that remained was a blank message.

I couldn't even send a fucking email without my lust making me sound like a pussy. I doubted the traffickers would appreciate or sympathize that the girl they'd sent me filled the brief I'd given them far too well, and I'd been in a state of permanent insanity ever since.

They'd just tell me to fuck her and get it out of my system. Simple.

It's not fucking simple.

No matter my fucked-up decisions, I wouldn't break my rules. For anyone.

I didn't do weak, and I didn't do dangerous. And I wasn't such an egotistical maniac to know where Eleanor Grace was concerned...she was dangerous. I wasn't on the market for a goddess who had the power to make me forget about work, science, and all the other balls I juggled in my day-to-day life. I didn't want the mess of the aftermath.

All I wanted was a fuck toy to help relieve some stress.

TO: 89082@gmail.com
From: S.Sinclair@goddessisles.com
Subject: New Addition

Hello,

If your recruitment agency becomes aware of a short, blonde, preferably foreign employee who doesn't speak much English, and confirm that she is amiable, submissive to authority, and a diligent worker, please advise at your earliest convenience.

The other girl you sent is straight from Hades, and I'm probably going to have to kill her because she's the first to make me—

Delete.
Delete.
Delete.

Sighing hard, I left the email short and to the point. The exact opposite of Jinx would be a frumpy blonde who kept her eyes cast on the floor, her temper non-existent, her obedience in check, and her attractiveness not hardwired to affect me.

Whatever fate Eleanor had found upon my shores was my own affair, not the men who'd sourced her. I didn't like the thought of killing her just because I had a visceral reaction. I wasn't cruel without cause—even though humans had no such qualms with slaughterhouses. The methods of death and dismemberment used behind closed doors made me seem like a prince of philanthropy. Therefore, I had to decide if I was going to be a monster or magnanimous.

Eleanor was in sound health. Her value topped any of my current stock. She had plenty of years of servitude in her young body, and it would be a waste to destroy her, all because I couldn't keep my dick in my pants.

So...starting today, I would behave myself.

Starting today, Eleanor fucking Grace would never ask me *'why her'* again. Instead, she'd be asking why she suddenly meant nothing.

Nothing more than a girl purchased by ill-gotten gains.

A goddess who deserved a safe home, a merciful master, and firm guidelines to keep her world from colliding with mine.

Chapter Twenty-Three

KNOCK, KNOCK, KNOCK.

I stretched in annoyance where I lay beneath the sun sail on the deck outside my villa. I'd spent a leisurely morning hiding from giggly goddesses and tormenting assholes, doing my best to once again plot a way free.

I'd commandeered the stationery provided in the bedside drawer and sketched a map of the island from memory. So far, I'd found the central hub where the restaurant and main facilities lived—also the place to avoid, thanks to its welcoming nature for guests to mingle and Sully to reign like a tyrant.

I'd set out at dawn this morning and jogged down the remaining sandy paths, finding forks leading to more accommodation, dead-ends into the jungle, lanes to the beach, and a few tracks leading deeper into the island.

I had no interest in going into the heart of this prison. My freedom wouldn't be found there…it would be found out here.

I looked up at the bright horizon.

Home called to me past the watery cage and miles of twinkling sea.

The knock came again, wrenching a reluctant groan and swinging my legs off the lounger where I'd sprawled. The black bikini I wore winked beneath the open-style kimono. The lacy ivory material dappled my skin with sun patterns, browning a stencil onto my flesh the longer I stayed outside.

The knock rapped again, this time with impatience.

The urge to ignore whoever it was kept my body heavy and locked on the lounger, but the knowledge that ignoring the summons would just bring possible pain ushered me up.

This wasn't the real world where I had a choice. I couldn't keep hiding behind a locked door because the lock belonged to someone who had a key.

A man who had all the keys.

To everything.

My happiness.

My health.

My hope.

Dammit.

The floppy cream hat I wore blocked one eye as I stood and padded my way from the deck and across the pristine floor of my villa, leaving breadcrumbs of golden sand behind.

My heart skittered from its normal rhythm, worrying that my visitor wouldn't be the friendly girl who brought my breakfast this morning. I'd yet to ring for lunch. I'd cocooned myself in an oasis of loneliness and had no desire for an interruption.

Of course, I knew who it was before I opened the door.

Bracing myself for the inevitable buffeting of awareness, hate, and heat, I wrenched open the thick barricade and came face to face with my nemesis. *"You."*

He jolted, his gaze instantly devouring my body.

My nipples pebbled despite myself. My stomach melted against my control.

I should've changed.

Despite the tropical temperatures, I should wear jackets and sacks to hide myself as much as possible. I didn't want him looking at me. I didn't want him anywhere *near* me.

Ignoring the need to cross my arms and hide my figure, I snapped, "Leave me the hell alone."

His eyes found mine again. A lazy smirk twitched his lips rather than the fiery snarls from last night. For a moment, we locked in another battle of piercing proximity. The hair on my nape stood up. Whenever we were together, the island seemed hotter and cooler all at once. My body became overly sensitive and totally troublesome with its responses.

I blamed the first morning and the memory of elixir.

I blamed him for all of it.

With a noble incline of his head, he bowed graciously. "Good afternoon…Jinx."

His suit of choice today was light grey with the finest chalk pinstripes. His tie was silver. His shirt white. His shoes as polished and as perfect as any CEO who worked in a city rather than one who ruled over an atoll.

I hated that he once again managed to steal what little air I had left. I loathed that despite my rancour—that only increased the longer we interacted—I found him indescribably attractive.

Once again, his perfectionism made me detest him all the more. "It was good until you appeared on my doorstep."

His eyes flashed, but he swallowed back his temper. "You and I…we need to get something straight." He cricked his neck as if I'd interrupted his script on how this meeting would go. Whatever cordial response he might've delivered died beneath a whip of anger. "I dislike you as much as you dislike me." I froze as he planted his hand above my head on the door frame. "Actually, dislike is too gentle a word. I'd say what I feel for you is more like—"

"Disgust."

He clucked his tongue in reprimand. His gaze snagged mine, blazing blue. "If I disgusted you, I wouldn't be able to make you wet."

I sucked in a breath. "We discussed that. Don't mistake biology for—"

"I made you wet because there's something going on between us. Just like you make me hard because, for some reason, I have a morbid fascination with fucking you."

I struggled to stay standing and not punch him or run into the sea. "There's *nothing* going on between us."

He signed condescendingly. "Such a little liar." His hand slipped from the doorframe and traced gently down my arm.

Instantly, goosebumps sprang, shivers attacked, dampness gathered.

No.

Just no.

I was mortified.

I was horrified.

I hated myself…not just him.

Removing his touch, he raked his hand through his hair and leaned back, giving me space to breathe and room to drown in despair.

"*Something* is going on between us, and neither of us are

interested in the mess it's causing." He swallowed hard. "Contrary to what it seems, I despise arguments. I much prefer smooth waters, Eleanor Grace, and I'm willing to make a compromise to ensure our co-inhabitation doesn't end with one of us killing the other."

I blinked. *"Excuse me?"*

His jaw clenched as if battling against his next phrase, but he pushed on anyway. "I'm...sorry for giving you the elixir without a proper welcome on my island. It was reckless and has blurred lines that I won't fucking cross."

I would've choked if I had any saliva in my mouth.

Did he...did he just apologise?

"You are here to work for me. I won't jeopardise the value you'll bring to my business by...making you unhappy. These fights have to stop. This lust has to end."

I hugged myself, unable to stop the need to curl close and protect. "And how do you propose we do that? Are you going to let me go?"

He shook his head, his canines flashing as he smiled. "No, I am not going to let you go."

"Then...what are you saying?"

"I'm saying, I will no longer torment you, and you will no longer be given liberties to talk back to me. I am your owner. You are my belonging. I will treat you with civility and respect as long as you obey without question." His voice lowered. "Believe me...this proposition is much better for you, Jinx. I suggest you stop pissing me off, stop antagonising me, stop making me so fucking hungry, and we can return to a simpler relationship."

I laughed once. "You expect me to *bow* to you? To never answer back...even when you're wrong. To never question your behaviour, even when it's morally corrupt?"

"Yes. This is my island. You obey my laws."

"And if I don't?"

"Then I increase your contract from four a month to four a day." He delivered the sentence with such coldness, it glittered with icicles.

I froze.

Four a *day?*

Four men in a single day?

I wanted to throw up.

My stomach actually clenched to evict my morning breakfast of mango and perfectly cooked nasi goreng.

Sully slipped his finger beneath my chin, raising my gaze to meet his. Before, the blue held streaks of animalistic desire. Now, they were clear with ruthlessness. "Respect me, and I'll leave you alone."

I arched my jaw away from his control, narrowing my eyes to slits. "How can I respect you when you trapped me here?"

"Find a way." Clearing his throat, he commanded, "Now...I've failed in my welcoming duties. Instead of enlisting a member of my staff to show you around, I will personally ensure your orientation is complete." His voice turned arctic. "After all, today is your last day on vacation. Tomorrow, you begin work as an official goddess." Taking my hand, he jerked me from the villa, making me stumble beside him. "Might as well become familiar with your home before you enter Euphoria."

I twisted my hand from his, rubbing at the prickles left behind from his touch. "What's Euphoria?"

He grinned like the devil. "Euphoria?" He strode ahead, inserting hands into his slacks pockets and looking effortlessly suave. "Is where you'll find true freedom. Your *only* freedom. Euphoria is the only place you'll want to be...once you've tried it."

Sullivan

Chapter Twenty-Four

I MADE A CHOICE.

Maybe not the right one, definitely not the easiest one, but one that would ensure Eleanor would stay alive, and I'd remain sane.

Soon, I would be able to relieve my needs with a girl who didn't worm their way under my skin. But for now, I would wrap myself up in impenetrable self-control and conduct myself with the same detachment as I did all my goddesses.

For two hours, I escorted Jinx around my shores. I showed her the private swimming pool where the goddesses hung out during the day if they wished—away from the guests they'd fucked the night before and protected against any additional interactions that hadn't been strictly paid for.

The girls never took their eyes off us as I walked her around the perimeter of the boulder-lined pool that looked like a giant pond with a waterfall cascading from the roof of a sala where loungers waited in the shade and a swim-up bar served any delicacy and hydration they required.

Not once did she speak to me.

Not once did I talk to her.

We explored the facilities and travelled the distance of my island without so much as a cough.

It didn't mean the tension between us wasn't rife with rage

and frustration, but it was refreshing not to have to engage in a war each time I sought out her company.

By the time I'd shown her the spa where she could have a massage any time she wanted, revealed the air-conditioned gym just for the girls and the extensive library where computers could be used to order anything they wanted—books, clothes, vibrators—there was a thin veil of tolerance between us.

Jinx ran her fingers over the keyboard after I'd told her she could order whatever her heart desired. "There's access to the internet here?"

I laughed once. "My generosity only goes so far."

"So...that's a no."

"That's a reminder that any social media surfing or messaging of family and friends will have to wait until you are no longer sheltered on my shores."

She crossed her arms, her temper that I was fast becoming familiar with sparking in her gaze. "Four years is an eternity. Four years of no communication usually means a loved one has died and—"

"But you haven't died." I snagged a strand of her hair, unable to stop myself from stroking the silky weight. "You've just taken a little...detour."

She tossed her head, removing her hair from my hold. Her lips thinned as she stewed with a reply. But, with immense control, she swallowed down her fury and moved away, glancing at the books with emotional detachment.

It pissed me off but also...cultivated annoying respect.

I might not offer internet to the girls, but I stood by my word that they received whatever they ordered. The monitored connection ran via my own outside line. I scanned their requests every night and approved them all with a single click, if appropriate, or denied if they weren't.

The symbiotic relationship we had was provider and provided. I worked hard to ensure they had more than they ever had before. And they worked hard to ensure my business was the success it would always be.

We needed each other.

That was the baseline of respect.

I hoped, by the time the tour ended, Eleanor would understand that.

I followed her as she padded from the library, threw a disgruntled look at the two goddesses bobbing in the pool on two blown-up flamingos, and darted down a pathway into the shadows. The brightness from the pool area was instantly replaced with humid shade from palm fronds.

Even though her silence didn't fool me that she'd accepted my truce, I relaxed a little. If anything it made me even more aware of her seething temper.

I constantly fought the almost undeniable urge to shove her against a palm tree and fuck her. But...I behaved, she behaved, and we proved we could exist without destroying the other.

"What's down there?" she asked, keeping her voice low but unable to hide her stewing hate.

I looked to where she gazed. The pathway meandered off into deeper shadow, abruptly disappearing into thick jungle. "Nirvana."

She raised an eyebrow sceptically. "Nirvana?"

"The name of the waterfall."

"There's a waterfall?"

Nodding, I said, "Twelve stories high. It crowns this entire island."

I wondered if she noticed this was our first civil conversation. Discussing something as innocent as a natural phenomenon rather than cursing each other for the connection we didn't want.

"How...how far is it?" She swallowed as if hating herself for even talking to me.

"Not far. Twenty-minute walk. Six-minute run."

"Am I allowed to visit?"

"You are." I slipped my hands into my pockets, refraining from snatching her hair again, dancing in the muggy breeze. "You can go anywhere you want, do whatever you please. As long as you look after yourself and show up for your weekly session in Euphoria, I have no qualms about you living a full and happy life."

"No qualms, huh?" She snorted. "How about no decency?"

I stilled, doing my best to keep myself under strict control. "I don't see a problem in ensuring your health and well-being."

"No, you wouldn't, would you?" She stalked ahead, hands balled and steps rigid.

Everything inside commanded I chase her, grab her, strip and fuck her. Instead, I rolled out the aching tension in my spine and reminded myself why I was playing this role. Why I'd boxed myself into the corner clearly labelled 'celibate'.

No fucking until my personal recruit arrived.

And definitely no fucking Eleanor goddamn Grace.

Slowly, I followed, drinking in the sight of her ass peeking through her lacy kimono, marvelling at the leggy length and curvy handholds of her hips. The black bikini hiding her decency could be eradicated with one yank of the bows holding it together.

My mouth watered to make her come apart again. To have her beg me, worship me, rather than loathe me.

My ego wasn't bruised, but my cock sure was. It wasn't down with this denial of what it wanted. It didn't believe in keeping pleasure and business separate. It wanted her. Fuck...*I* wanted her.

I wanted her so much I hadn't slept last night. I wanted her enough to come up with this shitty, stupid plan to keep my distance.

Fuck it.

My stride lengthened. My heart pounded. I slipped a hand from my pocket, ready to fist it deep into her long hair, only for a girl to appear at the fork up ahead. A sexy little blonde with a matching barcode tattoo and sensual smirk upon her pretty face.

Two years she'd been in my stable, and for two years, she'd been a guest's favourite. She'd transformed from a sobbing little heathen into a highly sexual, hugely popular goddess who regularly enticed guests back for a second stay. She was the only one who didn't try to get into my pants each time she saw me. Instead, she preferred to lavish all her lust on the men who paid a fortune to lay their hands on her.

In short, she was the perfect role model for any freshly acquired goddess who struggled to accept her new place.

"Sullivan." She smiled her minxy smile, looking deliberately past Eleanor and doing what she did best. I'd named her after the emotion she inevitably drew from all the other girls.

Jealousy.

She moved with effortless sexual freedom. She glided over my sand as if this was her island and not mine. She'd dedicated herself to being the best...and she was.

The other girls were jealous of her.

In fact...she suffered the same affliction Jinx had been cursed with, just because I couldn't leave her the hell alone. Two outcasts from the main group of goddesses, just because they were different.

Eleanor stiffened as Jealousy swayed her hips and came toward us with a leisurely, sensual stroll.

Jealousy smiled invitingly at Eleanor, no animosity or curiosity, just welcoming acceptance to a place she wholeheartedly believed was utopia, then completely dismissed her as she slotted herself into my side and reached up to kiss my cheek.

I permitted the contact, purely because there was no ulterior motive. She was the rare commodity that was worth every penny I'd paid for her. She'd come from a shitty existence. An abusive family, raping uncles, and disbelieving parents. She'd run away, been snatched and sold, and found happiness in my captivity.

I couldn't remember what her real name was, but I did remember how much she'd earned me and what sort of bonus I'd pay her when her time here was done.

The moment the kiss was delivered, she pulled away, patting my chest lightly. "Pleasure to see you on this stunning day."

Eleanor never took her eyes off Jealousy. She seemed shocked that she'd willingly touched me, amazed that I'd permitted it, and totally flummoxed as to the obvious friendship between us.

I couldn't stop watching Jinx, searching for a sign that she was pissed another woman had touched me. Wondering if she suffered the same envy I did whenever I thought of another man touching her.

But only disbelief glowed in her grey eyes. Only disturbed distress painted her face. She acted as if she wanted to yank Jealousy away from me, so I didn't infect her with a disease.

With my eyes locked with Eleanor's, I murmured, "Jealousy, meet Jinx. Jinx...this is Jealousy. I highly recommend you befriend her...she'll probably be the only confidant you'll have here."

Jealousy quirked an eyebrow. "She won't fit in with the others?"

I shook my head, breaking eye contact with one goddess to stare at another. "No."

"Why ever not?"

I bared my teeth in a condemning smile. "Because she has something the others don't."

Her forehead furrowed for a second as she flicked a glance at Eleanor who stood prim and proper with her arms around her waist, her kimono tugged tight and propriety doing its best to make her untouchable, but then her confusion vanished with a flash of understanding. "She has your attention."

I nodded once. "Unfortunately for her."

"Yes, indeed." Jealousy grinned, leaving my side to go to Eleanor. She held out her hand, polite and willing to shake. "Hello, Jinx. I must say, it will be nice if you aren't accepted by the main pack. We can stick together."

Eleanor left her hanging, refusing to accept her welcome. She backed away as if finally meeting a girl who was kind and refreshingly transparent was the final straw.

"Be nice, Jinx," I growled when the pause became awkward. "Believe me...it will be better for you in the long run if you have someone to talk to." I chuckled coldly. "After all...who else will you complain about me to?"

Her gaze whipped to mine. "I'll just complain directly to your face."

Jealousy gasped, her blonde hair bouncing over her shoulders as she turned to look at me. She waited for me to reprimand her. I was known for generosity but also swift strictness. I didn't permit rudeness or insolence without severe punishment.

But my cock had drained me of my reserves.

Keeping my temper on a leash had made me snappish.

My lust made me far too primed for a fight.

If Jealousy hadn't arrived, I'd probably be cock deep in Eleanor in the middle of the pathway. But she had arrived...and it was for the best.

It was a sign.

A sign that I was doing the right thing keeping my body as far away from Jinx's as humanly possible.

Time to get some work done.

Time to forget about my latest employee.

"That will be the last time you speak out of line to me." Smiling tightly at Jealousy, I added, "Show her the ropes. You can finish the orientation on my behalf." Turning to face Eleanor, I mockingly bowed at the feet of the long-haired girl who didn't know the close call she'd escaped. I treated her like royalty because that was what she made me.

She made me a king because only a king could have such consorts at his beck and call.

But I was also a king who didn't allow dangerous vixens into his bed.

Taking one last look at the girl I wanted to destroy, I left.

Chapter Twenty-Five

"SOOOO...THAT WAS STRANGE." Jealousy smiled, moving closer so her voice didn't chase Sully as he disappeared. "I'm doing my best not to ask, but I've not seen him act like that around a goddess before. Who are you, Goddess Jinx?"

I side-stepped away. I wasn't opposed to friends, and definitely wanted a network of people I could talk to and plot a way out of here, but I didn't trust she wasn't like the other girls. Brainwashed and infatuated with their liege and master.

With a name like Jealousy, I doubted her sweet smile and welcoming appearance was real. She was probably a master manipulator.

"You know he's never let anyone get away with being rude to him, right?" she added, when I showed no sign of joining in her conversation. "But then again...I'm guessing you're not just anyone...are you?"

I shivered, still staring down the empty path where Sully had gone.

What the hell was happening here? To me? To him? To my stable, simple world?

"My real name is Jess." Jealousy waved almost shyly even though she stood right next to me. "I won't bite...honest."

Sighing, I turned to face her, ready to explore another odd relationship if it meant it could rescue me from the mess I'd found myself in. "I'm Eleanor."

She beamed. "Pretty name."

"Not pretty enough seeing as he changed it."

"Ah, Jinx and Jealousy, they're just masks for us to wear so the guests don't know who we truly are."

I crossed my arms. "But if they knew our real names, they could look us up, contact our families…help us escape."

Jess frowned and nodded slowly. "That's true. I suppose that would be bad for business."

I scowled. "You don't sound pissed off about the fact that we're prisoners here."

She shrugged. "I'm happy. This isn't a prison to me."

"Don't you want to be free, though? Free to go where you want? Free to fly away and be with your family?"

Her pretty face cast in shadow. "My family isn't worthy of my company." Her voice hardened. "If anywhere in the world is a prison, it's in that house with them."

Goosebumps scattered up my arms at the sudden knowledge that this girl wasn't like the others. She wasn't like me. She'd already suffered abuse, and our versions of mistreatment were vastly different. Without knowing her full story, I had no right to complain.

Whatever reason she'd been called Jealousy, I didn't think it was because of any pettiness or envy on her part. She might be short and blonde with a pixy smile, but there was a pillar of pure marble inside her.

"I'm sorry." I apologised for jumping to conclusions about her and for what she'd lived through. I didn't need to ask to guess. The brittle vulnerability in her voice painted a vibrant enough picture, but it also told me the truth. She *was* happy here. She was content to stay because it was a thousand times better than wherever she'd been taken from.

This was her adoptive home while it was still my unwanted cage.

Her blonde hair bounced with loose curls as she moved forward, expecting me to fall into step with her. "Don't be. It was a while ago, and I don't ever have to go back."

I walked with her, intrigued despite myself. "But what about when Sully lets you go?"

She looked at the sugary sand coating our bare feet as we moved toward the beaming sunshine and beach up ahead. "I'll deal with that in two years." She flicked me a look. "I wouldn't say that to the pack but you…" She smiled sadly. "I'm sorry to say, you will be an outcast here like me. So we might as well skip the stilted getting-to-know-each-other and slip straight into friendship. And…because we're friends, I can tell you the truth." She plucked an orchid from its long stem as we passed, stroking the bright purple petals. "Sully can barely stand the other goddesses because they all want something from him that he's not prepared to give. But me…he knows I want something different."

My heart picked up speed. "What do you want?"

"To stay."

"That's exactly what the other girls want." I didn't mention eavesdropping the other night, but I couldn't imagine that was news to her.

"No, they want to stay and be an equal ruler with Sullivan. They think of this island as theirs. They think of Euphoria as their own personal creation and can't imagine life without it."

I squinted as the sun grew steadily brighter as we left the shady heliconias, banana plants, and orchids behind, trading it for sparkling sea and the brightest turquoise I'd ever seen. In front of us rested a row of pristine, gleaming kayaks, oars at their sides, ready to be used. Loungers waited with crisp rolled-up towels for a guest, umbrellas dotted the scalding hot sand, and the sun caused heat mirages to dance around the array of small cabanas serving nibbles, drinks, and anything else high-paying guests could ask for.

Beyond that rested the helipad where I'd arrived. Black basalt lined the area of the manmade bay while the bamboo jetty looked glued to the calm tide.

Memories of arriving, just a few short days ago, had already faded under the intensity of this place. A view wasn't just a view here. It didn't just complete a backdrop for life to exist; it demanded your full attention.

It swallowed you up with all five senses, engulfing you with bird song, gentle breezes, and vibrancy. I felt the soft *hish-hish* of the sea upon the sand. I tasted the fragrant flowers on the air. The part of me that was terrifyingly aware of its own mortality drank in the island with gratitude because nature was absolutely surreal and granted a gift.

A gift of being *alive*.

Jess, or Jealousy—whichever name she preferred—pressed her shoulder to mine as we skipped over the hot sand and sighed in relief the moment we entered the shallows. Her touch drenched me in a sensation of kinship. Of belonging. I missed my friends from school. Ever since starting the travelling adventure with

Scott, we hadn't been in one place long enough to evolve single night acquaintances into long-term friends.

But there, standing in the warm, licking tide on the picture-perfect beach with our shoulders touching, I didn't feel so trapped. So lost. So confused.

"I can understand why you wouldn't want to say goodbye to this place," I murmured, unable to tear my eyes off the horizon as a pod of dolphins broke the glassy surface, gliding past like ballerinas of the ocean.

The water was so clear, the reef around the island danced and refracted, one moment glowing in sunshine and anemones, the next dressed in shadow from a passing shoal of fish.

It was hard to focus on the underwater universe. Hazy and hidden beneath the surface, it was so different to ours, governed by totally foreign laws where even gravity wasn't welcome. Yet just because we weren't adapted to live there didn't mean others didn't find their purpose and place within the towers of coral and carpets of sand.

Maybe there was wisdom in that.

Wisdom to know that while I didn't feel as if I could survive on this island—that I was totally a fish out of water—somehow others flourished and found solitude.

Jess sighed, shielding her eyes from the intensity of the sunshine. "It truly is magical. But it's not just the island that makes me want to stay. It's not just the ability of learning to grow your own food or the simplicity of living in the tropics...I want to stay because—"

I looked at her, doing my best not to seem overly eager. "Because...?"

I wanted to know.

I wanted to know why she'd stopped.

She caught my gaze and smiled lopsidedly. "I can tell you...can't I?" Her eyes narrowed, searching mine as if rifling through my soul for answers. Answers she approved of before she nodded. "I want to stay because Sullivan isn't what you think. He's a workaholic. He's a genius for what he's created. Yet...instead of enjoying his own creations, he just keeps working." Her voice quietened to a whisper. "He needs someone who isn't after his drugs, his body, or his legacy. For a while now...that was me. All I ask of him is that I can stay. I'll clean the villas or cook in the restaurant if he doesn't want me as a goddess anymore. I'll take any job he needs me to do. But most of all...I want to stay, because eventually, he's going to break, and someone he can trust should be there to pick up the pieces."

"Break?"

She nodded. "He's been on a path that isn't sustainable ever since I met him…and it's getting worse." She sighed, turning to face the sea again. "Before, he used to laugh. Now, he barely ever smiles. Before, he seemed human. Now…I'm not so sure."

Giving me a quick nudge, she sighed again, "I guess I just don't want him to crash and burn, that's all. We all have limits."

"And why do you think he's reaching his?"

"Oh, I don't know." She ran fingers through her hair, cupping her curls so muggy air could lick away the glistening sweat on her nape. "Just a feeling." Dropping her hair, she turned to me. "Anyway, that's a dark topic for another day. Let's talk about you. Anything you want to know? Anything you want help with?"

I wanted to talk more about Sully, but I refused to come across as those other girls—fascinated and fanciful, hanging onto every word about him. My concerns about Sully stemmed entirely from self-preservation.

Glancing down the beach, left and right, I stiffened as two men appeared from the pathway. Dark sunglasses shielded their eyes while one wore a baseball hat over salt and pepper hair and the other let his floppy blond mess stick to his heat-damp forehead.

"Oh, no." Jealousy grabbed my hand, linking her fingers with mine. "Guests."

"Are they not allowed to see us?" My stomach churned as the men waved and started toward us. One shorter than the other, both wearing board-shorts and t-shirts ready to be peeled off for a swim. Perhaps they would be more interested in water sports than two stranded goddesses.

"They are. Some nights we have mingles and mixers. But usually, Sullivan likes to keep us away, purely to ramp up the anticipation of Euphoria…for both parties."

"What *is* Euphoria?" I asked quickly, aware our time of privacy was quickly depleting with each of the men's flip-flopped steps. "I've heard about it so often but still have no idea."

Jess smiled, a knowing almost patronizing gleam in her gaze. "Euphoria is…euphoria."

"What's that supposed to mean?"

"It means it's a place created entirely by Sullivan. I told you he was a genius. He can take a fantasy and turn it into a reality.

Everything you think you know…is gone. Everything you think is impossible is suddenly the only thing that makes sense." She let my hand go after a tight squeeze. "Honestly, the only way to know is to try it."

"And if I don't want to?"

She gave me an understanding look. "You don't have a choice."

"Do you really have sex with four men a month?" The guests were drawing closer, making me rush.

"Yes." She nodded with no shame or hardship. "Once a week in Euphoria is more than enough. Sullivan looks after us in that respect."

"Looks *after* you?" My eyebrows soared into my hair. "He forces you to sleep with—"

"Elixir makes it anything but forced, Jinx." She smiled a secret smile. "You'll know what I mean when you try it. Nothing about your time with a guest will be anything but sheer, insurmountable bliss."

I chewed on my tongue, unwilling to tell her Sully had already fed me the nasty, noxious drug. That I'd found it an invasion of everything I stood for. That it was perverse and putrid and every other foul word I could use to describe something that shouldn't exist.

"If it's so good, why aren't you expected to serve more than once a week?"

My question dripped with accusation, but Jess just smiled her contented smile and said, "Because you need the week to recover. Your body is unbelievably sore. Your immune system depleted. Your energy levels non-existent. You live more vibrantly and more freely in the hours you're in Euphoria than you do in a year of your life outside." She wrapped an arm around me, hugging me quickly. "You just have to trust. Trust that it won't be terrible."

Letting me go, she slipped from honest confidant into sensual madam, welcoming the guests as they arrived in the shallows where we stood. "Hello, Mr. Grammer. Hello, Mr. Wordworth. I hope you're enjoying your stay so far."

One man grinned, carefree and handsome, making me wonder why he'd pay for sex when he'd receive it willingly from most. His salt and pepper hair made him distinguished while his trim body kept him attractive. "Hello, goddesses. How are you two beautiful creatures on this stunning day?" His face split into a broad smile as if he had a secret he couldn't wait to spill.

My hackles shot up. All I wanted to do was run in the opposite direction.

Jess bowed her head politely, smiling with invitation. "We're fine. How are you?"

"Never been better."

The man with the floppy blond hair couldn't take his eyes off me. He stripped me bare with his gaze. He pinned me to the sand with intensity.

I immediately disliked him.

Instantly disgusted that he thought he had any right to look at me like I was some highly expensive dessert to a main course he'd already devoured.

"Hello, Jinx." He smiled with smug satisfaction. "Pleasure to see you're looking well recovered."

"Were you ill?" Jess asked, true concern painting her tone.

"She was weak from her arrival, I believe," the man replied on my behalf. "But back to full fitness now." He looked me up and down. His sunglasses couldn't hide the lust or hunger on his face. "At least...I hope."

Why the hell was he so interested in my well-being? And how did he know I hadn't been feeling well?

When I didn't speak, he reached out and took my hand.

My skin crawled as he bowed over my knuckles and kissed them gently. He bowed low, lower still. The move wasn't mocking like when Sully did it. His bow was full of worship. The authenticity of his awe made me shiver with foreboding.

No.

Not him.

Don't let it be him.

Letting me go, he confirmed my worst suspicion. "I've been counting the hours for our date tomorrow night, Jinx. I wish it was tonight, I must admit." He whistled quietly, drinking in my black bikini and lacy kimono. "You are the most gorgeous thing I've ever seen."

Never again would I wear such revealing clothes, even in the unbearable humidity and heat of this place. I would find the sack jumper I'd arrived in and never take it off.

The other man cleared his throat. "I might have to extend my stay, Goddess Jinx, and request your company a week from now...seeing as I lost the bidding war this time around."

"Bidding war?" The startled question squeaked out before I could stop myself.

"Yes." The salt and pepper gentleman purred. "We both requested the honour of sharing your first night in Euphoria. I was too slow to lock in the price that Sinclair offered."

A flurry of snowflakes landed on my shoulders, melting instantly and oozing icy fingers down my back. "What price?"

How much was my honour worth to that monster who'd bought me?

The blond man shook his head. "Money and pleasure are two separate things. We don't need to cheapen the enjoyment we'll find together by naming a number."

I backed away. "There won't be any enjoyment from my end. I assure you."

The guy grinned, flashing perfect white teeth. "That isn't the understanding I have. You will be under the influence of Sinclair's elixir, and he assured me that whatever we indulge in will be...mutually satisfying."

I wanted to be sick.

This couldn't be happening.

I should've been using every waking moment to find a way off this heinous place. Instead, I'd allowed Sully to fog my mind with wonderings about him. Permitted the beauty of this place to suck me deeper into its web.

How *stupid* could I be?

How could I forget my role here?

I stumbled in the sand.

The man's hand lashed out, locking around my elbow and giving me balance. I appreciated his help, but I couldn't stand him touching me.

Ripping out of his control, I swayed and looked at both of them with disbelief. I looked at Jess too. Unable to believe the puzzle that this girl and these men weren't enemies but...somehow symbiotic friends.

I wanted nothing to do with it.

I want to go home.

"Ex-excuse me." Swallowing back a wash of stomach acid, I bolted up the beach.

The bottoms of my soles burned from the hot sand. My breath caught in my tight chest. The air was too syrupy and heavy to stop my light-headedness.

By the time I got to my villa, tears plummeted down my cheeks, and I collapsed behind my door, blocking it with my body, creating a lock that didn't have a key so I couldn't be fetched, couldn't be taken, couldn't be used in Euphoria.

Chapter Twenty-Six

"SIR?"

I looked up from a text-heavy email full of theories, formulas, and questions from my scientists on where to go next with my latest concoction. This drug wasn't for pleasure or control. It wasn't for personal use or financial gain. This was purely philanthropic: a cure for cancer.

So many of the big pharmas spent more money on lobbying the giant industries that promoted food and lifestyle-causing cancer rather than investing in teams to cure it. In their minds, disease was great for their bottom line. Profit, profit, profit. In my mind...I owed a bit of good karma for everything I'd become.

Cricking my neck from sitting at my desk since dawn, I pinched the bridge of my nose and cursed the faint headache brewing. I couldn't blame dehydration or screen time because I'd worked much longer hours before. The pain behind my eyes was caused by the knowledge that in a few short hours, Jinx...Eleanor...would step into Euphoria and be fucked by another man.

Not just once.

Not twice.

Probably well over—

Don't fucking think about it.

He's paid.

He's owed.

She's serving him.

"What is it, Cal?" I dropped my hand and peered at him. He'd taken off his suit jacket, leaving him in a white shirt and ice blue tie. His cufflinks winked with silver stars as he passed me the dossier.

The dossier.

"Markus finished outlining his fantasy. Want me to input the parameters, or will you?"

My hands fisted around the folder. What sort of heathenous, wicked role-play would he have her endure? What world would I have to be the architect of to ensure he got his money's worth?

"I'll do it." My voice came out thick and black.

"You sure?"

I looked up, narrowed eyed and threatening. "I said...I'll do it."

"Fine." He held up his hands in surrender, then his lips twitched into a smirk. "It's an interesting request. A first, that's for sure."

I didn't like firsts.

I didn't like hearing about fetishes that I hadn't come across before. Especially fetishes that included Jinx being the main meal.

Waving him away, I waited until he'd exited and closed my office door before flipping open the file.

Markus Grammer.
Forty-four years.
Sexual health, clean.
General health, average.
Health and safety wavier, signed.
Agreement that he enters Euphoria at his own risk, signed.
Payment, in full.
Programming, ready to begin.

Gritting my teeth, I turned the next page.

A flurry of green and yellow shot through my open driftwood doors, followed by an indignant chirp.

"Ah, great. Just fucking great." I looked up just as Pika dive-bombed the file and started attacking the corners as if demon-possessed. "Hey! Oi. Stop it." Flicking the annoyingly energetic caique parrot off my reading material, I shook my hand, trying to dislodge his tight little claws as he wrapped around my middle finger, deciding to attack me instead.

Raising my hand, I huffed as he dangled upside down, his bright black eyes inquisitive, intelligent, and far too naughty to get away with the murder he managed on a daily basis. "Coconuts. Goddess. Sex! Sex. Sexxxxx."

God, why did I ever teach him how to talk?

"Pika...we've had this conversation."

He honestly laughed in my goddamn face and proceeded to gnaw on my fingernail. His little wings spread out as I shook my hand again, trying to break his tenacious grip. "Let me go."

He chirped. Then trilled. Then squawked and carried on a conversation as if I could understand every caw. After his noisy argument about why he never behaved nor did what I asked, he let my finger go, plopped onto my desk, and rolled onto his back, giving me his white fluffy belly and yellow chest.

"Hello. Please. Now!" His scaly legs waggled, just tempting me to scratch him.

"No way am I falling for that game again." Grabbing my pen, I poked him in the stomach, only for him to curl around the expensive limited edition implement and flap and squawk, biting and scratching as if he wouldn't stop until ink spilled in death.

Despite myself, a smile tugged at my lips.

Pika...was special.

I'd rescued him, like most animals that hid within my jungles on Goddess Isles. Some I brought to this island, so I could keep an eye on them, and others, I let loose on the more uninhabited shores, letting them revert to the way nature intended.

But Pika...he'd been an egg when we met. So had his sister, Skittles. They'd been born in the lab—totally random from the caique parrot my father's scientists had been testing acne medicine on. The parrot had lost all her feathers. She'd been depressed, lonely, and intensely sick from what humans did to her. No one knew she'd been fertilized before she'd been brought in from another lab.

I'd found four eggs in the bottom of her wire cage early one morning. Two had smashed. Two were whole. For the first time in forever, I'd felt the familiar empathy that'd gotten me in so much trouble in my youth.

Before anyone arrived, I'd scooped the eggs up, placed them in a disease incubator where Petri dishes grew sickness rather than nurtured life, then smuggled them home when no one was looking.

It'd been a full-on job looking after the eggs.

And then the hatchlings? Fuck me, they were even harder. I'd had to take the week off work to feed them every few hours until they left the naked, ugly alien stage and became pin cushions with quill-like feathers.

The week after Pika and Skittles came into my life...my parents died, and the company became mine.

The day I took control, I'd made changes to Sinclair and Sinclair Group. Lots and lots of fucking changes. I reclaimed a piece of myself again. I began to make up for all the shit that I'd done wrong.

Pika hopped away from annihilating my pen, knocked over the stapler, got his talons stuck in the tape dispenser, and ripped a laptop key out of the keyboard before I could stop him.

He was carnage on wings.

A little hurricane of nightmares.

"Pika." I tried to grab him, only for his cute green wings to snap open, shoot him into the air, and deposit him on the top of my head. There, he grabbed strands of my hair and hung upside down over my forehead, putting our eyes within millimetres of each other.

He squawked and bit my nose.

I gave up.

Slouching in my chair, I spread my hands the way I knew he liked and allowed him to distract me from the fantasy I had to code and the knowledge that Jinx was one hour closer to being consumed.

Pika flopped down my face, kept his wings tucked in total faith that I'd catch him under my chin, then lay on his back in the centre of my palm, rocking on his wings as I tickled his downy feathers. "Had a good few days, little nightmare?"

He blinked as if he understood everything I said. He chirped back with a very clear, "Yup!"

It never failed to astound me how quickly he'd learned to speak. Sure, I'd shared my life with him for almost fourteen years. Sure, his sister wasn't as friendly as him and preferred to live with the wild parrots in the palm trees with the occasional visit to me. But Pika had chosen me as his mate.

He was never far from my shoulder, disappearing for a few days only if the hibiscus flowers—which were his favourite—were blooming. He'd grow drunk on the nectar, pass out in some tree, and not come home for a while.

Those nights, I tried to convince myself that I didn't miss the stupid bird. That it would be best for all of us if he just reverted to his wild side and forgot about me raising his scrawny ass.

But...he always came back.

And he always made me a little bit better when he did.

Sighing heavily, I raised my hand until I slipped him onto my shoulder. There he snuggled into my ear, chirping and chattering, content and calm.

Bracing myself, I let my eyes fall unwillingly onto Markus Grammer's fantasy.

I read each page with my stomach coiled and my cock hard as a fucking rock.

I wanted to kill him but I also understood him.

Understood his fantasy because it was based in the roots of mankind. The need to dominate, manipulate, copulate.

It was a fantasy I could enjoy, if I ever let myself dabble in my creation.

Swallowing away inconvenient lust and violent possessiveness, I picked up my phone and arranged Jealousy to get Jinx ready.

Her vacation was over.

It was time to become a goddess.

Chapter Twenty-Seven

ALL DAY I'D EXISTED in a state of panic, terror, nausea, and claustrophobia.

The island no longer had the power to distract me with its sublime sea and comforting heat. After running from the guests on the beach, I'd curled in front of my door, and fallen asleep. Emotionally exhausted, I was determined never to leave that spot again.

However, when I woke up, a dinner tray with a carved-out pineapple holding delicious fried rice and tempeh had been delivered on the table outside. The knowledge that the door to my villa wasn't the only way in reminded me all over again how vulnerable I was.

How anyone could swim to the small beach in front of me or slither through the jungle and enter easily through the open driftwood sliders.

There was no point camping out in front of my door.

None whatsoever.

The only thing I still had control over was eating, so my body didn't crash again, and then I studied my hand-drawn map well into the night, racking my brains for scenarios on how to get free.

By the time the clock said three a.m. and I'd exhausted all concepts—both sane and insane—on how to escape, I made a promise to myself.

Whatever happened, I wouldn't let it affect me, just as I didn't let Sully affect me.

I sneered at myself.

He doesn't affect you?

I hung my head in my hands.

Sully was the secret I tried to keep even from myself. I hated him—there was no debate about that. But...I also couldn't deny that hate dipped into lust every now and again. His despised handsomeness somehow *did* affect me, and that was something I could never tolerate.

My promise evolved.

Whatever happens, do NOT let it affect you. You might have to sleep with someone, but remember what you said: it's just an activity...like skiing. And whenever Sully decides to torment you again, don't retaliate. Just be silent. Be remote. Be untouchable.

As dawn cracked the inky black of night, curling more and more fingers of light and ripping back the curtain of stars, I fell asleep.

I had nightmares of men surrounding me. Men touching me. Men lining up for their turn.

I woke with scratchy eyes and a chaotic heartbeat, knowing that today...was the day.

My fainting spell had bought me three days. Perhaps I should injure myself again and buy another week or so. Or maybe I should just swim out to sea and sink where no one could find me.

Sighing heavily, I looked out to the deck where yet another silently delivered tray waited on the table. I no longer had to ring for food to be brought, and I hauled myself from the bed, wrapped myself in a white sheet, then dragged it like drooping wings over the sandy floor to devour the island-grown vegetarian fare.

The scenery tried to cheer me up with a flock of seagulls landing on the azure flat ocean, a school of fish darting silver and fast through the surface, and a trio of parrots who landed in the palm tree beside me.

Heaven hiding hell.

Angels cloistering Satan himself.

A mythical story I couldn't escape from.

A knock sounded.

Polite and requesting…gentle even.

I sat lotus style in the middle of the woven grass mat in the living room. I wore the sack of a jumper, even though my skin grew clammy with heat. A staff member must've found it floating in the sea from where I'd stripped it that first day. It'd been freshly laundered, hung in the wardrobe, loud with its reminder of what I was.

If I was honest, my ears had been ringing with anticipation since noon. Waiting for that knock. Hearing an echo of it in the future. Trying to prepare myself for the inevitability.

It was a relief to finally face the real thing. To no longer tremble with apprehension, wondering when the summons would come.

It'd come.

I would be forced to swallow elixir.

I would be delivered to a man who'd paid to fuck me.

I tried to unfold my legs, to go and open the door, but all the power in my bones had bled out my pores, leaving me useless.

The knock came again, followed by a feminine, "Hello…Jinx?"

I gulped a breath, slouching.

It's not him.

Not Sully here to drug and deliver me, desperately gasping and horribly horny to that guest on the beach.

Another knock, but this time the handle turned, and the door cracked open. I'd left it unlocked after I came to terms with the falsity of my safety. Walls and doors couldn't protect me.

Not in this place.

It was better to just surrender to the knowledge that my body wasn't my own, my thoughts not considered, and my own desires totally disregarded.

"Ah…you poor thing." She came toward me, dressed in a lemony gown that hugged her petite chest and flared out to dance around her knees. Matched with her blonde curls, she looked like a lemon meringue cake—sweet and tart, satisfying and toe-curling.

Crouching in front of me, she balanced herself by placing both hands on my thighs.

The contact made a shudder wrack my body. My eyes remained dry, but it didn't mean everything else cried, begged, screamed that this wasn't happening.

"It's okay." She sighed gently. "The thought is more terrifying than the action." Tucking a lock of dark hair that'd escaped my ear, she added, "Sex is fine…isn't it? I mean, you've enjoyed it with the partners you've chosen in the past?"

I risked looking into her uncomplicated gaze. I still didn't trust her. After all, she loved Sully, even if she didn't lust after him. She might be an award-winning actress with her kindness and attempt at friendship. But she urged me silently to answer her, expecting honesty.

"Yes…" I licked my lips, lubricating my dry throat. "Sex with my boyfriend was pleasant."

She smiled, crinkling her eyes. "Just pleasant?"

I wanted some space, but I allowed her to stay balanced with her fingers digging into my legs. "What else is there?"

Stupid question.

Very stupid.

Jealousy's eyebrows shot up. "What *else* is there? To sex?" She swooned backward, landing in a fluff of lemon dress. "If you have to ask that, then you haven't experienced what it can be."

Shifting so I sat on my knees, I revealed, "Sully's already given me the elixir. He used it as a punishment on the day I arrived. The pleasure that awful stuff gave me was the most intense I'd ever felt before. But it also caused so, so much pain. If that's what it's like sleeping with a man while on that stuff…then…well—" I shrugged helplessly. "I'm terrified."

She nodded in sympathy. "You will be sore, I guarantee that. You'll be exhausted for days afterward. But, Jinx…while you're in Euphoria, none of that will matter." Her voice lowered with truth. "Honestly, the best piece of advice I can give you is…let go. Forget how you came to be here. Forget your friends, your life, your home. Forget even who you are. Just take my hand, come with me, and allow yourself to experience something no one else gets to in their entire life."

"No one? What about the men who—"

"Men who pay hundreds of thousands of dollars to worship us?" Her eyes glowed with past conquests and her own experience. "They won't hurt you…not in a violent way. They will give you their hearts while you are theirs. They will fall in love with you when you're in their arms. You will forever be incomparable for the rest of their godforsaken lives because they only get to taste ambrosia…but you, us, the goddesses on this island, *we* are that ambrosia. It's not the elixir. It's not Euphoria. It's *us* who makes this place burst with magic."

I climbed to my feet, rubbing my arms and needing to walk

on shaky legs. "It's still against my will."

She stood too, her eyes following me as I paced. "Isn't all work against your will?"

I stopped, glaring at her. "Going reluctantly to an office building compared to sleeping with a man are two completely different things."

"I suppose." She held out her palms. "But...the same too."

"I'm not arguing with you about the morality of employment versus slavery. Besides, plenty of people do work they love. Work that isn't against their will."

"Fair enough." She padded toward the door. The door she'd left open, revealing the sandy path and journey I had to take whether I wanted to or not. "Enough talking. I'll show you why you don't need to be afraid."

When I didn't uproot myself, she murmured, "Come. I'll be the one to guide you through getting ready."

"There's a process?"

"Yes. There are rules and techniques and a system that has to be followed."

"And if I refuse to leave this villa?" I crossed my arms, doing my best to be strong and brave—to be a female gladiator who would rip out the throats of any who touched her, but really, I was an imposter. A scared girl who'd been brought up with the ideals that her body was her temple and only those invited were allowed to enter.

"Then Sullivan would have to collect you himself." Her voice lowered. "And he wouldn't be as kind as I."

Drifting toward her, I asked despite myself, "Why does everyone idolize him? No one tries to kill him for what he's made us. No one tries to run away."

"Some do...in the beginning." She shrugged. "But Euphoria changes them."

"I don't want to be changed."

She came toward me, her eyes flashing. "Are you sure? Are you so sure you're the person you're meant to be with the limited life lessons you've learned already? Are you so sure you don't want to grow and evolve and experiment?" She leaned in until her body heat tangled with mine. "Are you so sure that you're not afraid because secretly, deep down...you *want* to let go? You want to know what it's like to be that raw, angry, wild little creature that society has forced us to tame?"

"I'm not some sexually starved beast who—"

"No." She wrapped an arm around my waist, one part threatening and all parts understanding. "You're a woman. And women have forgotten who we are because we give ourselves to others, over and over. Husbands, children, bosses, friends. We change to fit their ideal of us. We change to fit an ideal that *we* create. Tonight…just forget." Dropping her arm, she grabbed my hand and tugged me gently out of the villa. "Tonight…just be free."

⁂

"Holy…what is this place?" My mouth dropped open as Jealousy guided me through the double doors of a hexagonal villa I hadn't explored. If she hadn't guided me here, I would never have found it.

Nestled within a small glade, tucked at the end of a ten-minute walk from the residential area of the island, this new place held an aura of secrecy and temptation that dripped from the thatched roof, permeated the ground, and decorated the exposed rafters.

"This is where we play." She smiled, striding forward with familiarity while I stayed struck dumb as I drank in the majesty of such a place. The front foyer glowed with sun from the glass roof interspersed with thatch, five stories above us. Palm trees grew through the floor, stencilling the marble tiles with their fronds. The villa ached with opulence even though none of the usual garish strappings of glitz and glamour existed. The walls were a simple alabaster plaster. The wooden doors huge and left natural so their knots and grain were visible in their imperfection. Hinges of black metal were a feature, along with the simplicity of openness and no furniture.

It was like a church.

A church where no respectable god would reside.

A church of sex and sin.

"Come…this way." Jealousy opened one of the six doors all leading off the main foyer. Cracked open, the sense of space and sunlight continued bright and welcome, even as twilight cast the island in cocktail-happy hour.

Padding behind her, I drank in yet another offshoot of splendour. Unlike the grandness of the foyer, this space held furniture. A small nest of burnt orange chairs by the window, enjoying the babble and view of an exquisite waterfall splashing into a lily pad pond, and a lounger stretched by the wall with a rack of glossy magazines.

A waiting room.

A waiting room for a man about to have sex.

"This way." Through yet another door, the villa once again shrank. A building-size version of Russian dolls. Huge then large then medium then small…all fitting inside one another in a magic trick of cohesion.

This room needed no explanation.

A bathroom fit for a queen…or a goddess.

Part covered, part open, I drifted from the large vanity and stone-tiled shower to the private garden where a quartz bathtub waited filled to the brim with rose petal-dotted water.

Butterflies darted in the spiels of sunlight, their jewelled colours of blue and purple flashing like weightless gemstones.

Jealousy turned toward the vanity, touching the row of items laid out on fresh white towels. "This is where you'll bathe. Shower or bath, the choice is yours. Shave your legs, underarms, and if you shave between your legs, then do what you are naturally comfortable doing." She didn't blush talking about trimming pubic hair, far too confident and experienced in her own sexuality.

Giving me a kind smile, she tapped the wrapped toothbrush. "Clean your teeth, dry and brush your hair, dress in that dressing gown behind you, and when you're ready, join me behind that next door for the final preparations."

I eyed the door in question. Simple frosted glass leading to unknown horrors.

Was that where I would sleep with him?

Was that the bedroom where all of this would end?

"Any questions?" Jealousy asked, joining me by the bath.

Shaking my head, I dipped my fingers into the flower petal water.

Warm.

Fragrant with essential oils.

"No."

She squeezed my arm. "It will be okay…I promise."

I gave her a tight, worried smile.

Backing away, she added, "I'll be waiting, but take all the time you need. Don't rush." Blowing me a sweet kiss, she vanished through the smoky glass door and left me alone.

Sullivan

Chapter Twenty-Eight

IT TURNED OUT MY willpower was shit.

I found Jealousy in the VR room, sitting on the couch by the wall, reading something on her e-reader. "She ready?"

She shook her head, tearing herself from whatever material she found engrossing. "I left her in there about fifteen minutes ago. I told her to take her time."

Nodding, I deliberated just leaving.

I didn't need to be here.

The program code was complete. Jealousy had Jinx's cleanliness in hand, and my other staff knew their jobs backward. But...fuck it.

Without making eye contact with Jealousy, I marched to the glass door and pushed it open. The moment I entered the muggy, steamy bathroom, I shut and locked the door behind me.

Jinx wasn't there.

My stomach knotted, and I darted forward, searching the shower, the toilet, the little koi carp pond made from a huge porcelain pot.

Nothing.

Goddammit.

Tearing my phone out of my pocket, I spun around and brought up the number for Calvin. I'd get him to hop in the fastest speedboat and circle the island.

She can't have gotten far.

Just as I was about to connect the call, a caique parrot with the energy of a cocaine-snorting flea shot through the air and into the bathroom thanks to the open-air garden. He chirped and flapped around my head. "Not now," I growled.

He landed on my head and did his trick of hanging upside down, latching onto my hair to stare me dead in the eye, making me go cross-eyed if I wanted to look at him.

"Pika…" I bared my teeth. "If you want to be useful, find that damn goddess that's run away."

My hand curled around my phone. I'd expected the worst from Eleanor…but it was highly fucking inconvenient that she'd decided to bolt mere moments before having to serve Markus Grammer.

The tiny parrot did an acrobatic flip off my forehead and flapped noisily around my ears. I rolled my eyes, holding up my hand so he could perch on a finger.

He landed instantly, still cawing and cackling as if telling me all the reasons I shouldn't be here and why I should've done myself a favour and kicked Jinx off my island days ago.

"Yeah, yeah. I know." Bringing my hand to my face, I nuzzled into the little bird. Letting him peck my lips and coo into my cheek. He settled, still jumpy from my rage at finding an empty bathroom but content that I still loved him, and it wasn't him I was mad at.

A gentle slosh and a trickle of water ripped me around.
I blinked.
A wash of red-hot need fired through my veins.
She hadn't run away…after all.

Jinx sat up in the bath, water streaming over her face and hair, flower petals sticking to her bitter chocolate strands. The scent of sandalwood, orange, and vanilla coated her skin from soaking in a specially prepared blend.

The bath held so much water that only her face was visible, but it didn't stop my cock from thickening to a steel rod.

Her grey eyes flickered from me to Pika and back again. For the longest second, confusion blended with something akin to shock. Her tongue swiped on her lower lip, sipping the droplets left there. Her hands curled around the edge of the bath, white-knuckled as if my presence drove her to homicidal rage.

"You're still here." I stepped toward her, not caring that Pika flew from my finger and flapped around my face like a tiny annoying shadow.

She didn't look at me, preferring to follow the feathered fiend and his aerial acrobatics. "You have a pet?"

I shoved my hands into my pockets. "He's not a pet."

"Pet. Pet. Pet!" Pika shouted, darting to the floor and then to the ceiling. He knew he had her utmost attention, and he loved being the main event. He'd continue showing off until his wings fell off or he flew into a wall.

Which he had a tendency of doing.

"He can't be wild." Her eyes narrowed. "He talks and clearly adores you."

I shrugged. "He goes where he wants and hangs out with who he chooses."

"Sounds like he has more freedom than anyone on this island."

"He does." I ran a hand over my mouth. "Even more than me." For the first time in my life, I had no fucking idea what to say. The usual commands and curses would fit. I could order her from the bath, make her hurry; prove I was still in control. But...there was something different between us. Something languid and expectant...a pause in the next paragraph.

She didn't rush to fill the silence, and I drowned beneath white lightning possessiveness. Had I really agreed to let that asshole Grammer fuck her? What had I been thinking? It ought to be me with that right. She belonged to *me*, goddammit. And I wanted her. So. Fucking. Bad.

Moving toward her, I couldn't ignore the chugging of my heartbeat as lust I'd done my best to ignore smashed through my walls.

I'd thought keeping my distance would eradicate whatever curse she'd put on me.

It'd only made it stronger.

Fuck.

She huddled in the bath, sinking into the warmth until only her eyes were visible. The dark stone blurred her body, hiding her in shadows and illusion.

I fought against every fucking urge not to snatch her and take her for my own. Instead, I swallowed back starvation for sex, and grunted, "Why are you a vegetarian?"

A question that'd driven me mad. A question that kept me up at night and refused to let me masturbate in the morning. A question that could ensure her safety or her damnation.

She popped back up again, sucking in air, her eyes glowing grey with perplexity. "You want to know why I'm a...vegetarian?"

I nodded, gritting my teeth so I didn't do all the debasing acts currently running on a highlight reel inside my mind.

Slowly, she shrugged. "Why is that important?"

It's important.

Highly fucking important.

I shrugged, nonchalant and cold. "It's not. Just answer the damn question."

She flinched at my curt command. Droplets decorated her eyelashes like tiny diamonds. She blinked, scattering them onto her cheeks. "I've never liked the taste of meat. I just...one day, I decided I didn't want to eat it anymore."

I didn't like her answer. It revealed nothing about her. It didn't show me what I was beginning to suspect about her. The horrible conclusion that we shared yet another similarity. Our tempers, our desire to control until we couldn't anymore, our stupid morals that got us into this fucking mess.

"That's it?" I encroached on her, towering over her while she hunched in the liquid, water licking every inch that I wanted to.

"What else is there?" Her question was timid but also laced with fire.

"If you can't answer that, then—"

"It was a moral obligation," she blurted. Her gaze followed Pika as he hurtled himself toward a small orchid plant potted on the vanity. He slid down one of the slippery leaves, crashing into the centre of the foliage. "It's recognising that a life is a life. There is no difference between flesh, feather, or fur."

Well, fuck.

She'd just ruined any future she might've had.

"Stand up." I moved until my shoes clacked against the quartz bathtub.

"What? No. I'm naked." Her arms wrapped around her breasts.

"So? I've seen you bare. I've had my fingers in your cunt."

"But..." Her cheeks pinked as if there was a difference between letting me see her naked while under the influence of elixir versus now when she was innocent and safe in the bath.

My temper ticked tighter and tighter the longer she refused. My lust amplified until I shuddered with need. I should leave before I did something that would null and void the agreement I had with Grammer. I should fucking walk out that door and not come back.

But...

This girl.

This confusing, disorienting, *dangerous* girl.

I wanted a taste.

Just one tiny taste before I handed her over.

"You should've done what I said." My voice massacred each and every syllable. Before she could fight back or argue, I bent down, shoved my hand into the delicious thick wetness of her hair and jerked. I yanked her from the sweet-smelling water. I fisted her hair and used it as a rope to wrench her onto her knees in the bath.

And then, before I could stop myself, I pulled a little harder, bringing her mouth to mine, slamming our lips together with pain and pressure.

She cried out.

I groaned.

I hadn't kissed anyone in a very, very long time.

An eternity really.

And this wasn't a kiss.

This was domination. This was taking. This was beyond any fucking kiss that ever existed.

Her lips tried to stay locked against mine, but I'd never been good at asking permission. I took what I wanted. I carved out my own rules on a slate tablet and enforced every commandment.

This girl would obey me.

Fuck, she had to obey me. Otherwise...

I stabbed my tongue past her lips and into her mouth.

Her teeth tried to bite, but I jerked her head back, clamping my free hand around her throat. Trapped, I had her completely at my mercy as I plunged my tongue in, over and over, tasting her, destroying her, destroying myself.

Water sloshed all over my trousers as she fought to get free. Her chest pumped with erratic oxygen. Her body floundered in the bath.

But I didn't let go.

I just kissed her deeper.

I let myself have one thing of hers. To be the first to kiss her. To be the first to steal her soul.

Her hands clawed at my tie, forcing me to bend deeper.

For every attack she punished me with, I retaliated tenfold. I licked every dark place inside her. I wrapped my fist deeper into her hair, holding her forever. I tightened my hand around her jaw, feeling our tongues nudge against her cheeks as she fought to remove me from her mouth.

Only…our fight somehow turned into a desperate war. Her teeth caught my tongue, drawing blood. My teeth caught hers, threatening payback.

My heart pounded. My back ached. My entire bottom half was drenched.

And I couldn't get enough.

Jerking hard, I pulled her from her knees to her feet. She rose from the bathtub like some nymph from the sea. Water sluiced over her, swirling over tight nipples and gliding through trimmed pubic hair. Her flat stomach, her long legs, her delicacy and strength and—

I didn't stop kissing her, biting her, fucking *drowning* in her.

My hand dropped from her jaw to her throat and down to her breast.

I squeezed her hard, fingering her nipple until a deep-seated, feral moan escaped her kiss-bitten mouth.

I'd never been so fucking hard.

Our eyes locked as I continued slaughtering her mouth.

She not only battled against me but also herself. One second she lost herself, kissing me back, violently, explosively. The next she retreated, snapping and wriggling, trying to dislodge my control.

But no matter her disgust or her desire, I continued to take everything I could.

Dragging her from the bathtub, I plastered her to my body and thrust into her naked, wet body. My cock throbbed in agony, trapped behind drenched material and an unforgiving belt.

She snarled as I kissed her, then spun her around. Pushing her, she stumbled and automatically clutched the bath lip. She looked over her shoulder where I frantically scrambled at my zipper.

Every tattered heartbeat told me to claim her, fuck her…own her before another could.

Take her. Take her. Take her.

Mine. Mine. Mine.

Kicking her feet apart, I managed to pop my button and winced in torture as my cock pierced the top of my pants.

She shuddered.

Tears spilled down her cheeks, mingling with her bath.

And for the first time since I was nineteen, I let someone tell me what to do.

"Please...don't," she whispered. Not crying. Not begging. Just...asking me quietly not to rape her.

I stumbled back.

Life came crashing in.

How quickly I'd changed the vibe in this bathroom from sensual and humid to tense and treacherous.

Pika squawked and landed on her head, brandishing his little wings at me, his eyes bright and accusing. The flash of his green, yellow, and white feathers looked like a centrepiece of her invisible crown.

Condemning me.

Revealing just how far I'd been prepared to go.

Swiping both hands through my hair, I tripped to the door.

I couldn't even twist my tongue into dialogue. I couldn't remember how to talk.

She demoted me to nothing more than a beast.

Pika flapped again as I unlocked the door and tripped through it, slamming it shut behind me.

Jealousy jumped up from her reading nook, her eyes wide and face white. "Sullivan—"

"Get out! Get. *Out!*"

She dropped her e-reader and scampered.

And I slammed to my knees, digging a fist into my belly, trying to control the madness inside me.

Chapter Twenty-Nine

WHAT THE *HELL* JUST happened?

My knees gave out.

I crumpled to the floor, holding onto the bath as I did. The little parrot called Pika perched on my bare shoulder, his tiny talons digging into my skin. He twittered and squeaked, grooming my hair with his beak.

All I could do was sit.

Stupefied. Stunned. Shocked to my very core.

He'd *kissed* me.

He'd used violence to take what he wanted but…violence inside me had responded. Something I'd never known that lurked within me had ignited in an explosive gust of power—black power, erotic power—a power laced with cyanide and dynamite, poisoning me…or perhaps, poisoning him?

Poisoning both of us.

I'd gone from holding my breath under the water, giving myself the biggest pep talk in history, preparing myself to just get the sex over and done with, to being snatched by some demon and given a kiss to end all other kisses.

I brushed a shaky hand over my mouth.

Swollen and sore from his teeth and five o'clock shadow—extremely aware that I'd never been kissed like that before. That I'd been kissed by a man who wasn't Sullivan Sinclair: island mogul and trader of women. The man who'd kissed me had been an unhinged, highly sexual being who'd escaped his leash of self-control.

His fist banged on the glass door. "Hurry up. I've been patient long enough."

I jumped.

He didn't come in, but his shadow moved behind the frosted glass, pacing like a caged tiger.

What the *hell* was that?

That kiss.

That...awakening.

I shivered, doing my best to corral my legs into obedience.

Why had he kissed me?

And why did I feel completely lost? As if he'd shoved aside the old Eleanor—the girl loyal to Scott and fixated on escape—and called forth a coquettish goddess who'd just woken up.

Just been born.

Just felt the touch of someone who surpassed all other's touches. A touch belonging to someone who *fit*. Someone who, deep, deep beneath circumstance and control, was the very creation of magic and mystery I'd been searching for.

Stop it.

I crawled to my feet, wincing a little as the parrot dug his claws into my shoulder for purchase.

Don't be stupid.

I swayed and touched my bruised mouth again.

My stomach had chiselled itself into a chipped piece of stone. My heart hadn't remembered how to beat properly. And my body—under no manipulation from elixir or chemicals working against me—was heavy and wet and achy.

The damn man had drugged me just with a kiss.

Pika flapped around my head, landing on the floor and fluttering his feathers in the spilled water. He preened and nibbled at his belly, coating himself in the deliciously scented liquid.

Sully's fist came again.

Knock.

Knock!

"Get your ass out here, Jinx. Don't worry about clothing. Naked is your new uniform."

Searching for a towel, I grabbed one and huddled into it.

He might've have stolen me with a kiss and tossed me into a universe I could no longer understand, but it didn't mean I was okay with any of this.

How *could* I be okay when my enemy had the power to cinder me to ash but also incinerate me into flame? How could I survive, knowing that something was between us? Something he felt, I felt. Something that was mortally alarming and oh, so deadly.

"What do I do, Pika?" I whispered, towelling myself off and picking up the brush to run through my wet hair. The little bird chirped and flew to sit on the vanity tap, slipping on the chrome. "Pet. Pet, Pika!"

I tried to smile, yet another catastrophe hit me.

Sully was heartless and haughty and held the view that all humans were as disposable as any other living, breathing creature. That man I found terrifying. A man with such black and white ideals that there wasn't a single shade of grey in his entire soul.

But the man who'd stood before me when I'd come up for air in my bath, the man nuzzling into a tiny parrot and smiling such a soft, sincere smile…he made my heart pound for entirely new reasons.

Unsafe and unhealthy reasons because it made me thaw toward him just a tiny bit. To know he had a heart, after all.

"*Jinx!*" His snarl shot through the glass.

I dropped the brush, letting it clatter to the vanity. The noise made Pika squawk and launch into the sky, circling my head indignantly.

For a second, I allowed a glance at my reflection in the mirror. I'd avoided looking at myself much since I'd arrived. I didn't want to see the girl I knew, trapped and alone, homesick and afraid. I didn't want to see the pain in my eyes or the helplessness.

Balling my hands, I caught my gaze.

And once again, my heart scrambled to find a lifesaving beat.

Who *was* that girl?

Who is this total stranger?

As I touched my cheek with a trembling hand, my reflection mimicked me, but I didn't recognise the woman staring back. Her skin glowed a golden hue instead of the permanent snow of white heritage. Her hair seemed longer, darker, coils and ropes protecting her back and shoulders. Her breasts seemed bigger, her limbs leaner, her stance like a warrior ready to battle.

But it was my eyes and mouth that betrayed me the most.

My eyes were wild but also surprising clear. Two grey crystal orbs full of bad omens and concerning premonitions. And my lips looked exactly what a vixen who served men would look like.

Bright red, plump and bitten, thoroughly well used by a man who hadn't been given permission.

I'd never been a superstitious girl. I'd always accepted facts and made conclusions based on reality, but standing there, with a parrot landing on my shoulder and a body I no longer recognised, I felt like a seer suffering some awful clairvoyance.

Sully Sinclair will change my life. My world. Me.

In so many more ways than I feared.

With a gulp and a shudder, I broke the trance between me and the mirror, squared my shoulders, and strode toward the door.

Chapter Thirty

THE DOOR OPENED.

A naked goddess stepped from the humid bathroom with her neck arched, her body braced, and a flitting little parrot flying beside her.

I had more than a visceral reaction.

I had a full anatomy incineration.

I didn't know this girl.

We'd barely spoken.

Hardly touched.

Yet...fuck me.

She was *different*.

Different to anyone I'd ever met.

Only she made me act like a monster and a moron all at once. Only she made my pulse pound and sweat soak under my suit. Only she made me fucking rage at the weakness and sexual starvation she caused.

Why?

What made *her* special?

And most importantly...how did I fucking stop it?

I couldn't speak as she padded toward me. Her jaw clenched and damp hair still releasing glistening droplets on the tips, allowing moisture to temptingly roll down her flawless skin.

Snapping my fingers, I backed away, guiding her toward the

centre of the room.

Tearing her gaze from mine, she allowed curiosity to win, scanning the space, faster and faster as she noticed the pulleys and wires, the netting and strange contraptions.

To her credit, she didn't try to hide her nakedness. She owned her flesh. She moved as if she wore a gown made of impenetrable silk.

Pika, the little traitor, remained by her side as she drank in the odd facilities. His little wings tucked up tight as he landed and stole the crook of her shoulder and neck as his new home.

It did things to me...seeing an animal I'd raised, loved, and told my every secret to glare at me from the care of another. It made me jealous that he'd accepted her when he was fussy on which people he liked. It pissed me off that he wasn't as loyal as I believed.

And it made me angry...because what the fuck was I doing? What the fuck was I feeling? How the fuck did I *stop*?

"What is this place?" Her voice never rose above a whisper.

I swallowed the growl permanently living in my chest around her. "This is Euphoria."

She looked at me, causing my cock to throb and heart to stop. "I don't understand."

Raising her hand, she waved at the equipment that looked better suited for a Cirque du Soleil troop rather than a sex destination. "Why do you have aerial harnesses? Wires? Pulleys?"

"A fantasy is a fantasy." I shrugged as if it made total sense. "How can you fly if you're stuck on the ground?"

Her forehead furrowed, unable to figure it out.

And she wouldn't be able to.

Not until she'd experienced the essence of what I'd created.

The transformative power of this place.

She glanced at the bare tiles—sandstone for purchase with no carpets or rugs. "Where's the bed?" She frowned. "You say this is where people come to..." She trailed off.

I finished for her. "My goddesses and guests come here to fuck. And they have the best experience of their lives."

"But..." She frowned. "There's nothing soft about this place."

"Yet." Snapping my fingers again, I clasped my hands behind my back as two staff members scuttled in. Two young men who kept their eyes averted from Jinx's bareness and rushed to open the numerous cupboards bordering the room. Grabbing armfuls of furs, tawny and grey, white and speckled, they ran to us in the centre and tossed the armfuls at our feet.

Another trip and a pile of fur later, they vanished as seamlessly as they'd arrived.

I arched my chin at the scattered sea of furs and raised an eyebrow. "There is your softness."

They were in keeping with Markus Grammer's fantasy.

Props as it were.

She nudged a foxy looking pelt with her toe. "Fake, I presume?"

"Of course." I nodded.

"But why? Why not linen and mattresses and the usual play dungeon that people expect in a whorehouse or club?"

I moved toward her.

She stepped back.

I advanced again, stepping onto the pile of plush fur. My sodden clothes stuck wetly to my overheated flesh.

This time, she didn't move. Her stomach fluttered with breath, and she balled her hands as I touched her cheek. "Because that's normality, Eleanor Grace, and I deal in myth."

She flinched as I ran my thumb over her bottom lip.

Her breath caught.

And I almost broke my control again.

I bled with a need so vicious, I struggled to breathe.

I almost threw her to the floor of hides and fucked her.

But I wasn't going to throw away everything I'd created. She'd stolen enough from me. She wouldn't have anymore.

Backing away, I pressed a button on my phone.

A small whirring sound appeared as a fine wire attached to delicate harness descended from the ceiling. Catching it, I allowed one final study of her otherworldly beauty, then growled, "Come here. I'll show you how Euphoria works."

Chapter Thirty-One

I HESITATED.

I was off-balance from his kiss. I was confused by the bareness of the room. I was scared of what was about to happen.

"I won't ask a second time." His teeth flashed between shapely lips. His five o'clock shadow framed his mouth, narrowing all my attention there.

Against my will.

Against all common-sense.

Pika snuggled into my chin, rubbing me with his little head as a cat would their favourite person. He jolted me from my horrid fixation.

I swallowed hard and moved toward Sully.

Just the two of us.

No one else.

No Jealousy, no staff, no guests.

The aura between us hummed with anticipation. My heart collided with my ribs.

His jaw worked as I stopped in front of him.

He didn't speak as he undid the small clasp of the harness then wrapped his arms around me, imprisoning the device around my waist. The webbing was soft but fortified. Strong and utterly tamperproof. Buckling it loosely around my hips, he brought two other pieces up and over my shoulders, positioning them between my breasts to cinch into the harness around my middle. With his teeth gritted, he bent and reached between my legs, bringing two remaining thin straps to loop around my inner thighs and attach to the centre buckle.

God.

My skin broke out in goosebumps from his touch. His breathing remained shallow and short as if fighting his own battles by having me so close. I dared look down, swallowing again at the tented arousal of his wet trousers.

I closed my eyes as he tightened the straps, brushing my nipples and pussy with his hands.

Unlike the other day when he pushed me against the boardroom table and threatened to make me wet, he didn't have to make it a challenge to prove a point.

He'd succeeded in making my body a traitor the second his tongue had touched mine.

And I hated it.

I hated that I stood before him, nude and unprotected, and instead of scratching out his eyes and kicking him in the balls, I obeyed, I swayed, I *wanted*.

I'd become a horrendous clone of his brainwashed goddesses.

"Open your eyes."

My eyelashes flashed open. Our gazes connected. I grew dizzy looking into him.

Piercing blue.

Suffocating blue.

Drowning, drowning, dead—

A door to the back of the room slid open. "Sir?" Jealousy stood on the threshold. Nervousness painted her face, but she held her ground. "Would you like me to finish the process?"

Sully looked over his shoulder at her, breaking our stare, allowing me to live again, reincarnating me into yet another traitorous existence. "I'm capable of preparing her."

"Yes, of course. I didn't mean—"

"Leave."

She nodded and vanished.

Without looking at me, Sully strode toward the cupboard to our left. Opening it, he pulled out a trolley already stocked with whatever items he needed. Wheeling it to me, he locked the wheels beside me, then paused. He chewed on indecision before swallowing with determination.

Without a word, he scanned the trolley and its many boxes. Six in total. All black with a purple orchid stencilled on the top. Selecting the first, he pulled out a vial of glistening pearly oil.

I waited as he unscrewed the top, placed the vial down to put thin gloves on his hands, then poured a generous amount into his palm.

"What are you going to—"

His hands landed on my shoulders, dislodging Pika, who flew away with a snippy squawk, only to find mischief on the trolley, nibbling at the boxes, muttering to himself.

I stayed as stiff and as carved as the mermaids in his water fountain outside his office as his large, strong hands smeared oil over my shoulders, down my arms, over my hands, between my fingers, and back up to my throat.

He kept his eyes on my body, tipping more oil into his palm and going behind me.

I swallowed a moan as he massaged my back, ran his touch down my spine, staining every inch of me with the slippery stuff. My legs pressed together as he kneaded my ass. Dumping more oil into his hands, he ducked to his haunches and spread the coating down the backs of my thighs, my ankles, to the tops of my feet. When my back half was sufficiently covered, he returned to my front, kneeling in front of me to smear my front thighs, shins and bottoms of my feet.

Rising to his tall height, he smeared the remainder over my lower belly, up my ribcage, breasts, and collarbones, continuing his torture until my brow, cheekbones, and chin also shone.

Only once every part of me glistened a pearlescent hue did he place the vial back into its box and snap off his gloves.

My voice was rough and full of hunger. "What did you just put on me?"

"Something that will hijack your sensitivity."

I scowled. "What does that mean?"

"You'll see." Taking the next box, he pulled out a sheet of skin-coloured dots. Peeling one off, he ordered, "Give me your hand."

Hesitantly, I placed my palm in his. His long fingers kept me trapped while he very carefully positioned the dot right over my fingerprint. He continued until all ten fingers were covered with the fleshy toned sticker.

"Will you tell me what these do?" The latex-type material deadened my ability to feel when I pressed my fingertips together.

He gave a half-smile, tight and cool. "They change your sense of touch."

"Why?"

"You'll find out."

Swapping boxes, he opened the third. This one held a small bowl and a bottle the size of a travel mouthwash. Inside rested a blue liquid. Cupping my chin, he held me steady while he tipped the bottle against my lips.

Immediately, I reeled backward, only to remember I wore a harness locking me to the ceiling.

I couldn't run.

I couldn't refuse.

"It's not elixir," he murmured. "Not yet at least."

"What is it then?"

His features turned dark with annoyance, as if he wasn't used to being questioned. But he sighed impatiently, granting me an answer. "It warps your sense of taste."

"Why?"

He shrugged. "My answer will be the same for all your questions. You'll see." Pressing the bottle to my mouth again, he added, "Now, swill. Don't drink. Just swish and spit." Holding up the bowl, he waited for me to obey.

I allowed the liquid to splash past my lips. Swilling like I would after cleaning my teeth, I spat out into the little silver bowl he held. Placing both discarded items on the trolley, he brushed Pika away from the swirling blue liquid, giving him the lid of the bottle to play with instead.

He did it subconsciously. So comfortably. A flicker of a genuine smile on his face watching the antics of the tiny terror. It spoke of a relationship between man and bird far deeper than I'd thought.

Once again, something tenacious and vicious kicked my heart. Something that said *he's different. He's not what you think.*

Stupid kick.

Stupid thoughts.

Sully was exactly what I thought. A dealer in sex using bought and trapped women.

Don't forget that!

Don't be that stupid.

The fourth box opened. Sully pulled out a thin tube. Unscrewing the lid, he crowded close to me and cupped the back of my neck. I tried to lean away, but he brought the tube under my nose and smeared something cool and astringent under my nostrils.

It didn't smell.

It didn't destroy my olfactory abilities, and I still drowned in Sully's unique scent of sea, sunshine, and coconuts.

"If that's meant to ruin my sense of smell, it hasn't worked."

I didn't know why I gave him a heads-up that it hadn't done what I suspected. In fact, none of his tricks had. My skin still felt like mine. My sense of smell still operated. My fingertips didn't like the coverings, but it didn't truly stop my sense of pressure or heat.

"It will do. When you step into Euphoria."

I scowled. "You said I'm *in* Euphoria."

He tossed the tube into its box, opening the fifth. "You are. But it's not what you think. You're standing in the room where Euphoria takes place but...the location isn't physical."

"I don't understand." I wanted to keep repeating that phrase.

I don't understand.

I don't understand.

You.

But Sully lost any magnanimity about answering my questions and held up two small buds. I guessed they were for my ears before his electrifying touch brushed aside my hair and inserted one into my ear canal.

Goosebumps sprang down my arms and spine, pebbling my nipples and ensuring he saw, rather visibly, what his touch did to me.

He chuckled under his breath as he moved behind me, pulling my damp hair over my shoulder and kissing the shell of my ear with exquisite tenderness. "I might have found your weak spot, Eleanor." His teeth grazed the sensitive skin, clamping down on my lobe.

I shuddered.

A flush of wetness.

A knot of desire.

I shook my head in defiance as he inserted the second earbud. "Don't fool yourself."

He laughed again, rolling and velvety, black and unforgiving as he ensured both buds were tight and blocked my hearing.

They blocked my hearing as any earbud would, but I could still hear, still make out everything I needed to.

What was the point in all of this?

He's masking your senses.

My attention shot to the final box just as Sully picked it up, cracked the lid, and lifted out a small container with two separate screwed dishes.

Contact lenses.

My sense of sight.

The final one.

Touch, taste, sound, hearing, and sight.

"I don't want anything foreign in my eyes." I backed up a step, jiggling the apparatus keeping me tethered.

"It won't hurt you." He unscrewed the left container, careful not to spill the contents.

"I still don't want it."

"You don't have a choice." Looking up, he presented the small holder to me. "If you have experience with inserting lenses, be my guest. Or...I can do it for you."

"I've never put anything in my eyes."

"Well then." He reached in and plucked out a flimsy lens from the solution it bobbed in. Placing the other one down safely, he eyed Pika to make sure he was still entertained with a piece of cardboard he'd shredded from an empty box and moved closer.

His hand cupped my nape again, bringing me close to him.

I tried to fight it, but my stupid, stupid body tingled from having his so close. I struggled to breathe as he brushed aside some hair on my cheeks with his knuckles, then pulled my head back a little. "Relax."

"Relax?" I sneered. "How can I relax in this place?"

"You'll learn to." His face stayed stern with concentration. I focused on his fingers as they came closer and closer, looming over my eye. "You'll learn to love it here. You'll beg to return."

"That will never happen." I wanted to close my eyes and refuse.

"Never is a challenge." He repeated our previous conversation, and sensing my intention to disobey, he let my nape go and slid his control to my eyebrow and delicate skin beneath, holding my vision wide open. "Hold still."

I flinched as he plopped something wet and awful over my pupil. My eye boycotted the obstruction. Natural instinct made me blink over and over again, trying to get it out.

He let me go, allowing me space to come to terms with it.

My hand raised to rub, to smear it from my sight, but he caught my wrist, clucking his tongue. "Take that out, and I'll tie your hands."

Slowly, the sensation faded, my eyeball accepting the intrusion. It stung slightly and felt way too big and gritty, but I endured...because I had to.

Sighing in discomfort, I permitted him to insert the second one, cursing the blurred vision. The nastiness of something I didn't want blinding me.

"I can't see."

"You will."

A few more blinks and finally my eyes figured out how to see through the film.

Huh, he was right. I was still aware of them, but they no longer obstructed anything.

Again, I wanted to ask what was the point. I could still see and hear, touch and smell. Why go to all this effort to take away my senses when none of them had been stolen?

He stepped back, assessing me, drinking in my nakedness.

With lewdness that ached with masculinity, he readjusted his hard-on, wincing a little in pain. If it'd turned him on so much to be around me...why was he preparing me for another man? Why not have one of his countless minions do the task? Why not enlist one of his many willing goddesses to put him out of his misery?

He caught me watching him touching himself. His throat worked as he swallowed hard. "Want something, Jinx?"

I tilted my head, finding it hard to breathe. "Why do you do that?"

"Do what?"

"Call me by two names?" I licked my lips as he throttled his cock, his suit rustling with damp material. "You said I wasn't Eleanor anymore...I was Jinx as long as I belonged to you. Yet..." I bit my lip as he let himself go and stormed into me.

His big hands cupped my cheek, smearing oil deeper into my skin. "I keep asking myself that same question." He pressed his forehead to mine. "You aren't a girl anymore; therefore, you don't deserve your name. You are a goddess; therefore, you should respond to the title I give you." He sighed with a growl. "Seems even I break my rules."

My lips sparked for his. I didn't want to kiss him. I wanted him to back away and take all his sinning need with him. But I also wanted to see if what'd happened in the bathroom was real. If it was a one-time crazy insane moment, or if such a connection continued smouldering between two people who should never have met.

We stood there, locked against each other, both waiting for something.

Waiting for what?

He was a demon, a monster, a god of sin, emperor of lust, and undisputed king of danger. And I wanted him to prove to me that whatever I'd felt in that bathroom was *wrong*. That I'd been intoxicated by a violent, vibrant kiss that confused my nervous system into thinking it meant something unbelievable rather than something I should be inherently petrified of.

With a gruff groan, Sully pulled away and reached into his back pocket. His hand came up with a familiar bottle.

A bottle holding the worst witchcraft I'd ever had to endure.

"No." Immediately, I tripped backward, clanging against the wire that held me captive. "I'm not taking that."

He moved slowly, methodically, planting himself directly in front of me while I strained against the harness. Never looking away, he unscrewed the tiny vial and held it up. "This is going down your throat, one way or another."

"I'll spit it out."

"I'll suffocate you until you swallow." His eyes flashed dark denim. "Or are you forgetting our first meeting and my previous methods?"

"I don't want it."

He ran a hand through his hair as if my fight for control bored him. "That's not a valid argument."

"Please." I settled for sweetness—for a different tactic other than war. But unlike the last time, when I'd begged him to stop in the bathroom, driven to the pinnacle of fear, knowing without a doubt that he was seconds away from taking me, he didn't react.

My voice didn't hold the vulnerability of before. My please wasn't from the heart but calculated.

Tapping the bottle with his finger, he cocked his head, his gaze dark and turbulent. "This will make it all bearable. I promise."

Prickles broke out over my skin. Frustration and claustrophobia. Fear and captivity. *"Please..."* This time it wasn't so calculated, it echoed with my rising levels of panic.

"Shush." He reached out, digging his fingers into my drying hair, a slight shake showing he wasn't as calm as he portrayed.

Did he feel it too?

Was he growing drunk on the raw chaos between us? The feeling of no longer being human, but a vessel for bottled up need.

Need and fear and turmoil.

"Don't think about what will be...just focus on what is now."

I trembled as he once again brought the elixir to my lips, hovering the poisonous liquid over me. I clamped my mouth shut, shaking my head.

"Everything has an expiry date, Jinx. Happiness or hardship. It's all the same. Nothing lasts forever."

Our eyes locked again.

For a second, it looked as if he'd tear me from the harness and take me somewhere where he could finish what he'd started when he dragged me from the bath. His control frayed at the edges, showing the cost this preparation had taken. But then ice froze his lust, and cruelly, he pressed the bottle between my lips and tipped.

The splash of flower-infused, sugary liquid coated my tongue.

He pinched my nose and prepared to slap his palm over my lips.

I managed to spit out a small amount. Just a tiny bit. It oozed down my chin as his anger exploded, and his hand suffocated my face with fury.

I didn't wait until I almost passed out from lack of oxygen this time.

I knew I couldn't win.

I'd been taught this lesson.

I'd rebelled a little by spitting out a few measly millilitres.

Who knew if it would make any difference to the longevity of the drug, but I'd won a tiny victory, and he'd win his.

Narrowing my gaze, I arched my chin and swallowed.

Instantly, he let me go as if I burned him from the inside out.

He stood ever so close, his chest pumping with breath. His suit looking rumbled and dishevelled from bathwater splashing him.

His gaze locked on the trickle of wasted elixir on my skin, smearing with oil, destined never to poison me.

A blackness descended over him.

A split-second decision that derailed both our lives and made them immeasurably harder.

"Goddamn you." Launching at me, his fingers weaved into my hair just as his mouth crashed against mine.

Sullivan

Chapter Thirty-Two

A SECOND MISTAKE.

A second kiss.

Come on, be honest.

It wasn't my second mistake where this damn girl was concerned. I'd been fucking up ever since she arrived.

But did it stop me?

Fuck no.

Dragging her into me, I yanked at her hair—the hair I couldn't seem to stop fisting—and kissed her deeper. She didn't retaliate or respond, too shocked by my pounce, too stunned to fight.

Piercing her lips with my tongue, I finally woke her up. Finally shattered her shock that she was being kissed. And thoroughly.

The strange taste of elixir on my tongue.

The smear of rebellion that she'd tried to spit out.

I didn't know what my intention had been. To lick it off her chin and shove it into her mouth with my tongue? To feed it to her? To ensure she drank from me until she savoured every fucking drop?

But...it'd backfired.

I didn't take my own medicinal creations purely for one reason. My system reacted too well. And fuck me, this latest version was strong.

Too strong.

I could see that now. Taste it. *Feel* it.

Fuck, I could feel it.

It soaked into my tongue, mingling orchid extraction, aphrodisiacs, hallucinogens, and a complex blend of chemicals with her own intoxicating, mind-numbing flavour. It saturated my blood. It shot around my veins. The tingling, fiery, snarling power branched off to attack my heart, my belly, my cock.

Potent.

Powerful.

It made every part of me a machine just for sex. To fuck until I couldn't move. To consume everything about this girl until neither of us existed.

While my mind raced, doing its best to outrun the minor trace of elixir already hijacking my body, I ground my hips into Eleanor's oil-smeared nudity.

She'd been sufficiently prepared.

She was ready to play.

Yet...here I was destroying her.

She fought a little, her head vying for space while my mouth continued to condemn hers. I kissed her wetly and hotly, desperate for everything all at once.

I wanted that perfect reward when she kissed me back in the bath. When she forgot herself just for a second and gave in.

I waited.

I kissed.

I thrust into her, unable to stop myself.

The elixir's strength magnified, making me lose myself to lust. Pulling away, I panted as I held Eleanor's cheeks and studied her.

Desire-wet lips. Glazed gaze. Pebbled nipples.

Her body had already undergone the insidious pull of elixir. Yet she fought it. Her face screwed up as she shook her head, denying the licking, whispering tugs of need.

She'd been able to fight the elixir in my office for a good six or seven minutes.

Today, it wouldn't be that long.

The more you took it, the faster its effects.

I could be patient.

Fuck her.

Okay, so my patience had died the second I'd made the mistake of licking her.

She shuddered in my hold. The muscles in her belly

contracted. Her legs pressed together. Her hands balled as her head fell forward, sending a cascade of hair over my suited arms.

"Don't fight it. There's no point."

"There is. There is a point," she snapped through gritted teeth.

"You can't win."

"That's not the *point!*" Her grey gaze glowed with fury. "I hate you."

"I don't care." Planting my mouth over hers again, I swallowed up her hate. I ate her fury. I drank every drop of loathing she could conjure.

And finally, fucking finally…the rigidity in her body turned to liquid invitation.

Her spine relaxed, her hips rocked, her mouth opened with a sigh of disbelief and disturbed passion.

I groaned.

She moaned.

We attacked each other.

A kiss was just a kiss…but this?

It was fucking explosive.

Her hands clutched at my lapels, dragging me into her. My fingers slid from her strands, dropping down her spine to knead the fullness of her ass. I hoisted and jerked her into me, aggressive and possessive, driving the rock-hardness of my throbbing cock into her.

I wanted to be inside her.

I'd never needed anything more.

Her tongue tangled with mine, sending another electrical storm through my belly and into my balls.

Fuuuucck, she could kiss.

Just as violent.

Just as messy.

Sliding and nipping, plunging and taking.

We were perfectly matched. Her height to my height. Her tenacious desire with my wrathful hunger.

She crawled up me, whimpering and squirming, rubbing her clit against my leg.

Splaying my hands on her hips, I rocked with her, encouraging her to smear my exceedingly expensive suit with her wetness.

Her head fell back as I dropped my fingers between her legs, spearing two deep inside her.

"Oh, *God!*" She went tense and floppy all at the same time. Bowing into my touch. Giving herself entirely to me.

She was no longer frigid. She was fully participating.

I bent to bite her nipples. To suck. To claim.

My thumb found her clit, pressing cruelly as my lips tracked quick and questing back to her mouth, finding her panting and delirious.

I kissed her brutally hard as I drove two fingers deep into her.

She cried out into my mouth. Opening wide for my tongue, she focused on my touch, allowing me to do whatever the hell I wanted.

She tried to climb me, coil around me like a snake, unashamedly using me for her own pleasure.

I fucking loved it.

I loved the feeling of having such a willing, demanding woman. A goddess who knew exactly what she wanted and wouldn't waste time playing coy or bashful. She wanted to come. I smelled it on my fingers. I tasted it on my tongue. She wanted to come around my cock just as much as I wanted to come inside her.

Her fingers latched on to my belt, yanking at the strap and fumbling with the buckle. She got it undone.

I grunted.

She gasped.

My fingers thrust harder into her wet body in encouragement. My hips were possessed, arching and rolling, phantom fucking her even while apart.

"Ah, shit, Sinclair!"

The shout came from outside our drowning, damning world.

A whistle came after, piercing and sharp.

Ripping my mouth from Eleanor's, I struggled to focus my gaze over my shoulder.

Calvin.

He stood with his hands spread as if he couldn't explain my actions. His mouth set into a steely line. His face black with annoyance.

"Fuck off." I snarled, my entire body quaking as Eleanor unzipped me and her small hand inched into my trousers.

I wanted to know what it would feel like to have her fist me. To have her touch me, hold me, suck me, fuck me.

"Markus is in the next room." Cal crossed his arms as my eyes went cross-eyed. "He's under the impression his goddess is ready for him."

Everything screeched to a halt.

I snatched Jinx's wrist, stopping her from grabbing my aching, excruciating erection.

If she touched me, I was done.

It would be impossible to stop.

She mewled and whimpered, trying to plaster herself against me, to use me for friction, licking her lips for more.

It took everything I had, but through some magical power of restraint, I stumbled backward, away from her, too far for her to follow thanks to the harness and wire trapping her.

Every molecule inside howled to return to her. To get as naked as her and hoist her into my arms. To slide home. To fuck guests and obligations. To ignore responsibilities and contracts. But with fresh air and a disapproving manservant, the small droplet of elixir I'd ingested lost its tenacious pull. Its claws weren't as sharp. Its need not as influential.

I inhaled a shuddery breath.

I rearranged the pounding pain of my cock.

I raked a trembly hand through my hair as I turned and faced Calvin.

He scowled. "I know you've got a thing for that one but, mate...have some fucking respect."

I pointed a finger in his face, my anger on a furious ledge. "Stop before you say something stupid."

"How about you stop before you—"

"I stopped, didn't I?" I smoothed my blazer, buckling my belt with as much decorum as I could.

"Another two seconds you would've been balls deep in that girl." He looked behind me, seeing her naked for the second time since she'd arrived. I followed his stare, shocked at the change in her.

In a way, elixir stripped humanity and left just an animal behind. She didn't have a tail or pointy ears or soft fur but from the sinuous way she moved, the way she bared her teeth, and the explicit roll of her hips, she was a creature in heat.

Nothing more.

Yet another reminder that humans were no more special than a dog or bird or dolphin. When it came to mating, we were all unhinged.

"Sully...God...*please.*" Her words slurred and thick with hunger. Her tongue struggling to talk when all it wanted to do was taste and lick.

"Leave, Sinclair. I'll load the program." Calvin pulled out his phone, logging into the extensive system I'd paid intelligent nerds to create from a concept I'd dreamed about.

A crazy, consuming dream that was the nucleus of how Euphoria had been born.

I held up my hand. "I'll do it."

"You sure?"

I gave him the finger and fished my phone from my pocket. It took a moment to log in, pull up the code I'd programmed this afternoon from Markus Grammer's dossier, and hover my thumb over the load button.

I looked up, drinking in the sight of Eleanor, disgraced and trapped, starving for something that I wouldn't be the one to give her.

Markus would.

He'd feed her his cock.

He'd drink down her cries of ecstasy.

Christ.

Could I do it?

Even now, this close to time, I didn't know if I could go through with it.

But what choice did I have?

It was too late.

I'd committed.

The deal was done.

Without realising, I stepped toward her, drawn against my will, unable to differentiate if my feral attitude toward her came from the traces of elixir or whatever curse she'd put on me.

"Sully." Her eyes flashed silver, drunk on desire. "Don't give me to someone else." Her hips moved. Her arms wrapped around herself, squeezing tight. "Give me to you."

"You've had as much of me as you ever will."

Otherwise, I'll end up killing you.

She suffered a full-body quake. "But I want you. I'm...I'm losing myself. I need...I need you inside me. *Please.*" Frustrated tears fell down her cheeks. Already her skin had lost the golden hue from swimming in my sea and gone a concerning white. "I hate this. I hate feeling like this. I hate having no control. If I have to sleep with someone...let it be you. You made me this miserable. It's your responsibility to *help* me."

Help her?

I'd *ruin* her.

Just like she'd fucking ruined me.

"You'll forget about me the moment I press this button."

Her forehead bunched as her hands crept to her breasts, clutching both with tight fingers. "I won't. I don't want to be given to a guest. Please..." She moaned, her knees trembling and body swaying in the harness. "I don't want to be like this. Make it stop. *Please* make it stop."

My stomach pierced with mirroring pain.

I didn't want to be like this either.

I didn't want to feel things outside of my control. I didn't want my mind transfixed on her or my body obsessed with hers.

I'd given her a drug to make her come undone.

All she'd done to make me unravel was fucking *exist*.

More tears splashed down her cheeks as she forcibly removed her hands from her breasts. She shook until her teeth chattered. She looked sick. Positively feverish and broken.

Shit.

Would her system handle another round with elixir? Would she cope being used, over and over, begging for something that could ultimately kill her?

Worry sprang sharp and nasty.

An emotion I wasn't familiar with these days after I'd efficiently learned how to stop that heinous fear.

Empathy.

That was my weakness.

Too much empathy could kill a person. Not enough could kill someone else.

I'd learned to kill others, rather than myself.

And if Eleanor couldn't cope. If her system shut down in Euphoria...well, that would release me from this curse, and I could hopefully forget about her.

It didn't matter my heart lashed with pain.

It didn't matter my stomach coiled against my wishes with worry.

This was business.

She was my possession.

I had a contract to fulfil.

With my thumb over the button, ready to send her far, far away, I walked into her embrace. I let her snake around me. I permitted her wet pussy to grind against my thigh. I cupped her cheek and kissed her sweetly on the forehead.

She moaned. "Please, keep me for yourself."

"I can't," I breathed.

"Why not?" She tried to dig her way into my suit, her body blazing like wildfire, her skin damp with sweat and sensitivity-switching oil.

"Because I don't trust myself around you." I nuzzled her ear. "I don't trust you."

"Trust me. Take me." She kissed my cheek feverishly.

Pika shot off the trolley, finally bored with his game of shredding cardboard and flipping lids, fluttering around our heads as if searching for a way to join.

I looked from the free bird, flying whichever way he wanted and back to the woman tethered in hell. And I whispered the truth that I'd tried to keep even from myself, "You're dangerous, Eleanor Grace. You have the power to ruin me."

"I don't. I won't. I'm yours. You *made* me yours."

"Yes, I did. I made you mine." I pulled away. "And that's perhaps my biggest mistake of all."

Stepping back, I pressed the upload button. My phone paused for a second, then the success screen showed.

For a moment, nothing changed.

Eleanor still stood in front of me. Beside herself with lust. Miserable and wet.

The next, her body jolted in the harness.

She went lax.

Her legs buckled.

She hung from the ceiling as if dead.

I knew it was just the initiating process. That in a couple of heartbeats, she'd be standing upright and breathing, but…I wouldn't be there to see.

Markus would.

Markus would be the one she begged.

While I went fucking wild with regret.

"Goodbye, Eleanor."

Turning, I forced dead legs and reluctant heart to leave her for my guest.

Chapter Thirty-Three

EVERYTHING WENT BLINDINGLY WHITE.

It all disappeared.

The need.

The heat.

The hunger.

Sight, sound, smell, taste, touch.

I was sucked into a vacuum of nothingness.

I died.

Is this what death is?

Just…emptiness?

Everything deleted, including you? Including all your thoughts and feelings, your triumphs and tragedies?

I tried to breathe, I couldn't.

I tried to move, nothing obeyed.

Panic grew.

Terror overflowed.

And then…the white exploded in colour. A palette of bleeding pigments as if splashed on a virgin canvas, smearing and dripping, painting a masterpiece in its wake.

I blinked.

I struggled to understand.

I was in a cave.

An earthy, rustic cave with charcoal drawings of a mammoth and sabre-toothed tiger. A cave with damp coils from underground springs staining the walls. A cave with furs piled on the floor, a crackling fire in a stone hearth, a tower of hand-smoothed wooden bowls and utensils, and the scent of roasted meat almost ready to eat.

The moment I smelled the charred flesh, my heart bucked.

Smell!

I smelled everything.

The mustiness of the dirt floor. The sourness of tanned hides. The smokiness of the fire.

Along with smell came sensitivity.

I felt the warmth of the fire. I wanted to crawl closer, to soak up the flames because the cave was cold. Icy breezes kept sneaking in around the large fur pinned on a frame against the entrance to whatever landscape existed outside.

My eyes noticed every detail. The groves on the floor where sleeping holes had been dug with primitive tools. The broken chips from the cave walls from someone trying to create another entry. This place wasn't made up.

It was *real.*

As real as the island had been with Sully Sinclair.

But the tropical heat had gone.

The scents of pineapple and salty sea no more.

The inherent sixth sense of knowing you were surrounded by water was replaced with the undeniable reality that I was now deep in some savannah. Surrounded by land, locked by plains and terrain.

But how?

How was I here when I'd just been there?

How could I bend and scoop up a handful of dirt and have it trickle through my fingers? How could the fire hiss and spit when I threw the remaining grains into it?

I stepped forward, panic plaiting with the horrible sensation that I'd lost my mind. That I'd had a stroke, and this was the most vivid dream of my life all while I lay in a coma somewhere.

Something stopped me.

The slither of leather against earthen floor.

I looked down.

A tear rolled down my cheek.

A heavy cuff latched around my ankle, trapping me to this cave. I followed the leather rope, picking up it and tracing its length until it vanished into the floor.

No.

I looked around for a knife to cut myself free. Suddenly very aware of the coiling desire still prominent in my belly. The wetness smearing my inner thighs. The hunger that'd been kind in a tiny reprieve of my surroundings had now returned in full force.

My breasts tingled and throbbed for touch. My clit begged to be played with so I could come. Walking caused friction. Friction caused desire.

Who cared if I was in a cave?

Who cared if none of this could be explained?

My body was hungry for something only a man could give. No amount of food or liquid could sate me. Only pleasure. Climaxes. Orgasms.

Sully.

I *needed* him.

He'd made me like this. He could fix me. He *had* to fix me because I couldn't survive this again.

I can't.

I can't do it.

Already my heart galloped at an unsustainable beat. My stomach gnawed on emptiness, doing its best to chew its way to my core so I could come over and over again. To use the last of my reserves, hurtling me into death on a rain of climaxes.

My teeth ached as a full-body shudder tried to make me come from air alone.

My legs wobbled as I stumbled forward, tearing at my hair, wishing I could crack open my skull and pour out the elixir that broke me.

Stop it.

You can fight it.

I collapsed to my knees, moaning in despair as my hand went between my legs. I *couldn't* stop it. I couldn't fight it. My eyes rolled back as I played with my clit. I moaned as my tease became vicious and violent, desperate to eradicate the bubbling, pressuring lust.

"No!" I ripped my hand away, launching to my feet. The leather cuff almost made me trip as I paced wildly, trying to figure out a way to stay sane.

Another couple of minutes and I would revert to what I'd become a few days ago—a poor girl who sobbed in her villa, screaming in ecstasy over and over as she came a thousand times.

I need him.

I needed his cock.

I needed to be filled and ridden and—

Almost as if I'd conjured him with my explosive desire, a foot scuffed against the ground, ripping my attention to the mouth of the cave.

Sully—

My body melted further. My core clenched hard.

The fur was pulled back, and a man appeared.

A man I'd never seen before.

Not Sully.

Not the guest Grammer from the beach.

No one I had ever met.

Who...

He was tall. Exceedingly so. He was built like the predators of this prehistoric time with big arms, a flat, ripped stomach, and hugely muscular legs. Nothing about him said softness. He carried a spear, sharpened by fire and stained with blood. His naked chest held the meltings of snowflakes as he stepped fully into the cave and closed the fur behind him.

He shook like a dog, his long hair tangled and knotted with debris from living a rough and rustic life. His skin was weathered. His flesh scarred and well-used.

He looked as if he'd stepped from the history books and somehow stumbled into my world.

My coma.

My strange, erotic death.

He noticed me, standing crazed and cuffed to the floor.

Instantly, the aura in the cave changed.

Gone was the sensation of shock and pity. I no longer worried how I'd gotten here and what this all meant. I no longer pined for a man who was the devil incarnate. I no longer fought the treachery and betrayal of the elixir.

I'd reached my limit.

If I fought the basic instinct to mate another moment, my heart would explode.

All I wanted...all I *needed*—the only thing that would keep me alive was *him*.

I didn't care who he was.

I didn't feel shame that I wanted him or horror that I would willingly fuck a complete stranger.

I was done.

The moment I accepted my nightmare, my pulse calmed a little. It knew it would be rewarded soon. That the tingling, tangling, twisting coils in my belly would soon shatter outward in shards of light and lewd delight.

The man's nostrils flared, smelling my need, reacting like a hunter who'd scented blood.

His chest rose and fell as he licked his lips.

I tried to look away.

I tried a final time to *wake up*.

But I had nothing left, and the same terrible, troubling pull inside me affected him. The same instinctual magnet to fuck and fuck and die in each other's arms.

His large hands fell to the loincloth around his hips. A scraped and cured hide fell from his huge body, revealing an equally, terrifyingly large cock.

Flaccid but rapidly filling with blood, rising as if from a bow, standing to attention to please me.

My stomach melted.

I was a slave to the primitive urge to join.

I wedged a fist in my lower belly, biting down on a moan.

I didn't want this.

But I did.

I didn't want this man.

But I did.

I wanted to stop all of this.

But I also couldn't deny if I didn't have him touch me, fuck me, help me release this debilitating need, I wouldn't exist.

It wasn't a dramatic stupid promise.

It was the truth.

I would die.

Surely, surely die.

My heart raced, ricocheting more desire around my veins. My skin prickled to be touched. My hand raised in invitation, shaking and sweaty.

And the man nodded and came toward me.

He took my hand. Cold power. Calloused touch. Possessive control.

Even if I didn't want this, I wouldn't have had a choice.

In one touch, he showed me the truth—the truth that he might've just stumbled upon me. That he might have nothing to do with this strange fantastical world I was trapped in. But regardless of how he'd found me...he'd take me.

He'd take me even if I belonged to another. He'd fuck me even if I said no.

Blistering panic broke through my heady haze. Somehow, I

shook my head, backing up a step. "No…"

His jaw gritted, and heavy eyebrows knitted over raging eyes. Jerking my hand, he wrapped it firmly around his now steely hard cock.

I flinched.

I shuddered.

I gushed more wetness.

Keeping my fingers around him, he yanked me forward by my wrist. He drank me in, sniffing my throat, licking my skin, pushing my hair away and sending a wash of electricity over my cheek with his scarred knuckles. He threaded his fingers to my nape, bringing our foreheads together.

"Mine." His voice was guttural and achingly low, as if he'd only just learned how to speak. As if vocabulary was as foreign as walking on two legs. As if he'd transformed from a beast and shed his animal skin purely to come and ravage me.

I shuddered at the mental image.

Another trickle of wetness oozed down my thigh.

My inner muscles clenched around nothing, and I finally broke.

Sully hadn't given me what I needed.

But this man…this overly endowed caveman would.

A wave of gratitude filled me. Displaced and manic, but it was gratitude just the same. Immense relief that someone cared enough to save me. To help me through this crippling pain.

His dark eyes sparked with a hunger that matched mine, and his hold on my hair became a fist around a rope. Without asking for permission or telling me his plans, he jerked me around until I faced away from him.

I suffered a full-body convulsion.

He wrapped my long strands around his wrist.

I cried out.

He pushed me down and down until I kneeled on the dirt floor.

I landed on all fours, digging fingernails into the dirt like an animal, arching my back, mewling in need.

He crashed behind me.

He bent and bit my hip.

His teeth sank painfully into my flesh.

I squirmed to get away only for his powerful hands to clamp around my hips and yank me backward.

He soared up behind me.

He positioned.
He mounted.

PRE-ORDER TWICE A WISH
Book Two in Goddess Isles
Releasing 24th March 2020

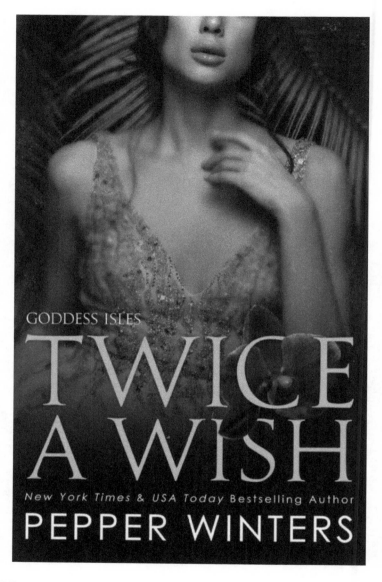

GODDESS ISLES

TWICE A WISH

New York Times & USA Today Bestselling Author

PEPPER WINTERS

"There was a monster once. A monster who bought me, controlled me, and took away my freedom.
There was a man once. A man who dealt in myth and secrets, hiding behind his mask, making me hunger and wish to know the truth."

Eleanor Grace belongs to the man and the monster, hating him but unable to deny that something links them together. Something she doesn't want to feel, something that traps her as surely as the sea surrounding the island where she serves.

Sully Sinclair belongs to his past and the black and white script his life has become. He views his goddesses as commodities, possessions to be treated kindly but firmly. Only problem is…Eleanor is different.

She's jinxed him.

Cursed him.

Awakened him.

A goddess with the power to ruin him.

PREORDER TWICE A WISH : Release Date: 24th March 2020

PREORDER THIRD A KISS : Release Date: 21st April 2020

PREORDER FOURTH A LIE : Release Date: 19th May 2020

PREORDER FIFTH A FURY : Release Date: 16th June 2020

PLAYLIST

Imagine Dragons - Nothing left to say
Imagine Dragons – Thunder
Rihanna – Stay
John Legend – All of me
Rag 'n' Bone Man – Human
Titanium – David Guetta
Imagine Dragons – Demons
Bastille – Pompeii
Bastille – The Draw
Halsey – Graveyard
Halsey – Haunting
Billie Eilish – Bad Guy
Imagine Dragons - Monster

ACKNOWLEDGEMENTS

Thank you to YOU

Thank you to bookstagrammers, bloggers, tweeters, facebookers, goodreaders, reviewers, and book worms for all your hard work providing feedback, graphics, and buzz.

Thank you to my beta readers (Melissa, Heather, Selena, Effie, Tamicka, Vickie, and Nicole), for reading along and joining in on my excitement.

Thank you my editor, Jenny for murdering those many typos.

Thank you to my audio narrators, Sarah and Scott for keeping pace with my schedule and providing such great narration.

Thank you to Amazon, iBooks, Nook, Kobo, Draft2Digital, and Googleplay for the platforms that allowed my dreams to come true.

Thank you to my horses for keeping me sane, my rabbit for being my writing muse, my husband for keeping me based in reality, not fantasy.

Thank you to every reader who has taken a chance on my work and has come along for another Dark Romance adventure.

I couldn't do this without any of you.

Buckle up…this series is going to be a fun one.

CPSIA information can be obtained
at www.ICGtesting.com
Printed in the USA
LVHW041543280220
648531LV00003B/495

9 781653 889860